"Let's live dangerously and take a dip in the spring," Ariel said

"If I get love-struck I may never go home." Rex rose, pulling her up with him.

"Why do I feel like a guinea pig?" she asked.

"Because I'm a born scientist. I need to explore every inch of my subjects." He smoothed her dress down, feeling the warmth of her skin beneath the soft curve of her belly. "If Romeo's in the water," he promised, nuzzling his face against her neck as they began to walk toward the spring, "the outcome could be very dangerous."

"That's my hope," Ariel said. "And because you've already gathered all your samples and the bug only stays in the bloodstream a week, things could work out perfectly…."

Rex knew he was acting uncharacteristically, but surely that was only because she was so gorgeous.

"A week of sexual bliss," he murmured.

Sexual bliss indeed…

Blaze™

Dear Reader,

I hope you're ready for a hot, wild, sexy read!

West Virginia, with its lush mountains and deep river valleys, seemed just the place to set a humorous story with a taste of mystery. At first, sexy Rex Houston, a doctor from the Centers for Disease Control and Prevention, isn't that thrilled about taking a trip to the tiny town of Bliss, but everything changes when he meets Ariel!

Enjoy their love story!

Jule McBride

Books by Jule McBride

HARLEQUIN BLAZE
67—THE SEX FILES
91—ALL TUCKED IN…

SOMETHING IN THE WATER...

Jule McBride

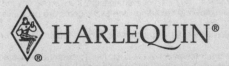

HARLEQUIN®

TORONTO • NEW YORK • LONDON
AMSTERDAM • PARIS • SYDNEY • HAMBURG
STOCKHOLM • ATHENS • TOKYO • MILAN • MADRID
PRAGUE • WARSAW • BUDAPEST • AUCKLAND

ISBN 0-373-79230-1

SOMETHING IN THE WATER...

www.eHarlequin.com

Printed in U.S.A.

1

"TELL US ABOUT Matilda Teasdale again, Pappy," urged sixteen-year-old Jeb Pass. He blew blond bangs from brown eyes, then glanced at his gangly dark-haired buddy, Marsh, who was seated next to him on a fallen tree limb, staring across the dying campfire at Jeb's grandpa. Pappy tugged his beard and petted his gray mutt, Hammerhead; the dog was curled up, his tail twitching in tandem with a red bandana around his neck, as if he were chasing rabbits in his dreams.

"Seems to me," Pappy mused, "by now you ought to know all the stories about Matilda by heart. You boys were born and bred in Bliss, and with Jeb being a history buff and all, too."

"C'mon, Pappy," Jeb insisted. "Was she really a witch?"

"Or just some weird lady from England?" Marsh squinted.

"I bet she *was* a witch," said Jeb. "I even bet they tried to burn her at the stake, the way everybody said. That's why she came to America in the first place. Huh, Pappy?"

Pappy considered, surveying the star-studded night sky. "I reckon no one really knows, seeing as Matilda came to Bliss in the 1700s. She'd brought enough money to the one-block mining town to build the house overlooking the spring. People claimed she'd come with only a Native American guide to help carry two worn leather trunks. It was said he was a Cherokee medicine man who'd offered Matilda safe passage across the mountains in exchange for her secret blends of curative teas. Some said she wasn't a witch at all, but that she came to Bliss because her teas could only reach full potency when blended with the world's finest water." Pappy smiled. "And that means from Spice Spring."

"But how'd she hear about the spring if she was living in England?" Marsh asked.

Pappy shrugged. "Your guess is as good as mine, kid."

Suddenly shuddering, Jeb stared across the spring, settling his gaze where the surface glimmered under moonlight. When his eyes found the opposite shore, they floated up the stone steps carved into the mountainside and stopped at the top of the hill, on the old Victorian house that local kids had nicknamed Teasdale's Terror.

The women who lived there now each went by the last name of Anderson, not Teasdale, but they were related to Matilda. Anderson was a name that one of the women—no one really knew which one—had gotten by marriage. How summer visitors managed to stay in the huge house, now a bed-and-breakfast, Jeb would never know. The place looked about as homey as Dracula's castle. He wondered if Michelle McNulty had really bought magical teas there last summer, the way she'd claimed. Every year, Michelle came from Charleston with her family and rented a cabin on the water, but this year she seemed...well, grown up.

It wasn't just that she'd gotten a job waitressing at Jack's on Bliss Run Road, then had started moonlighting by helping to construct booths for the upcoming Harvest Festival, taking place at the end of the week. There were other changes, like how she'd filled out under her T-shirts more than most soon-to-be high-school freshmen. When she fixed Jeb a pie or soda, he could see her breasts sway under cotton and even make out her nipples pointing out, thanks to the air-conditioning Jack blasted in the diner.

This summer, Michelle had quit holding Jeb's gaze, as if she'd realized her looks were affecting him and couldn't handle it. Not that Jeb could offer any advice, but he did have fantasies of sitting beside her in the Bliss theater, the only place in town showing first-run movies. Afterward, he figured he might cup her knee with his hand, then run it ever so slowly upward on her thigh....

"Ah," murmured Pappy, following Jeb's gaze, "The Teasdale Terror House."

"Now, are those witches really related to Matilda?" asked Marsh, speaking of the Andersons—the great-grandmother and two generations of daughters. A fourth Anderson, Ariel Anderson, had flown the coup years ago. "Maybe they really did kill their husbands," he added darkly. "That's what some people say."

"I don't think they're witches," Pappy chided. "When you see them in town, you know as well as I do that they're always polite."

"A cover," assured Jeb.

Pappy chuckled. "They do dress weird."

"All in black," added Marsh. "Like someone died."

"Their husbands." Jeb nodded with assurance. "The

oldest one's got to be a hundred years old. They say she still moves like lightning, and uses a broomstick, instead of a cane. None of them ever go to the movies or take vacations."

Marsh looked vindicated. "And they sell those teas."

Pappy smiled. "The ladies do own a tearoom, boys."

"They don't have friends," Marsh continued.

"And no one will go up there in the winter," added Jeb, although he'd done so on a dare once. It had been a snowy night, and when he'd reached the wraparound porch and prepared to ring the doorbell, the wind had picked up, howling in his ears, and he'd wrenched around, staring toward the woods where Marsh and their buddies had sworn they'd wait. He'd seen only evergreens, which he'd figured sheltered everything from ghosts to bobcats.

Just as he'd been about to press the doorbell, Jeb had heard a branch break. Wolves in the woods, he'd thought, then leaves had rustled, and Jeb had realized, someone—or some*thing*—was pushing aside the underbrush, moving toward him, steadily.

That's when Sam Anderson—Sam was short for Samantha—had swung open the heavy front door so swiftly that it had snapped backward on its groaning hinges; the heavy brass demon-head knocker clanked and wind ruffled a white apron Sam had worn over a long black dress. She was Granny Anderson's daughter and Ariel's mother. "What are you doing out there, Jeb Pass? Why, you'd better come in. It's colder than a witch's—" Chuckling, she'd cut off her speech and scrutinized him through devilish eyes.

Spinning around, he'd run all the way down witches

mountain, sure that whatever he'd heard chasing him was huge and hairy, with claws that could shred him to pieces. Of course, that had been years ago. Way back in seventh grade.

"In the winter, all they do is read books from the library," Marsh was saying.

"Giblets is the only one they ever talk to. *Miss Gibbet,*" Jeb corrected. Elsinore Gibbet, the librarian, was well past sixty and as scrawny as a chicken, with extra skin under her chin and a chirpy voice that had inspired local kids to call her Chicken Giblets. Jeb continued, "At the library, she showed me a history book that says weird stuff's always gone on in Bliss, Pappy. Starting in the 1700s—"

"After Matilda came to town," Marsh put in.

"They say there started to be periods of time when…"

"Something goes…well, buggy," Pappy suggested.

Jeb nodded. "And because of it, Miss Gibbet said people used to come from all over the place, just to swim in Spice Spring."

"From as far away as China," continued Marsh.

"Especially during summers like this one," Pappy added. "When the water's been chilled by a series of cold snaps, then the weather heats up again. And during such a summer, when the sun, moon and stars align just right, they say a dip in Spice Spring can change your life. Especially your love life."

Jeb thought of Michelle and felt his cheeks warm.

Pappy went on. "At the end of the summer, folks used to come here from bigger towns to bottle the water. And of course, they'd head up the hill, to the Andersons', for medicinal teas."

Jeb thought of the mysterious book of tea recipes said to have been handed down by Matilda. According to rumor, the book had a cloth cover and pages so yellow and brittle that it had to be kept in a safe in the witches' root cellar.

As every kid in Bliss knew, the Anderson women had taken to hiding from the public and wearing black. Except for the youngest one, Ariel. When she'd kissed the witch house and tearoom goodbye and roared out of Bliss on her Harley Davidson motorcycle eleven years ago, she'd been wearing red fishnets, a tight leather miniskirt and a top that had looked more like fancy underwear. Jeb had only been five years old, but it was the sort of moment no one ever forgot.

Later, he'd heard all the hot gossip about the sexy things she'd done with Studs Underwood, years before he'd gotten elected sheriff. Even now, Jeb's face colored, since some of the local guys could get pretty descriptive when it came to tales of Ariel.

"When the moon's just right and the stars align," Marsh began again. "And they make teas with water from Spice Spring...is that when you get cured from whatever's bothering you?"

"Not so much illnesses," said Pappy. "But matters of the heart. You know, sadness. Loneliness. That sort of thing. At least, that's what I always heard. And of course, those women make love potions." Pappy raised a bony finger. "But don't you start getting ideas about stealing that book of theirs. Attempts have never been successful."

"I'd hate to get the widows mad," admitted Marsh.

"I remember," Pappy continued, "just a couple years

back, the sheriff got called up to the tearoom. Somebody had taken a hatchet to the root-cellar door, tied a rope around the safe and tried to drag it up the steps."

"Guess they couldn't get it open," Marsh offered.

"I heard about that," said Jeb. "It took three men to haul it back downstairs." He followed his grandfather's gaze over the water. The source of the spring was deeper than Jeb and his buddies could dive, although they'd spent summers trying. Once, Jeb had gotten close enough to feel the heat bubbling from beneath; it was as if a hole had opened onto the earth's fiery core.

The spring's source was directly under the mountain on which Terror House was perched. It was as if the spring itself had given rise to the steep, conical, lushly vegetated hill, as well as the house that sat on top, like a dark cherry. It was weird, Jeb thought, how the spring, rather than coal, had become the town's black gold. That, and the visitors summering there.

"At least the Core Coal Company didn't wind up strip-mining here," Jeb said.

Pappy nodded his agreement. "If they'd done that, you wouldn't see a spot of green left in these hills."

Jeb had been studying that piece of town lore, so he knew that, in the late seventies, when the economy had been at its worst, the Lyons family had begun to buy land, promising to develop the area as a summer resort. Later, everyone had found that the consortium they'd belonged to was actually planning to strip-mine, which would have left the hills barren. Without vegetation to filter rainwater, the crystal spring would have been destroyed.

Jeb sighed. None of that had happened, thankfully. Eli Saltwell, now a crotchety old recluse pushing ninety, had uncovered the plot and told everybody in town. So, Bliss had become a summer resort, but one run by locals, not the consortium. It didn't have the promised fancy hotels, but then, most people felt that was just as well, since out-of-towners came anyway.

In another week, after the Harvest Festival, the summer visitors would be gone, though. *Michelle* would be gone. Jeb's heart squeezed in a way that was both unwelcome and unfamiliar. He'd give anything to kiss her once. Maybe even slip his hand under her shirt and cup a breast. His throat tightened as he imagined her sweet pink lips parting, asking for more....

Pappy's voice drew him from the reverie, and before Jeb could concentrate on the words, he was conscious once more of the thick, dark blanket of air around him, and of the red-yellow glow of logs crackling on the fire, not to mention the pup tent and his unrolled sleeping bag. He heard the hoot of an owl, the whine of crickets, and then stared up at the impossibly yellow globe of a full moon hanging in the sky, bisected by the turret.

It was pure magic.

"It really is one of those special years," Pappy mused. "We've had a series of early cold snaps, and now summer's back in the air. Once—I guess it was way back in 1790—not long after Matilda arrived, they say we had this kind of strange weather. Unpredictable. Cold then hot, with a few electrical storms thrown in for good measure. They say, for about a week, everything in Bliss..."

Jeb and Marsh scooted on the log, as if to get closer to Pappy. "What?" Jeb said.

"Went silent," Pappy continued. "A woman named Nellie White was supposed to travel to see her mama over in Buchanan, but never went, as she'd promised. And they say Archibald Evans, the blacksmith, didn't get out of Bliss to shoe some horses, even though he had an appointment. The local paper—it was only one sheet long in those days—wasn't delivered the way it was on most Fridays."

Pappy paused. "They say it happened again, not long after that, too, back in 1806."

"I heard a train came through. They'd built the tracks by then," said Marsh. "But it didn't leave the station for a week, and the conductor would never say why."

"And in 1865, right?" added Jeb, his voice quickening. "That's what Gib—uh, Miss Gibbet—told me and Marsh."

"Yeah," agreed Marsh. "She said it was during the Civil War. The North was coming one way, and the South was coming another—"

"But both sides laid down their weapons," continued Jeb.

"And no one knows why," Pappy finished.

Jeb nodded. "Miss Gibbet said the war picked right back up, though."

"And then she said that in 1943—" began Marsh.

"When the munitions factory was here—"

"It didn't deliver orders for guns," said Jeb. "There was a blackout, too. And no phone service. Planes flew overhead, and pilots said, from the air, the town looked totally dark."

"Now, if all that was true," said Pappy with a soft chuckle, "you'd think the U.S. government would get involved. Still, according to statistics, they do say a lot of babies have been conceived during those lost weeks.

In fact, my mama got pregnant with me during the blackout of forty-four, if you must know."

Jeb said, "No way!"

Pappy crossed a finger over his heart. "So I'm told. There's no pattern to when the town...well, goes silent. But they do say it happens when the weather's like this."

Marsh guffawed. "Wish it would happen week after next, after the Harvest Festival."

"Fat chance," Jeb said, trying not to think of the festival, and his last chance to get closer to Michelle. "That's when school starts."

"A blackout the first week of school. You two should be so lucky."

Lucky. Warmth flooded Jeb's cheeks. He sure wished he could get lucky with Michelle. Leaning, he lifted his canteen, unscrewed the cap, then took a deep swig. One thing was certain—the springwater that was purified in the reservoir then pumped into local homes was the best stuff Jeb had ever tasted. It had none of the aftertaste Jeb had tasted in city water—not the hints of metal, nor the soapy texture he couldn't stand. Nope. Despite the heat that came mysteriously from its hidden source, Spice Spring always stayed as crisp as a winter morning, and the water seemed to bubble when it hit your tongue. No doubt, the spring delivered the champagne of water. Jeb took another deep draft, and just as he did, he imagined spending a lost week in Bliss with Michelle McNulty.

"Earth to Jeb," said Pappy.

"Ditto that," said Marsh.

But Jeb was gone, lost in Michelle McNulty's open arms.

Peru

A WORLD AWAY, Angus Lyons gathered the strands of his shoulder-length silver hair into a ponytail, then he lifted the receiver of a field phone and stared through the open canvas flaps of his tent door, wondering who was bothering to call him in the rain forest. "Yeah?"

"Where are you? Sounds like you're a hundred feet under water that's been electrified with static."

"That's about right," Angus admitted, fingering his thick silver beard and wondering if he should trim it, in deference to the heat. Gazing into a spray of morning mist, he took in vaulting curtains of green leaves and mammoth trunks of trees untouched by civilization. And never would be, if Angus had his way. As he considered the losing battle to preserve places such as this, Angus wished he was younger. At sixty, his time wasn't exactly running out, but he didn't have his whole life in front of him, either, and there was no one to carry on his mission. Since his wife Linda's death two years ago, he'd felt like a buoy cut loose on the open sea.

"Aren't you even going to ask who this is?"

Angus laughed. "Why don't you just tell me?"

"Jack Hayes. News director at WCBK TV in Pittsburgh."

"Pittsburgh?" He didn't know anyone in—

"We went to school—"

Now it came to him. "Harvard, class of sixty-five. Hell, I haven't seen you since the last reunion, Jack. What can I do for you?"

"Well…I've got an employee named Ariel Anderson, who's from Bliss, West Virginia. She's keen to do a human-interest story about her hometown, and we gave her the go-ahead. But in the pitch, she mentioned your name, and the possibility of including information about your involvement with—"

"The Core Coal Company buyout in the late seventies," Angus muttered. "Attempted buyout," he corrected.

"I was surprised," Jack continued. "I always think of you as involved in nonprofit. And...well, aren't you out there saving the rain forests, or some such?"

"Trying," said Angus noncommittally, even though right now, his business associations, nonprofit or otherwise, were the furthest thing from his mind. He was remembering a long-ago summer and a pretty, young, small-town girl with strawberry hair, a great body and a smile to die for. Even now, he could still see her swimming in springwater so clear and deep that he'd felt he was looking into the core of the earth whenever he'd stared into the depths. Suddenly, with a stab of guilt, Angus thought of his deceased wife, Linda.

"I thought I'd better call," Jack continued. "I told Ariel to keep the town's business history out of the story since the piece isn't supposed to be a coal-industry exposé...."

"You wanted to see if dredging up past history would cause me any trouble," Angus guessed. Before Jack could answer, he continued, "I appreciate it. And yeah, I'd prefer to keep my name out of any story about Core Coal and Bliss. I did have some involvement down there." And now, when he thought of the place, his heart ached. It was the only place he'd ever seen that was as lush and green with vegetation as the rain forests he'd come to tend and love. "You say the woman's name is Ariel *Anderson?*"

"Uh...yeah. Why?"

"No reason. Just curious."

"I don't know much about her," Jack offered, "except that she came from Bliss and wound up at the University of Pittsburgh. After grad school, she came onboard at WCBK, and she's been here three years. So, she's still young. Thirty, tops. A tough cookie. Ambitious. One of those people who's out to prove herself."

Angus knew the type. He'd been well into adulthood before he'd realized that the phantoms from which he'd been running had only existed in his own imagination. "And she's from Bliss?" he said, soliciting a chuckle from Jack.

"A town that's aptly named, I'd imagine. I don't know why, but most women I've ever met who've come from those West Virginia hills are gorgeous, and she's no exception. Tall and blond, with incredible skin and a smile that stops every man in his tracks." Jack laughed. "Not that she bothers to use it. A yuppie with a heart of steel, with a Southern twang wrapped in a throaty voice that sounds just like Kathleen Turner's. I think her boss, a guy by the name of Ryan Vermere, has got a hopeless crush on her."

"If I ever meet her," Angus said, "I'll keep all that in mind."

"No chance, Angus. This one's made for glass and concrete. Two-martini lunches. The kind of girl for whom nothing's ever going to be enough. Definitely, she's not the type to stop and smell flowers, so I doubt you'd ever bump into her in a rain forest."

That was exactly why, thought Angus as he hung up the phone and reached for his suitcase, he was heading for Bliss, West Virginia.

Atlanta, Georgia
Centers for Disease Control and Prevention

"THIS BETTER BE GOOD," Rex Houston muttered good-naturedly. Holding out his arms, he let a tech disconnect the air hose attached to the white suit, then Rex went next door where, once more, he held out his arms and let another tech hose him down, then help him strip off the gear.

Butt-naked, he headed for yet another shower, then for a locker room where, without bothering with underwear, he shoved long legs into jeans, and sockless feet into leather Dockers. He was still buttoning a white shirt as he strode down a hallway toward his boss's office.

Behind him, somebody wolf-whistled. One of the techs called out, "Sexy Rexy." He was used to the teasing. Tossing a bemused smirk over his shoulder he pushed open a door. He stared at his boss and said, "You called?"

"Come on in. Sit."

"Nothing like your bedside manner." Sauntering into the room, as if he'd had nothing better to do today, such as be suited up in the bio-level-four lab, he seated himself in one of the leather roller chairs. Not bad, he thought, his eyes taking in the plush office, for a lady who'd never seen field action. Nope, Jessica Williams—an upper-crust type from South Carolina who'd been born and bred in a navy suit—would never get her lily hands dirty with viruses as deadly as Ebola or hantavirus.

"I have an assignment for you."

The words were pure bliss, and Rex's pique evaporated like water under a hot sun. "An assignment?" Already, in his mind's eye, Rex was packing...traveling to one of the world's hot-spots, probably some small town in Africa. Already, he could hear the chopper blades beating and the clipped tone of a pilot as he put the bird down while filling in Rex's team, regarding the number dead, the course of some new unknown disease. "What's the bug look like? Has anyone identified it?"

Jessica shook her head. "Actually, nothing's really happened yet. We just got a call from a local."

Rex's mind was racing. "Only one call?" That was hardly enough to interest the CDC, much less to get people such as him—known in the field as cowboys—involved in a case.

"Homeland Security," Jessica reminded.

Since 9-11, anything that vaguely smacked of bioterror needed to be checked out thoroughly. "And you don't have any information?" That would make the case even more interesting. Rex was part of a team that had traced more than one virus back to its native origins. "My shots are up to date," Rex assured, "and I'm ready to go. I can be on a plane within the next hour."

"Glad to hear it."

Now that he knew an assignment was involved, he was relieved to be getting out of the lab in Atlanta. "Where to?"

"Bliss."

That stopped him cold. He stared.

"Bliss," Jessica repeated, now looking as if she were bracing herself for a fight. Not a good sign. "West Virginia. An overnight trip," she added quickly. "To be honest, we got a hysterical call from an elderly woman named Elsinore Gibbet—"

"Since when does the CDC respond to hysterical calls from elderly women?"

"Careful or I'll cite you for sexism. She called the World Health Organization and the Department of Homeland Security," Jessica continued.

He sighed. If anything really happened, Jessica wanted to make sure CDC got dibs. "Let me get this right," Rex muttered. "Some lady called and—"

"Look, I just want you to go test the water. You're in, you're out. Overnight. If you don't find anything, World Health won't go down."

"I'm not a fireman who chases kittens up tree trunks."

"I need an M.D., not a tech. If you go, the other organizations are covered. Besides, there might be something to the complaint. There have been times when something odd happens in this town. Like unexplainable blackouts." Pausing, Jessica shoved a file across her desk. "It's all right here."

Rex didn't reach for the case file.

"I'm thinking you might find evidence of the virus we've nicknamed Romeo," she prodded.

"Why me?" Rex groaned. According to office rumors, the virus to which she was referring had only been documented once, in South America, two years back, and then the documentation had mysteriously been lost. Most people assumed the bug had never existed, and that the references to it had been created as a joke. "You're sending me to look for the love bug," he said flatly. "You've got to be kidding."

"The bug makes people lose inhibitions," Jessica countered. "And we've not yet seen it in the States. It can cause temporary euphoria, a high that's said to result in increased sexual behavior. Given the patterns of unusual activity in the town, dating back to the 1700s, as well as the local reliance on a spring, as in the South American case—"

"The case is not documented."

"It was, but the documents were destroyed."

"I don't believe in documents that don't exist."

"Well then, take some that do," Jessica said, pushing the file toward him. "We have pictures of the bug, drawn by people who saw it."

He considered. The last thing he wanted to explore was a love bug, and not just because people all over the world were dying of real diseases that deserved his attention. There was also the matter of Janet Kaston. She'd been a tech at CDC when he'd met her a year ago, and like no other woman he'd ever known. She'd come to the city from a farm in the backwoods of Georgia, and she was pretty in a girl-next-door kind of way. As nice as pie, too, and the first woman he'd dated whom his mother had actually liked.

Within months, he'd found himself engaged. He'd let himself get roped into hours of conversations about kids and mortgages, too. And his folks, who'd despaired of him ever settling down, couldn't have been more thrilled. Hell, he'd surprised himself when he'd proposed. And he'd liked sex with Janet. It wasn't the down-and-dirty, no-holds-barred kind he usually sought out. She'd been all hearts and flowers, and while she'd left him cold, on some physical levels, her seeming lack of experience had conned his heart. *Seeming* and *conned* being the operative words.

Just two weeks before the wedding, Rex had found his soon-to-be bride in the kitchen pantry of the country club where their rehearsal dinner was to be held. As much as he'd tried to block it from his mind, he could still see her clearly, down on her knees, delivering more than catering orders to their chef, who'd frosted a hard-on with cake icing from Rex's own wedding cake.

The betrayal had hurt more than anything. As it turned out, she'd been a wild child with a string of boyfriends back in Georgia, whom she'd never told Rex about. He'd been part of her plan to straighten up her act by landing a doctor husband who could give her a soccer-mom lifestyle.

He'd walked out of the pantry and never looked back. Which was why a trip to an Ebola-ridden desert town would have been welcome. There was nothing like living in a village devastated by disease to keep a man on his toes, and his mind in the present.

Romeo—otherwise known as *generis misealius*—had never even killed anyone. If it had even really existed.

"It's an order," Jessica said.

Bliss, West Virginia, he thought. Without even seeing a map, he knew what the town would look like. Two blocks long and probably in a dry county. With any luck, though, there'd be a Hooters the next town over. Rex sure didn't need a love drug to tell him he was horny. It had been months since Janet, and while he never intended to engage his emotions again—he could sure use some sex. Against his will, he reached for the folder. "Did you book a hotel?"

"None in the area."

"Don't tell me. I'll be sleeping in a tent, right?"

"A bed-and-breakfast," she corrected. "The fanciest place up there. It's called the Teasdale Teahouse."

So much for Hooters. "A teahouse," he echoed.

She smiled sweetly. "A car's outside. It'll take you

by your house and to the airport. Your plane leaves in an hour." She glanced at her watch. "Forty minutes," she corrected.

His return smile matched hers for sincerity. They eyed each other a long moment. "Well then, as much as I hate to leave you, Jessica, I guess I'd better go." With that, he rose, lifted the file, then strode from her office. He'd just crossed the threshold when, from behind him, he heard her wolf whistle.

"Careful," he tossed over his shoulder, "or I'll charge you with sexual harassment."

He could still hear his boss laughing when he hit the stifling August air. "Bliss," he muttered. And a teahouse, no less. Now, why was he so sure he was headed for the tenth rung of hell?

2

ARIEL SPUN THE DIAL of the Honda Accord's radio. On the local station, the Beatles were crooning, "Love, love, love…" Was this a joke? The previous song on the local station had been "Moon River", and the one before, "Every Breath You Take."

She blew out a sigh, clutched the wheel with both hands and stared anxiously from Bliss Run Road to the spring, which she could glimpse between the trees, then to the distant hill. Her heart constricted. At the top, she could just make out bits of the house where she'd grown up—tips of turrets, flashes of mint-and-lemon trim. Despite the colors visible under the blazing sun, the shape of the place was foreboding.

Her gaze returned to the road. Tied between phone poles, a white banner flew overhead, announcing the Harvest Festival. "Now, that's odd," she murmured. The Bliss theater was showing only black-and-white romantic movies this week. Tonight, *Casablanca* was paired with *Bringing Up Baby.* Glancing upward, she glimpsed the teahouse again and punched the gas. She was running hours behind schedule, and God only knew what was going on at the proverbial ranch. She'd gotten a call from Great-gran this morning, saying that someone had broken into the root cellar, opened the safe and stolen the book of Matilda Teasdale's tea recipes. They'd had to call the sheriff, which meant Ariel was going to have to talk to Studs Underwood.

Feeling sure her blood pressure was skyrocketing, Ariel took a deep breath. The last person she wanted to see was Studs. Oh, she'd heard the rumors about all the sexual things she'd done for him. She'd given him tongue baths, made love to another woman in his presence and worn crotchless panties—when she'd bothered to wear any underwear at all. Oh, yeah. And what else? Allegedly she and Studs had been the hottest couple ever to hit Bliss.

That he was now married to Joanie Summers hardly helped matters. Ariel glanced into the rearview mirror. Thankfully, she looked great. The eleven years since she'd left Bliss hadn't aged her a bit. She could still afford to go light on the makeup accentuating her blue eyes. Her straight, long, wild blond hair was pulled severely back, and turned neatly into a tight French roll, the pins of which were starting to give her a headache, if she was honest about it.

Not that she'd give in to temptation and let down her hair. She'd brought mostly suits, all of them more expensive than she could afford, and the one she wore now—a pale pink silk skirt and jacket, with a white silk blouse beneath—made her look impossibly demure. She couldn't wait until tonight, since she planned to wear it into Jack's Diner, and give the town something to buzz about. It was a far cry from the fishnets and miniskirt she'd worn the day she'd left Bliss. She'd been home in the many years since then, of course, but usually, she'd kept out of sight, staying put in the teahouse. When she had ventured onto Bliss Run Road, she'd never sported a total makeover.

This outfit hit the right note, with matching pumps that gave just enough lift to accentuate her calves but not so much that she looked like she was inviting attention. Yes, she thought, her hands tightening around the wheel, her long-awaited plan to restore her good name was definitely going to work. Color flooded her cheeks as she thought of how she'd roared out of town eleven years ago, on the back of her flame-red Harley. No doubt about it, back then she'd been hell on wheels, with the world's worst reputation to uphold. But once she'd gotten out of Bliss, she'd been able to start finding herself. Not Ariel Anderson, youngest of the four weird, witchy, widowed Andersons.

Now she was about to put Bliss on the map, nationally. And that would make people in town finally respect her. Her heart squeezed tightly. Her family, as well. Her mom, Gran and Great-gran weren't nearly as strange as the young kids always made out. No stranger than Chicken Giblets, really. But the three women did keep to themselves, wear dark clothes, and keep mum about their mysterious family history, especially Ariel's mother when it came to answering questions about the identity of Ariel's father.

Her lips tightened. She couldn't dwell on that right now. Nor on the fact that she was going to have to talk to Studs, since the recipe book had been stolen. "We've got to get it back before the festival," she muttered. Not only was the book of deep sentimental value, but she'd hoped to include shots of it for the feature spot she was putting together for WCBK. She'd considered mentioning the near buyout of the local land by Core Coal in the seventies, but the news director, Jack Hayes, had pushed the story in a more human-interest direction. Her more immediate boss, Ryan, had agreed.

Just the thought of Ryan made her lips go dry, so she reached for a bottled water and took a sip. He'd been asking her out, and if the story went well, and she got a transfer to another department, and without the taint of her adolescent reputation still hanging over her head…

She'd start to loosen up. Feel more free, sexually. Ryan was everything she wanted. Which meant the opposite of every man she'd ever met in Bliss. Of average build, with sandy-brown hair and brown eyes, he was the type to open doors and pay for his date…inclined to wear suits even when he didn't need to for an occasion. Still, it was hard to imagine introducing such a normal guy to her family. But she'd cross that bridge when she came to it. She hadn't even dated him yet, much less slept with him.

Her gaze narrowed, and she did a double take. Something was different about Jack's Diner. "New curtains," she decided. From a distance, it looked as if the fabric was printed with hearts. That was very strange, since Jack's tastes ran to keg parties, hunting up in the mountains with his buddies and decorating with American flags.

His sister, she suddenly thought, solving the mystery. She was a seamstress. Probably, she'd taken it upon herself to spruce the place up. Which would make the town eatery even more photogenic for her piece, Ariel realized.

She wished she'd been able to bring her own cameraman from Pittsburgh. Instead, Jack Hayes and Ryan had arranged for a stringer to come down to Bliss from nearby Charleston. This way, she could spend the week vacationing and refining the text of the spot by considering possible camera shots and interviews. She'd have the man shoot a day's worth of tape, and when she returned to Pittsburgh, she'd edit it herself.

No matter what happened—whether locals teased her or Studs referenced all that past business—she'd hold her head high. No one in town was going to see so much as a hair out of place. Her story might get picked up nationally, too. That was her biggest hope. She'd taken great care to create just the sort of piece—a small-town festival—with which the networks always ended their evening newscasts.

"What the—" She didn't finish, but wrenched her head around. "What's Great-gran doing in town?" She never left the house. Ariel slowed, intending to stop and offer her great grandmother a lift, but she was standing in front of the hardware store, having a heated debate with Eli Saltwell; no one ever talked to Eli, especially not Great-gran. She'd been feuding with him ever since Ariel could remember. As far as Great-gran was concerned, Eli was responsible for everything from rising taxes to bad weather. The source of the conflict had remained a mystery. Her great-gran spit and crossed the street whenever she saw Eli, and on the rare occasions she'd gone to town, she'd always refused to enter any local store when Eli had been inside.

She was still considering whether to pull over when Joanie Summers—now Underwood—exited the hardware store, raised a hand and waved. Stunned, Ariel turned toward the windshield again, half expecting to see someone else. Surely, Joanie wasn't waving at her, not when Ariel and Joanie's husband, Studs, used to be the talk of Bliss! But no, Joanie really was waving at her, and Great-gran really was deeply immersed in a conversation with Eli. Realizing someone had stepped in front of her car, Ariel gasped once more, then simultaneously pressed the horn and depressed the brakes.

A hand came down hard on the hood. And Ariel, her heart now beating out of control, clamped a hand to her chest. It was Chicken Giblets.

Elsinore Gibbet swiftly circled the car, at least as quickly as an octogenarian in a floral-print housedress and blue-rinsed hair could, so Ariel began powering down the passenger-side window, but it was too late. Already, Giblets had wrenched open the door, lunged inside and slammed the door shut, while saying ominously, "I'm so glad you're here, Ariel."

Realizing Jack was behind her in the diner's truck, Ariel had no choice but to depress the gas pedal again. As she drove, she fought the feeling that her well-planned trip to Bliss had just nosedived and was heading in a southerly direction. Doing another double take, she saw a man she didn't recognize and who didn't look like one of the summer visitors. He was deeply tanned, with long silver hair tied back in a ponytail and a silver beard.

Not that she had time for more than a glimpse. "Uh…Miss Gibbet," she began, since she'd never known what to call people who'd been in positions of authority when she'd been younger, such as teachers or librarians.

"It's okay, honey," she said, as if reading Ariel's

mind. "You're old enough to call me Elsinore now. Head on up to your place, and I'll fill you in on all the details."

Details? "Fill me in?" Ariel echoed.

"You're a reporter, right?"

"I'm here working on a story, yes."

Fighting a sense of foreboding, she turned off Bliss Run Road onto Mountain Drive, a narrow two-lane stretch of incline. She cast a glance into the rearview mirror, still unable to believe her great-gran had been speaking with Eli Saltwell.

"Your great-gran and Eli aren't the half of it," assured Elsinore, as if reading her mind once more. "The Bliss theater is only showing romance movies, you can only get romance songs on the local radio, and Jack's introduced an early-bird breakfast special for two. But don't worry. I called the CDC."

"The CDC?"

"The Centers for Disease Control. In Atlanta."

"I know what the CDC is," Ariel managed to say.

"Then why did you ask?" returned Elsinore, looking miffed.

Ariel gaped at the librarian. It was bad enough that the recipe book, Ariel's relatives' pride and joy, not to mention a feature element in Ariel's news story, had been stolen, but… "Why did you call the CDC?"

"Well, you know the stories about the spring…." Elsinore began.

Ariel had no idea where this was heading. "Uh huh."

"Well, it's rumored that Pappy Pass and his ex-wife, Maime, are getting back together. Then, there's the fact that Eli and your great-gran are talking. Ever since Matilda—" Elsinore paused. "Nothing against your family, Ariel," she began again, "but ever since she came, there's been nothing but trouble. First, the town went dead in 1790, then in 1806."

Ariel's heart was sinking as her childhood home came into view. What if the town really had…well, shut down in the past? "Those are just town legends, Elsinore," she said uncertainly.

"There's proof in the history books, and you know it."

"Local history books, mostly," Ariel pointed out. "And those are full of fanciful folktales."

Elsinore pursed her lips primly and Ariel looked at the cars in the lot. Seeing her mother's old black Cadillac, and Gran's silver Eldorado, Ariel wondered how her great-gran had gotten to town. The rest of the cars—about ten—belonged to guests. There was one huge black RV that looked more like a military vehicle. Figuring she'd unload the Honda after she said hello, she pulled in front of the wraparound porch. "Let's go inside. I'll bet Mom's got some iced tea made," she said cordially, as she moved to get out of the car. "Don't worry, Elsinore, we'll get to the bottom of all this."

"I've already gotten to the bottom of it," Elsinore said, "and your family is responsible. It was Matilda who brought this on us, and now, it's all happening again. I predict that, within a week, all industry in Bliss will shut down."

"Uh-huh," Ariel couldn't help but say dryly. "And that would be…what? Jack's Diner? Oh, right," she added. "I forgot. The ice-cream truck."

"And the canoe-and-bike rental stand," Elsinore put in.

Taking a deep breath, Ariel shut her car door, wincing at the stifling heat, then she went up the porch stairs, with Elsinore on her heels. As she pushed through a door, foyer, and into the living room, she inhaled audibly. What was going on here? A shoulder duffel was near the door, as if no one had bothered to check in a guest. Next to it was a six-pack of bottled water and a thick manila file. Slowly, her eyes followed a trail of black clothes—shoes, stockings...

Feeling off balance, she quickly swiped them from the Chinese rug, terrified a guest might see them. It looked as if one of her relatives had started disrobing in the public rooms, while going toward the back of the house. Ariel scanned the terrain and saw another hint of black through some French doors.

"A slip," she whispered, lifting it from the doorknob. Outside, the air was truly unbearable, making her miss the air-conditioning in the car. Through a thicket of trees, she could hear splashing in the pool to her left. It sounded as if most of the guests were swimming, but she had a suspicion that...

Her pulse ticked fast in her throat as her eyes trailed down the flight of steps carved into the mountain, to where a black dress flew on a pole near the dock, waving like a flag. Ariel shut her eyes. Counted to ten. Opened them again—only to find this was not her overactive imagination. Her mother was swimming in the spring, and judging by the trail of clothes, she was only wearing a bra and panties. As she heard Elsinore gasp, Ariel realized that there were no scents of dinner in the house, even though it was nearly two o'clock. Her relatives did the cooking, and often, because of the Southern fare they served, beans or stewed tomatoes would be on the stove by now.

All the fantastical stories she'd heard in her youth suddenly came racing back. Swiftly, she whirled, feeling panicked, thinking she'd better return to the porch.

She gasped. She'd run right into something hard and as dripping wet as the spring. Just as she glanced up, big sexy-feeling hands closed around the sleeves of her pale pink jacket; seemingly, the move was meant to steady her; instead, her hips locked with a male stranger's, and her cheek hit a pectoral smelling of chlorinated water. Something else, too. Something more intriguing, less definable. Even though he felt cold from the water, he was hot, too. Yes, he was pure burning fire, sizzling out of control and searing every inch of her. Unbidden, her hands reached, landing naturally on his waist, and she could feel the skin alive beneath her fingertips.

The second her fingers touched his wet skin, the whole world seemed to slide off-kilter. She could almost believe she, herself, had just drunk a gallon of Matilda's love tea made with springwater. Or as if she, herself, had just plunged into the spring during one of those freaky end-of-summer nights when the water was reputed to be most pungent.

Knowing she was losing her mind, she made herself step back and stared at her soaked suit. As she slipped swiftly out of the jacket and shook off the water, she looked up. "Oh, no," she murmured, her dismayed tone coming more in response to the man's good looks than anything else.

His gaze had landed on her chest, too, and while she'd thought the aversion of his eyes was due to embarrassment at their collision, she now realized her silk blouse had gotten as wet as the jacket. Silently, she cursed herself for removing her jacket, since despite the summery air, her nipples had been affected by the icy water and constricted. Heat vying with the August humidity flushed her cheeks.

His gaze didn't hold an ounce of apology, either. In fact, his eyes looked hot and predatory. Feeling strangely faint, but not about to let him unbalance her, she stared right back. Surely, her weakening knees had less to do with him than the fact that the temperature had to be hovering near ninety.

She realized he was blond. It was hard to tell what kind of blond—light or medium, since his hair was wet. Nor could she tell how long it was, since dry, she imagined it might have some wave to it. But it was hard to tell. Either way, it was slicked back and tucked behind his ears. His red swimsuit was tight and wet, and his strong chest was tanned the color of chestnuts.

She sighed deeply, willing away unwanted sensations. Fate couldn't be this unkind to her. Two hours ago, she'd been on top of the world, ready to put Bliss on the map by covering the Harvest Festival. Now, the recipe book had been stolen, and Elsinore was convinced Bliss had gone…well, *buggy* for the first time in sixty years. Even worse, Ariel had now run right into a man who'd threaten any decent woman's reputation, not to mention her sanity.

"Sorry," he murmured.

Recognizing he must be a guest, she forced a smile. She'd been trained from childhood that the customer was always right. Besides, if he was staying at the teahouse, she'd be dealing with him at every meal. "Uh," she managed to say. "Me, too. I'm Ariel Anderson.

"Anderson," he repeated, recognition entering his voice. "I couldn't find anyone, so I left my duffel by the door, put on a suit and came out to cool off."

Not much of a suit, she thought. From the drawl, she could tell he was a big-city guy, not from one of the nearby West Virginia towns, such as Charleston or Huntington. It hit her that she'd lost all track of time from the moment their bodies had connected. Only now did the sounds from guests playing in the pool drift back into her consciousness—laughter, the bat of a ball, the pounding of the diving board. "I'm sorry," she repeated. "No one helped you?"

He shook his head. "I've been here for an hour."

"I'll be glad to check you in," she said, even though she ranked the task right up there with talking to Studs about the stolen recipe book. She added, "That is, if you're ready to get dressed."

His eyes blazed into hers. They were the bluest she'd ever seen. Arresting. Captivating. She realized the double entendre in what she'd said, and quickly added, "I mean, if you're finished swimming." That was a better way of putting it, wasn't it?

"Of course," he murmured.

She couldn't help but wonder what he did for a living. It would be something that required intelligence. He had the sharply assessing gaze of a brainiac. His eyes dipped again, settling on her damp blouse, and she knew he was taking in her lace bra and nipples. When his eyes found hers again, it felt as if a thousand years had just passed. His voice lowered during that time and now it sounded husky and suggestive. "You might want to change, too."

She hadn't felt so completely unbalanced in her life. She'd totally forgotten that Elsinore Gibbet was standing beside her, witnessing the exchange. At least until Elsinore said, worriedly, "I thought it was all happening again. Now I'm sure of it."

The man thrust out a huge damp hand that, just a moment ago, had been curled around Ariel's upper arm. Then he said the last thing she expected. "I'm Dr. Rex Houston, CDC."

3

SHE DIDN'T MOVE A MUSCLE, not even to take his hand. And to be honest, Rex didn't want her to. The way she was standing, with her back to the sun, he was enjoying how the rays shone through her skirt, illuminating a great pair of legs. Blood surged in his groin, and he could only hope she'd get him checked into his room before he started sporting a full-service erection. Maybe this trip to Bliss was going to work out better than he'd thought.

After all, this had been the longest stretch without sex he'd ever endured in his adult life. Wishing he'd grabbed a towel at poolside—less to dry than cover himself— he tried to train his mind on something other than the woman in front of him.

Not that he could. He just wished she didn't remind him of Janet. Just like Janet, Ariel Anderson had a small-town, girl-next-door kind of appeal. She was fair, with perfect skin, and eyes as clear, big and blue as the crystal waters of the spring below. Her hair was drawn back, in a way that on another woman would have been called severe, but that didn't mar her features in the least, but instead enhanced them. She didn't wear much, or need, makeup. And that fresh-faced look, coupled with a tall, thin, leggy body clad in see-through clothes was doing him in.

As if coming to her senses, she took his hand, making him wonder just how long he'd been standing there with it extended. Minutes? Time seemed to have slowed. As her long, slender fingers traced the back of his hand, he offered a squeeze that sent heat dancing through him.

"Look," she began as she abruptly headed past him and toward the house, gesturing for him to follow. "I know Elsinore called you, but we really don't need the CDC…."

He wasn't sure what annoyed him most—her determination to push things in an all-business direction, or the fact that the nutty old bat who'd phoned the CDC was still on their heels, which meant he wasn't alone with Ariel.

Just looking at her, he felt all tangled up inside. Maybe he even wanted her because she was so much like Janet. As much as he hadn't wanted to take it personally, seeing his fiancée with the chef had been a blow to his ego. As Ariel breezed through a French door, he caught the edge and held it open for her and Elsinore.

"Thanks," both said over their shoulders.

"No problem." It was only Ariel's voice he'd really heard. She had a remarkable voice. Low and throaty, it was the sort that a man expected to find in bars, back alleyways and cathouses…in forbidden corners that catered to the midnight side. It sounded like she'd smoked too many cigarettes and drunk too much booze, although Rex was sure she'd never touched either.

They'd reached the staircase when an elderly woman appeared, wearing an apron over a black dress. She was short, probably just five feet, if that, and about seventy years of age. Apparently, three women lived here——he'd gleaned that much from guests at the pool——Ariel's mother, her grandmother and her great grandmother. Thankfully, at least one of them cooked. The house had filled with the aroma of food.

"Ariel!" the elderly woman was saying as she rushed forward, spatula in hand, and encased her in a quick, tight hug. "We've been waiting for your arrival for hours."

"Hi, Gran." Ariel kissed her cheek, then glanced toward the French doors again. "Uh…what's going on?" she continued, stepping back. "I thought I saw Mom, swimming down in the spring, and Great-gran was in town. Since both your cars are here, I couldn't figure out how she'd gotten there——"

"It's a long story," her grandmother said. "Everything went haywire today! We went to talk to Sheriff Underwood about Matilda's book. I guess you know him by the name of Studs, since you're the same age. And you know how we hate to go to town."

Ariel's mind strained to keep pace with her grandmother's monologue. With a nearly naked man beside her, especially one who'd felt so good pressed against her, it was difficult. "Are there any leads?"

"The sheriff found a red bandanna near the safe, and there were dog prints outside. I think he was going to question Pappy Pass, today, since his dog, Hammerhead, usually has a red bandanna tied around his neck."

"Pappy would never——"

"I think his grandson, Jeb, might be the culprit. Youngsters may have wanted to take the book for a lark. You know how they do. It wouldn't be the first time, after all. We're all beside ourselves with worry, as I'm sure you are, too. It's one of our dearest possessions and two centuries old."

"Surely whoever took it knows it's valuable."

"I hope. If anything happens to that book, it will be so upsetting. We've just got to find it before the Harvest Festival, otherwise we'll have to make all our tea blends by memory, and…" Her voice trailed off and she laughed, her eyes twinkling as she patted her granddaughter's cheek lovingly. "As old as we're getting, I hate to think what might happen if we made up love blends from memory, then tried to sell them."

"Lord have mercy," whispered Elsinore, speaking for the first time. "If your potions got jumbled, that really would be terrible, wouldn't it? All the wrong people would be falling in love, and so forth."

"Why, Elsinore, I didn't see you," said Ariel's grandmother. "Come into the kitchen with me. Let me pour you some sun tea. I made it during the day with fresh springwater. It'll cool you off while Ariel takes this gentleman upstairs to get him settled. As soon as Ariel's mother comes in from her dip, she can run you back down the mountain and pick up Great-gran." Gran nodded toward the staircase. "That's your duffel?"

Rex nodded.

She inclined her chin. "Everybody calls me Gran," she said. "So, you can, too. All the women in the house used to use proper names, but the guests can't remember. So we just have them call us Mom, Gran and Great-gran. It lends a homey feel, and nobody has to struggle too hard to remember things such as Samantha, Sylvia and Christina." She chuckled. "Now, the locals know our first names," she added. "And before anyone tells you otherwise, you should also know that some of the young kids in town believe we're witches."

"You certainly look like one," he agreed.

She smiled, delighted. "Whatever the case, it's good for business."

"You might want to throw in a ghost."

"I'll consider it," she assured. "Now, you two skedaddle. Even as it is, dinner's going to be late. And before you ask, I don't want help in the kitchen, Ariel. Your job is to entertain the new guest until dinner." The elderly woman flashed him a wide smile. "Ariel will take care of your every need. I can assure you of that, sir."

Trying not to take the words as a double entendre, Rex felt glad the sun had dried him well enough that he wasn't dripping on the woman's floor. "Sorry I'm not dressed," he apologized, glancing around at the stately living room, with its hardwood floors, Chinese rugs, marble-top tables and chandelier. "But when I couldn't check in…"

"You won't be punished this time," Gran assured with mock severity. "But next time, we'll bring out nails and chains. Thumbscrews."

"I thought that was for the people who tortured the witches."

"Exactly. As a witch, you pick these things up."

"Don't feed the rumors," Ariel said, the teasing seemingly bothering her.

Heeding the words, her grandmother continued, "Usually, you're to change in the deck house, but Ariel will explain all house rules." She glanced at Ariel. "He's in the Overlook room."

Looking startled, Ariel parted her lips in protest.

"It's the only room available."

Lifting his bag, he shouldered it, then picked up the rest of his belongings. He was still wondering what exactly was wrong with his accommodations as he preceded Ariel upstairs. He couldn't help but wonder if the view of his tush affected her, too, since it clearly did the women with whom he worked. As they entered a long upstairs hallway, Ariel pointed left, and when he reached the end of the hallway, he understood her objection. The Overlook room was right next door to one with a sign affixed to the door that read Welcome Home Ariel.

"We're neighbors," he said as she showed him into his quarters. He could swear he saw her throat working as he took in the door between their rooms. There was a lock on his side and probably one on hers as well....

He pulled his mind to business. The room was great. He would have chosen it for a personal vacation. To be honest, he hated small towns, unless they were riddled with some contagious disease. Otherwise, he got bored in under ten minutes flat. Living someplace like Bliss was akin to slow death by torture, as far as he was concerned, but when Jessica had said this was the fanciest place in town, she hadn't been lying.

"Nice," he said.

She seemed to soften. "Glad you like it."

She did, too. He could hear her love for the place in that maddeningly throaty voice. He took in the bed—a king-size, masculine affair covered with a nautically inspired duvet—facing a picture window overlooking the steep, lush-green incline to the spring. Everything reflected the sailing motif—from a shadow box illustrating boating knots, to ships-in-bottles that the women had placed on tables.

He strode to the bathroom and glanced in, feeling his heart skip a beat. The room was spacious, and mirrored, with a sunken tub of navy porcelain; the dark cabinetry, with its brass knocker-style pulls, made the place look like a captain's quarters. With the tub full of white suds, a man would feel he was bathing in the waves of the ocean.

Her folks might be rumored to be witches, or just crazy old widows who'd killed their husbands, but they knew how to make a man feel like a man. "Spacious," he commented, deciding not to mention the mirrors as he moved into the room again, and toward the picture window, to stare down at the spring. "Wow."

"It's my favorite view," she said, coming to stand next to him. "Mine's the same."

Definitely, he liked the fact that she was next door.

He realized her eyes were full of questions, and he raised his eyebrow. "Hmm?"

"What exactly is the CDC doing here? I mean, I know there are stories about how Bliss is said to have had…well, strange spots of time where business seems to shut down. Such tall tales add…"

"Spice to the town?"

"Exactly. The summer people love it."

"The source might be a bug called Romeo. Also called *generis misealius,*" he said. And then he plunged into an account of the history of the virus. He was more pleased than he should have been when she didn't glaze as he spoke about the difficulties of tracing viruses.

"You're serious?"

"Absolutely." He continued, his voice quickening with excitement as he spoke about the possibility of solving the town's long-standing mystery. At least until he mentioned the World Health Organization.

"They can't come here!" she said, dismayed. "This is ridiculous. Really Dr. Houston—"

"Rex," he corrected.

"This is all local myth. It really is."

"A possibility," he agreed, moving nearer to where she stood by the window. "You're related to Matilda Teasdale, right?"

She lifted her gaze from the spring, her crystal eyes looking wary and startled once more. "You know about that?"

He glanced toward the file on the bed. "Your dossier."

Now she looked mortified. "My..."

He frowned. Suddenly, she became even more interesting, if that was possible. "What could a woman like you have to hide?"

She shot him a long look. "A woman like me?"

He fought the urge to touch her—and lost. He knew better because just one touch would be enough to electrify his whole body and there would be no point to it, except to leave him craving more. Lifting a finger anyway, he glanced it off her cheek. "Proper."

That seemed to please her. "You think so?"

"Yeah." He knew his eyes were disrobing her.

Her expression shuttered. "You don't even know me."

He wanted to, at least for tonight, and he felt the urge, like a call to something wild and undeniable. "You could let me get to know you."

Her eyes darted away. "I don't think we'll have time for that."

"Really?" he returned mildly.

She wanted to back away—he was sure of it; he could feel it in his bones—yet she didn't. "The dossier doesn't say much about you, specifically," he found himself admitting. Surprised at the huskiness of his own voice, he went on, "But it does talk about the history of the house. Everyone seems to think Matilda and the women who've inhabited the place since are witches." His eyes locked into hers. "Are you?"

"You're a doctor. A scientist. You should know better."

"So, you think my framework of knowledge is limited to microbes and cells?"

Her lips suddenly twitched, as if the banter was threatening to make her smile against her will. "That was my hope."

It was a risk, but he inched closer, near enough to catch a whiff of her perfume. "The way you seem to affect me, you're testing my deepest convictions."

"A man should always keep his convictions."

He kept his voice steady and bemused, even though she was doing wild things to his blood. "Why?"

"It shows character."

Chuckling, he shrugged. "An overrated virtue."

The scent of her perfume was soft, faint and floral, but he could smell something else beneath it that stirred him. He could sense so much in this woman. Old wounds that ran deep. A river of pain, maybe. But he wanted to ask her a thousand questions, starting with how it felt to grow up in a place that was apparently considered to be the local haunted house.

Taking a deep breath, she blew out an audible sigh. "To be honest," she murmured. "I don't want the CDC here." She frowned. "Really, it's nothing personal."

"It's always personal."

"I don't know if it was in your…uh, dossier."

"It's not a dossier. Just so you know, the CDC doesn't really keep files on citizens. It's America, and we do have civil rights, you know."

"I work for a Pittsburgh TV station," she began. "And next week, during the Harvest Festival, a cameraman's coming from Charleston, to help me tape a feature spot. It's a big chance for me. I don't want anything blowing it. I definitely don't want the World Health Organization coming into town during the shoot, much less the military."

He was impressed. "The plot thickens."

"Meaning?"

"I thought you were home for a family vacation."

"That, too."

But she had ambition.

"And in addition to keeping you off my turf," she continued, "I need to find a missing recipe book. It's old, treasured by my family. It contains all Matilda's recipes, was written by her own hand. People have tried to steal it for years, as my grandmother suggested downstairs, but now, someone's broken into the safe, and taken it." She paused. "So you see," she finished, "I don't have time for flirtation."

His heart missed another beat. "Flirtation wasn't really what I had in mind."

"No?"

He slowly shook his head. Primal heat flared inside him. Barely able to believe he was doing it—he was usually a little more suave—he glanced pointedly toward the bed. "Flirtation," he murmured, raising a finger to touch her cheek once more. "It does seem like a waste of time."

She blinked, as if she couldn't quite believe the conversation they were having, then answering desire sparked in her eyes and she said the very last thing he expected. "Then let's not waste any more of it."

Scarcely believing his ears, Rex leaned across the scant remaining foot between them, circled an arm around her waist and drew her against himself, almost gasping as they made contact. She had a strong body. Probably, she worked out, and the muscles and bones felt equally hard, and yet she yielded to him, too, with a female softness. He arched to her, and as his mouth covered hers, she lifted her hands to his shoulders.

His tongue pushed apart her lips, and belatedly, he realized his kiss was too hard, too demanding. He didn't even know her. They'd met only moments before. Maybe Romeo was in the water, after all. Maybe he'd become infected as he'd splashed in the chlorinated pool. Why had he gone swimming? Usually, he was much more rigorous at a possibly infected site. But it had seemed so hot, and the proprietors hadn't been around, and...

Jessica would kill him if she knew.

But right now, he didn't even care. His hands tightened around Ariel's back, urging her closer, as her tongue moved against his, feeling silken, hot and delicious. Her fingers dug into his shoulders, then he felt them on his bare back, moving toward the elastic band of his trunks.

He wanted to remove her jacket again. And as he imagined using his teeth to unbutton the flimsy silk blouse, and his tongue to lick inside the lace of the bra, blood engorged him.

When she broke the kiss, he was half-glad. At least one of them had come to their senses. Except that, honestly, he wanted to spiral back downward into the whirlpool of the kiss and spend all night drowning in it.

"I'm sorry," she said, breathlessly. "I don't know what...came over me."

If he reached for her, she'd let him kiss her again, right now. He knew it and she knew it. Even as she took another self-protective step backward, she was licking her lips, tasting his moisture.

"I do," he managed to say huskily, slowly shaking his head, barely able to believe the kinetic heat that had ignited between them. "We want each other."

Her skin was flushed, her breath short. "Like I said," she continued, her voice holding a quiver that indicated she was just as shaken as him. "I'm worried about my project. And you're only here overnight. Before dinner, you can take your samples of the water." She pointed through the window. "Those steps take you right down to the spring."

"I have to take them from other locations as well," he found himself saying, the words seeming strangely inane in his mouth. Why were they talking at all? The way she'd felt in his arms, and tasted on his lips, they should have wound up in that huge bed making love.

Tonight, she'd come to him. He knew it like his own name. And right now, if someone told him he'd become clairvoyant, he'd have believed it. He could see her in his fantasies, naked and sudsed in the bathtub…how he'd slowly dry each inch of her before pulling down the duvet and laying her on sheets.

Her voice still held that crazy-making quiver. "You've got a few hours until dinner."

With that, she turned to go. He could only watch in disbelief—and need. Every swish of her hips felt like sheer torture. His hands ached to mold the curves of her hips. Instead, he said, "I'll be leaving in fifteen minutes. Think you can be ready?"

At the threshold, she turned. Everything in her gaze said she felt they'd better stay as far apart as possible. "Ready?"

Determined to ignore the fact that he was standing there, barefoot with a hard-on, in nothing but wet trunks, he said, "In case the World Health Organization really does wind up involved in this. It might affect your story."

Looking torn, she considered the truth of it. "Okay," she finally said. "Fifteen minutes. I'll meet you downstairs. We'll take my car. It's the silver Honda Accord."

4

As Rex leaned over the edge of a dock on the out-skirts of town and filled a test tube, he tried to strike up a conversation, saying, "Romeo's reputed to thrive in places like this."

A breeze was gaining momentum and, as waves of sticky air came her way, Ariel pressed a hand to the hem of her dress, holding it against her thigh. She'd hardly anticipated an outing like this, so she'd had to wear clothes from her old closet at the teahouse. Most were racier than she'd be caught dead in nowadays, but she'd managed to find a white sundress with an empire waist and spaghetti straps. Or at least she'd thought it was suit-able until the breeze had begun lifting the hem. Since the dress gathered beneath her breasts and had a built-in slip, the air threatened to lift it all the way over her head. Every time she looked at the man in front of her, she was stunned that she'd let him kiss her, and with such aban-don. She didn't even know him! But she wanted him....

"I think it might storm," she said when the fabric bil-lowed like a sail once more. She was determined, like him, to play it cool, as if nothing had happened. But it had. She could still feel the heavenly burgeoning pres-sure between her legs. He'd been so aroused....

She forced herself back to the present once more, as he said, "It's supposed to later."

Supposed to? For a second, she couldn't even remember what he'd been referring to. Then she thought, *Supposed to rain. Right.* Picking up the earlier conversation, she continued, "Um. What do you mean, 'places like this'?"

Still acting as if their kiss were the last thing on his mind, Rex slid another test tube into a tray he'd brought down the steep embankment, then he glanced at her. Wearing a T-shirt and jeans, he looked every bit as good as he had in his swimsuit. He was just as aware of her as he'd been in the Overlook room, too, judging by the glint in his eyes. "At this time of year," he explained. "And in weather like you've been having in Bliss, an environment may have been created in which the virus could best grow."

"And it doesn't hurt people?"

He shrugged. "Doesn't seem to. But like I said, the South American documents were lost, if they ever really existed."

She was still wondering what had happened to them in the Overlook room. One moment, she'd been shaking hands with the man. In the next, they'd been kissing in a way that could only lead to bed. "You don't think they did exist?"

"Your guess is as good as mine."

"Why would anyone lie about something such as that?"

He eyed her a long moment. "A love bug," he reminded her. "You've got to admit the idea is pretty funny."

Intriguing, anyway. She couldn't help but smile back, even though his presence threatened everything she'd hoped to accomplish in Bliss this week. "Are you saying scientists have a sense of humor?"

"Only if the jokes involve dreaded diseases," he assured her.

He was filling a last tube. "If the bug's in the water, and that's the cause of the town shutting down in the past," he continued, "and if the increase in births is true, after those periods, then it follows that there would be rashes of death, as well. If the bug had long-term lethal effects, that is. And there's no such documentation in town records."

"That's a relief."

Being with him wasn't, however. She could only hope the night passed uneventfully. With him next door, she couldn't trust herself. In the morning, he'd be gone, though, and then she could concentrate on finding the recipe book. On the way to this area of the spring, he'd insisted on stopping at the sheriff's office.

Still, she'd reasoned, she was bound to run into Studs Underwood eventually, and she did want to see if he'd made any progress. Besides, it wouldn't hurt to have a man in tow for her inevitable showdown with Studs. She hadn't seen him since a visit three years ago, but she wasn't about to con herself into thinking the man had changed.

"That figures," Rex had said dryly when they'd found a sign on the door, indicating Studs was out.

"It's a small town," she'd offered. "The police station's not exactly teeming with employees. There's a woman who's here when Studs is out, but it looks as if she ran out for coffee or a snack." She'd debated telling Rex of her past association with the sheriff, but had refrained. "Is it really that important that you talk to him?"

"It's protocol," Rex had returned. As he'd stared at the door, considering his next move, he'd explained the CDC's rules regarding contacting local law enforcement officers before conducting tests in an area.

"Maybe he's at Pappy Pass's," she'd suggested.

Since Pappy's was on the way, they'd driven there next, only to find Studs hadn't bothered to question him yet. Pappy had been sitting on his front porch, smoking a cob pipe and reading a hunting magazine, and he'd looked surprised to see her.

"Hello," he'd said, eyeing her with seeming approval. "Why, Ariel, you look…good."

As much as she hated how he'd implied that she'd once looked bad, she'd thanked him. After all, she really had blazed down Bliss Run Road at least a thousand times, looking like the worst kind of tramp. Even now, she cringed when she thought of the tight shirts she'd worn. She'd gone braless, too, so the outlines of her ample breasts had been there for all the world to see.

When questioned, Pappy had said Hammerhead's red bandanna was missing, so it might be the one found at the crime scene. "But that's a long way for him to roam, Ariel," Pappy had pointed out.

And it was. Besides, if the truth be told, Hammerhead seemed happiest curled at his master's feet, and the few times Ariel had seen the mutt, he'd been sleeping in the back of Pappy's pickup. He wasn't exactly frisky, and Mountain Drive was a hike, both from Pappy's and town. "Maybe he was in a car with Jeb?"

"I thought about that," Pappy had said, "but Jeb swore he didn't take the book. I was in town when I heard about the break-in, so I asked him. You know how kids…"

She'd nodded. Ever since she could remember, kids had dared each other to visit Terror House at night. Ariel knew people wanted to get their hands on recipes for the love teas, too. Some thought there were secret teas in the book never made available to the public by the Anderson women. And, well…about that much, they were right. So, heaven only knew what somebody was home-brewing today.

"You might try talking to Jeb yourself, Ariel."

"Maybe I will. Thanks for asking him, Pappy," she'd returned, wondering if he really had. Not that Pappy was the type to lie. His reputation around town was every bit as good as hers was bad. Still, he loved his grandson, and if he suspected any wrongdoing on his part, he might cover for him.

Sliding the last tube into the tray, Rex stood. "I'm going to run these up to the lab and grab some slides. I forgot to bring them down. I'll be right back. Mind waiting?"

She shook her head, then watched him walk to the end of the dock and uphill, his long legs easily making a path to the road. He really was a fine specimen of a man, and just watching him made her throat tighten, especially since she could still feel his hot mouth on hers.

Driving would have calmed her nerves and made her feel more in control, which was why she'd suggested they take her car, but as it had turned out, he'd flown into Charleston, picked up a mobile lab unit in a hangar there—it was the big, black RV she'd seen in the lot—then he'd driven to Bliss. Apparently, such vehicles were kept all over the country, for use by the CDC and military.

Now her nerves still felt jittery. It didn't help that they were standing on a dock near Panty Point, the town's best-known make-out spot. On the opposite side of the spring, she could see the teahouse, and to the left, she could see the town. Definitely, Panty Point was the most isolated spot around. Though, she'd expected to see kids at least, exploring the bike trails that snaked across the rocky terrain and strip of muddy beach.

She watched sunlight dappling the magical waters. For a moment, she almost felt at peace, despite how Rex was unsettling her. The spring always calmed her. Maybe it was the only thing on earth that really could. Trees rocketed toward the sky, and the hills were vivid with color from the wildflowers. For all the pain it had brought her, she'd always felt Bliss was the center of the earth. Just like the spring, Ariel had come from it, and the town—for better or worse—was her source.

Nothing had ever made her feel so grounded. Except maybe Rex's kiss. Her knees had weakened when he'd kissed her, her skin had burned, but she'd felt grounded, too, even as her mind had floated far above the room. She'd been flying yet solid on her feet. The kiss had felt so right, like part of her homecoming.

While they'd kissed, the weight of the past had been lifted, and she'd forgotten how she'd felt growing up, teased by kids who thought her family was weird. Adults, too. She'd forgotten how she used to beg her mother for information about her father, how her mother would only say she'd had an affair that hadn't worked out. She and the man had never been married, leaving Ariel with the impression that he'd been a visitor who'd skipped out, leaving town quickly, and that the rejection had deeply wounded her mother.

Later, in adolescence, she'd quit asking her mother

about him. What man would want a child by a woman he'd rejected? Besides, she'd never been able to bear the pain that came into her mother's eyes whenever she'd brought up the subject. Gran and Great-gran knew more about him. Ariel was sure of it.

But as time went on, she'd decided her mother knew best. And sleeping dogs were better left to lie. Ariel had started concentrating her energies on making her great escape, leaving town and making a different life for herself.

Hearing Rex behind her, she took a deep breath, bracing herself before she turned around. At the house, it had taken all her resources not to simply lock the door, strip and get down to business. She'd craved a man like Rex Houston for so long. Wasn't that what this trip was all about? Coming to terms with the past? Sure, she wanted to show the town that she wasn't really the sexpot they'd assumed, but only to better help her claim her sexual self. Her reputation had been hurtful, but she'd worn a brave face, and in doing so, had lost touch with the sensual woman she was meant to be. For so long, she'd felt her unfinished business in Bliss was in the way of moving on....

With her boss, Ryan? That had been her idea hours ago. But now... Yes, tonight maybe she really would let go with this man, enjoy just one night of abandoned sex. One kiss, and she knew he could give her more pleasure than anyone ever had. Just as she turned around, the breeze lifted her dress and she gasped, not catching the hem in time. The dress fluttered, flying nearly over her head, exposing white bikini panties. Embarrassed, she batted down the fabric, pressing it against her thigh, fighting a blush. "Damn," she mouthed as she looked up—and then felt the breath leave her body, entirely.

"Studs."

"Did I surprise you, honey?" he said, his dark eyes lascivious. He was wearing tan shorts with a uniform shirt; a gun belt was around his waist, a hand on his weapon.

He knew he had. And it had been intentional. "The name's Ariel."

"Who'd know that better than your lover?"

She wasn't proud of it, but she glanced toward the hill, half hoping she'd see Rex. No such luck. And when she glanced to her right, she realized Studs had come down to the water by a different path, judging by the mountain bike lying on its side a hundred yards from the dock. The word Police was emblazoned across the bike's top bar.

"Already," she said, "I can see you haven't changed a bit."

"And from what you just showed me, sweet girl," he countered, "you haven't, either. Nice panties."

"Don't start," she warned, backing up a fraction, until she hit a pole behind her, so she could use it to steady herself. Why did she let this piece of trash get to her?

"You're not happy to see me?"

"Hardly."

He flashed a grin—bright white teeth in a tan as dark as his personality. "Could have fooled me, the way you lifted that skirt."

She started to say the breeze had lifted it, but that was what he wanted, to push her into defending herself. "So I guess you haven't been doing anything useful," she said. "Like your job."

"I figure I can handle my job just fine."

"Guess not. Gran called me this morning about the recipe book. She said it was stolen last night, and I just talked to Pappy Pass—"

Now he was moving toward her. "You can't breeze into town and start questioning my suspects, Ariel."

"Apparently somebody has to," she said hotly. "That book's been in my family for years, and we all want it found. It's valuable. It could be destroyed."

He stopped in front of her. In high school, he'd been good-looking, a strapping, dark-haired jock. Quarterback of the high-school football team, as well as prom king with the woman he'd married, Joanie Summers, at his side as queen. But that had been years ago. Joanie had held up better than him. Even after three kids, she'd kept her figure. Studs had put on weight, though, and the broad, once-handsome, wide face that had dazzled schoolgirls was now creased with lines. He had a beer belly and looked ten years older than he really was. The nickname, Studs, was no longer fitting. That was, Ariel decided, at least some small satisfaction.

He was leering at her. "Miss me?"

"You know better."

Edging closer, he dropped his voice to a near whisper. "Oh, c'mon now, Ariel, when you're up in the big city, I bet you wonder about me all the time, don't you? Lying in bed, you still think of me. Admit it. You dream of the good old days."

"There were no good old days."

"What did you get, amnesia?"

"If I had, I would have forgotten you."

"You mean to tell me that you don't remember how

I loved you so good in the back of my daddy's pickup truck? Why, everybody in town knows what went down in the parking lot of Jack's Diner, and how we drove to Charleston and got a motel room, so I could watch you getting it on with that woman. I told Joanie I hadn't wanted to. But then, everybody knows you can be damn persuasive, Ariel. You had it bad for me, didn't you, Ariel? Everybody in town knew you were my fantasy girl. And it made Joanie so jealous. My, oh my. How she hated you...."

And turned all the other girls against Ariel, out of spite. On the school bus, which had picked her up at the bottom of Mountain Drive, no one had ever talked to her. Thanks to him.

Too much of the past was flooding back. She hated him...just as she hated how she used to fantasize about a father who never came to protect her, and a mother who'd never been able to understand how the teasing was affecting her daughter. "Oh, you're right, Studs," she muttered, stepping toward him and offering a shy smile. She put her hands on his waist. "Maybe I did miss you more than I admit. Those stories about you and me got so out of control...." His eyes widened as she traced a pink fingernail down his chest. "But they got me to thinking..."

"They did?"

"But you're married now...."

"Uh...yeah."

"But we won't let Joanie get in the way. Now, will we?" Broadening her smile, she grabbed a fistful of his shirt, then spun. "You sick bastard," she whispered, then flattened her hand on his chest and pushed hard.

He was facing her when he flew off the dock, and if

she hadn't been so furious, Ariel might have laughed. His eyes were bugging, his arms were flailing, and under the circumstances, even a saint wouldn't be sorry that the dunking would ruin the fancy, animal-skin cowboy boots on his kicking feet. She leaped back as he hit the water, but not in time. She groaned as a freezing wave of springwater drenched her. "Twice in one day," she muttered.

"You could stand to lose a few pounds," she said to Studs. "That splash could have hit Bliss Run Road. In fact," she added as he came back up, sputtering, "I think it's started a tidal wave. Whoa! Call in the coast guard!"

Deciding she'd better reach the mobile lab before Studs got out—after all, he was packing a weapon—she whirled, intending to go down the dock, then saw Rex standing in front of her, a small briefcase-style kit in his hand and an uncertain expression on his face.

"Old boyfriend?"

She wanted to die, right then and there. It didn't help that yet another outfit was soaked, or that it was white and she was braless. Or that Studs was having difficulty hauling himself out of the water. He was going to catapult over the side of the dock any second now, dripping like a creature from the blue lagoon.

She wanted to laugh, but fury was coursing through her. Everything was going wrong. When he'd kissed her, Rex had seemed different. Unconnected to the town, but in under two hours, he'd been roped into her past. If only for a moment, he'd felt like a part of her here-and-now, and maybe even her future.

He raised a hand. "Sorry. It's none of my business."

"He's not an old boyfriend," she assured.

Disbelief clouded Rex's eyes.

"You heard everything?"

"I didn't want to interrupt. The conversation seemed kind of…"

Intimate.

"But…" He considered. "When it looked like things were getting out of hand, I figured I might step in and toss him into the lake. And then…" He looked toward where Studs was sloshing in the water. "You beat me to the punch."

She swallowed hard, trying to fight her pique. "So, I guess you're the kind of guy who believes everything he hears." She paused. "Some scientist."

"Believe everything I hear," he echoed, as if his mind was trying to catch up.

Just like everyone else in this backwater that always knotted up her insides! One minute, she loved this town. The next, she wanted to run as if the hounds of hell were on her heels and never look back.

"He's not my boyfriend," she said again.

"Who is he then?"

"Studs Underwood," she said. "The sheriff you were looking for."

She hated seeing the mortification on Rex's features. She didn't blame him. He'd explained that local law-enforcement officers sometimes gave the CDC trouble. A visit from the organization was one of the bigger events in a small-town sheriff's career, sometimes, so the CDC had to be diplomatic and make a show of involving them. And Rex really did have a job to do.

Studs was rising to his feet, his uniform shirt and shorts jeans plastered to his body. "Sheriff Underwood," she found herself saying, once more slapping down the hem of her dress, "this is Rex Houston. Dr. Rex Houston. From the CDC."

Somehow, she wasn't surprised when Rex moved quickly forward, his hand outstretched. "I know we're meeting under real strange circumstances, Sheriff," he began. "But I want you to know I stopped in town, at your office...."

The words propelled Ariel forward. She didn't look back, but kept her eyes fixed on the top of the hill, in the direction of the mobile lab, which was her destination. This was too much. Had it been only hours ago that she'd driven into Bliss, wearing her beautiful silk suit?

Ariel was breathing hard when she reached the mobile lab. Opening the passenger side door, she got in and stared in back. The sides of the RV-style vehicle were lined with metal shelves, and two washing-machine style tumblers were visible, as well as other equipment, the functions of which Rex had explained on the drive. A roller chair was seat-belted to the side, so it wouldn't roll toward a makeshift desk.

Through the windshield, she could see a canopy of green leaves that made her long for the city. The encounter with Studs hadn't left her shaken. She felt dirty now. Like she wanted to get out of here and take a shower. And so, when she saw Rex had left the keys dangling in the ignition, she found herself saying, "If Dr. Rex Houston wants to make friends with local law enforcement, I think we'll let him." As far as she was concerned, he could catch a ride back to town on Studs Underwood's mountain bike.

Scooting to the driver's seat, Ariel turned the key in the ignition and then she simply drove away.

5

ANGER WAS STILL FLOODING Ariel when she reached her room. It didn't help that she'd gotten home just in time to see Great-gran getting out of Eli Saltwell's old jalopy, having clearly accepted a ride back from town from her archenemy, or that her mother was in the kitchen, openly admitting to swimming in her bra and panties, where she might have been viewed by guests. "Now, Ariel," she'd said, "I'm sure no one saw me. You need to loosen up, sweetie."

Loosen up? "This town's coming unraveled," she'd muttered. How to explain? Her mother usually wore black, long-sleeved dresses, even in summer. Even worse, Gran was chatting about how charming Rex Houston was, and what a good husband he might make for Ariel, which was why she'd put him next door to her, even though other rooms had really been available.

Ariel pulled the wet white dress over her head and laid it on top of a hamper near the window to dry in the sunlight, then strutted to the bed in her panties. With her luck, Romeo really was in the water. The only stranger pairing than Eli and Great-gran would have been Ariel and Studs Underwood. "That'll be a cold day," Ariel said, lifting her suitcase, opening it on the bed next to her garment bag and staring at the neatly arranged contents.

The springwater had made her skin sticky, so she figured she'd shower. There was still time before dinner. Hopefully, Rex would have a long walk back to the house, and she could avoid him for the rest of his stay. "Maybe he won't even make it before sundown."

Her heart pulled as she thought of the coming night. She hadn't been home in summer for three years, so she'd missed the events her relatives planned—bonfires and marshmallow roasts. Catching a glimpse of herself in the mirror on the back of the closet door, she groaned. She looked like hell. Totally mussed, but her body looked good. Given the kind of attention she'd always solicited from Studs, she didn't know whether to be glad about that or not. As her eyes flicked over her figure, her throat constricted. "What a waste," she couldn't help but say.

She was tall and leggy, with full breasts and a nicely nipped-in waist. When younger, she'd always assumed she'd be married by now—working at a dream career and in a relationship to which she could give her whole self. It never occurred to her that she'd be cresting twenty-nine and still alone.

She opened the closet door. As she did so, she realized her head ached. "The pins," she muttered, quickly removing them. As she stared at racks of clothes, she set the pins on a dresser top. She'd tried her best to look respectable today. But here she was, letting her hair down and contemplating wearing one of the outfits that had made her so infamous around Bliss.

She felt a rush of excitement. Maybe she'd put on

something racy for dinner, just to watch Rex Houston's eyes pop. She wasn't going to sleep with him now. Of course she wasn't! Not after the way he'd run right up to Studs and had shaken hands as if they were best friends. Yes…

She settled on a strapless leopard-print tube. Lifting it from a hanger, she tossed it to the bed. "Oh, yeah," she said. "That and a pair of skintight white Lycra shorts. Thong panties."

As furious as she was, it was tempting…damn tempting. She was going over some other offerings—a sheer halter, low-rise jeans, when the door flew open. She whirled, instinctively covering her chest, expecting to see her mom or Gran.

But it was Rex, and he looked just as shocked. He was frozen in the doorway, his hand on the knob, his widening eyes taking her in. Ariel was seized by a wicked desire to punish the man. "Don't bother to knock," she bit out, aware that every inch of her was laid bare for his eyes.

He had a totally dumb-guy expression on his face. "Huh?"

"You just burst into my room without knocking."

He was still in shock, especially since she wasn't even bothering to cover the rest of herself. "Uh…you stole the mobile lab."

"Boo hoo."

His gaze dropped down the length of her body. Clearly, she could have robbed him blind and he wouldn't have cared. "It's a government vehicle."

She could see his broad chest heaving, as if he couldn't take a deep breath. Her hands crossed under her breasts, both to indicate she was furious and to lift them for his gaze. Oh, yes…let him understand that she wasn't nearly as proper as he'd assumed. Let him dream of all those things she'd supposedly done with Studs.

He paused, looking exasperated, and as if he knew the gentlemanly thing was to leave her to dress, but he couldn't quite bring himself to do so. He eyed her panties. "Do you know what that vehicle's worth?"

"Nothing to me," she assured.

"Don't you have any…" He searched for a word, just as his eyes searched her body, and he settled on saying, "Morals?"

"Funny, coming from a stranger who kissed me senseless an hour ago." If people wanted to think she was a brazen hussy, without any morals to speak of, well she'd be happy to let them. A lot had happened since she'd driven into town with dreams of reinventing herself hours ago—like his kiss.

"It cost millions," he finally managed to say, as if still completely undecided about how to respond to the fact that she was standing there, taunting him with her nakedness. "It's not a car, Ariel. It's a science lab."

Unconcerned, she turned toward the closet and began to rifle through the rack. She made a show of slowly licking her lips, knowing she was asking for it…wanting him to charge over and kiss her again. "If it's so important to the government, you shouldn't have left the keys in it."

"I saw that goon down on the dock pawing you," he muttered, sounding thoroughly frustrated. "And I…"

She couldn't ignore the squeeze of her heart. So, he'd been rushing down the hill to rescue her from Studs? "I'm flattered." She pulled out a short dress that buttoned down the front and held it out at arm's length as if considering it. "It's nice to know protecting me ranked higher than a mobile lab, but I didn't need male protection."

"Obviously."

"I enjoy taking care of myself."

"I didn't know you knew him."

"Ah," she said turning to fully face him, loving how his eyes instantly glazed. She knew better than to play with fire, especially in Bliss. Wasn't she just acting out the past, since seeing Studs again? Wasn't this the most self-destructive part of her, which had gotten her into such trouble when she was a teenager? Why couldn't she just accept that men always wielded power over women? Always had, always would. For every decent guy, there were a thousand Studses.

"One minute, my knight in shining armor," she found herself saying. "The next, best friend to Studs Underwood. I figured you two wanted to get to know each other, and that he'd be happy to give you a ride. Of course, I didn't think you'd get here so quickly." She flashed him a smile. "But then, you had to race to your lab unit."

"Losing it could cost me my job."

She felt a twinge of guilt. "It won't happen again."

"On the way up here—" Interrupting his thought, he said, "The sheriff's car was right on the top of the hill, and while we were following you, he offered to arrest you."

Interesting. "You told him not to?"

"Yes. And he wanted to. He said you should have been arrested before now. In fact, it sounds like you have quite a reputation around here."

"Does that bother you?"

He looked torn. "Dammit," he suddenly muttered, thrusting a hand through locks of sun-streaked hair that hung almost to his shoulders. "The way you look now," he said hoarsely. "No."

"I thought you were a scientist," she purred, still unable to take in that he'd eaten up what Studs had had to say like candy. "What's a woman, after all? Just cells and microbes, right?"

Rex took a confused step forward. "What's gotten into you? When I got here, you were wearing that little pink suit, acting holier than thou. And now..."

She felt both hot and cold all over, trembling inside, and something dark and shivery, like beams of moonlight seemed to stream through her veins. "Well, you heard what kind of girl I am, didn't you? So, nothing should surprise you now."

His gaze traveled from the closet to the leopard-print tube on the bed, then settled on the open suitcase. Inside, her new belts were coiled around two-tone pocketbooks and matching pumps, and neatly folded T-shirts lay next to stacks of walking shorts. Beside the suitcase, her new pastel suits were visible through the clear plastic of a garment bag.

Suddenly, he slammed shut the door behind him, and her heart beat furiously as he came toward her. He looked none too happy now, his lips pursed grimly and his expression determined. "Look," he said, snatching the dress from her hand. "Just put this on. I don't know what the hell happened back there—" When she didn't comply, he lifted her hand, thrust it through a short sleeve. "But let's just forget about it. Let's just get a fresh start here."

Swiftly leaning, he reached for her other hand, urging it into the other sleeve, but as he moved, their bellies brushed. There was no way she could fight the response. Her flesh quivered, and her nipples constricted so quickly.

He stepped back, and when he did, there was no mistaking that he was breathing hard. His voice was gruff. "C'mon. Do a guy a favor. Button up."

Every nerve inside her was jangling like bells. When her eyes dipped over his jeans, she could see the visible evidence of his excitement. This crazy day had just gotten a whole lot crazier. Was she really standing here, in front of a near stranger, a dress open over her body, which was naked save for a pair of panties? "What if I don't take orders?" she said petulantly, her own ears registering the impossible throatiness of her own voice.

"C'mon," he said. "Quit playing games, Ariel."

"But you heard it all from the good sheriff, didn't you?" she taunted. "And now you know all about how the local bad girl likes to play games."

She watched his tongue inadvertently circle his lips, and as she sucked in an audible breath, her breasts swelled, the tips aching for the lips he'd just wet. She felt her knees weaken, as if a gale wind had just sapped their strength.

"An hour ago you were all too happy to kiss me," she whispered.

"Is that what you want?"

She knew she'd lost her mind, but it was the truth. "More."

He took another deep breath as if to steady his nerves. "Right now, I think you're mad at your boyfriend. Or old boyfriend. Or whatever he is—"

She barely knew what came over her. But she reached over and splayed her palm on his chest. "He is not my boyfriend," she said succinctly.

"Okay," said Rex, not about to argue.

"He has never been my boyfriend."

Again, Rex looked torn, probably because of what he'd overheard. Beneath her skin, his T-shirt felt as soft as silk. His bare skin was even softer, and the threads of chest hair softer still.

When Rex spoke, his voice sounded thicker with a slow Southern drawl. "For not being your boyfriend," he said, "the guy sure got you riled."

"Why don't you try to get him out of my system?"

Everything in his expression said he'd already been pushed beyond the limits of male endurance. "Could be difficult."

"Maybe you can innoculate me."

His voice caught as he angled closer, soliciting a shiver when the buckle of his belt pressed her bare belly. "Cure you of…"

"The heat," she murmured.

"I'd only make you hotter."

"Prove it," she whispered as he placed a hand on her back, near the small of her spine. Warmth from his palm seeped through the thin fabric of the dress. Already, her panties were wet; when he exerted pressure, she arched, uttering a moan when she felt the strain of his erection against her.

The house was too old to accommodate central air and the room was so hot. Besides, she'd always preferred fresh air to the window air conditioners that had been placed in all the rooms, but now her skin felt like a heavy coat, and she quickly shrugged out of the dress he'd just insisted she put on. She glanced over her shoulder, toward the bed, trying not to think about how long it had been since she'd had sex. And yet how could she forget? Nearly a year. And with a date she hadn't wanted nearly as much as she wanted Rex Houston. Ever since, during her and Ryan's flirtation at work, she'd been hoping something wild would happen....

Seeing the hopeless mess on the duvet, she urged him backward toward one of the overstuffed chairs, until his knees hit, curled over the edge and he sat down. Shrugging out of the his T-shirt, he tossed it aside, and as her gaze drifted over his chest, she blew out a long, quivering breath. He really was gorgeous. Broad-chested and tan, covered in blond hair.

The way he was looking at her was thoroughly unsettling, too. His midnight-blue eyes were steady, the gaze both hungry and self-assured. Like most people, he really thought she was a town bad girl, everything Studs had said. And right now, she didn't mind in the least. In fact, she wanted to play the part. Leaning, she grabbed his belt buckle and flicked it open.

He leaned back his head, his lips parting in ecstasy as her nails teased the skin near the waistband of his jeans. She toyed, tracing the space as if they had all day to play, until he made a strangled sound—something between a moan and a curse. His own hand quickly covered hers then, and deftly, he snapped open his jeans and dragged down the zipper. A tuft of his briefs was visible, and he released another sigh, this time of relief.

"I haven't even kissed you yet," she whispered, tucking her hands behind him, under the waistband, so she could slip off his pants.

"Then you'd better start."

Another wave of heat claimed her as her palms glided slowly downward over the smooth skin of his behind. "Would you like that, Rex?"

"Yeah," he muttered.

Sweat and desire mixed, and when she leaned closer, she caught mingled scents, the pungent aroma of need shooting into her like a dart. It must have affected him the same way, because he lifted his hips, so she could divest him of his pants. Then he slipped a hand under the waistband of the briefs, gasping as the clothes came free.

"You said you want to be kissed," she teased huskily, her heart hammering as she took him in. He was thoroughly aroused; she'd sent him over the edge with her taunts. "But you didn't say where."

"Where," he said huskily.

She ran a nail from the scrotum all the long way up to the tippy top, testing each ridge, then she lowered her mouth.

He groaned. Hands fell to her hair. She wondered what had come over her, and why she wanted him so badly. Hours ago, he'd been a stranger. But her mind clouded as she tasted him, and every thought went spinning into some black void like a whirlpool.

He was salt and spice, arching as she clicked teeth on the silken skin of the head, until he was uttering a long, unbroken sound of longing and gathering her hair in fistfuls. Slowly, she flicked the sensitive underside until he was about to come.

It hit her that she'd always longed to feel a man's

mouth on her… Why not now, she thought. With him. Rex would do it. Already, he was full to bursting, straining. He'd do any damn thing she wanted! She felt wild with lust, too, determined to send him tumbling into oblivion.

Need forced her to her feet. She stood before him, taking in what she'd done to him. He was dusky with promise, completely hard. She wanted to feel his tongue plunging hungrily between her lips, to let him slake his thirst while she explored every crevice of his mouth. She wanted to be swallowed by his long, tan muscular arms, too, to drown in their embrace until the sun went down and the moon rose. Maybe then, they'd run naked in the woods like nymphs and fall asleep on a bed of soft pine needles.

Slipping both hands inside the front of her panties, she pushed them down, now pretending she was a master stripper and teasing Rex with the view, until she'd removed the last barrier between them. Just as her panties hit the floor, he reached for her, and she was in his arms, her legs parting to straddle him. Nothing had ever felt so good as those arms, she decided, as they wrapped tightly around her back. He lowered his head and caught one of her nipples between his teeth, expertly nibbling, then suckling hard, drawing gasps of pleasure. A moment later, their mouths locked and tongues greedily thrust.

"Condom?" he whispered wetly against her mouth.

She veered back. She hadn't even thought of that, and didn't need to say so. The panic was in her eyes. It was too late now, she was too far gone. She didn't want to stop. As if reading her mind, he softly cursed. Her mind raced. Of course, they needed a condom. What had she been thinking? But the fact was, she couldn't think. "I don't have…"

A hand slid around her neck, pulling her mouth to his again, and as their lips covered each other, sizzling and burning, he urged her to the floor. Lying there, she looked up as he settled between her legs, his astonishingly big hands splaying on her thighs, his eyes taking their fill as he parted her.

As he slowly leaned, she felt his hot breath on her thighs. It whispered on her belly, and her tummy tightened. Then he kissed her, circling her navel with his tongue. Lower, she thought, suddenly crying and arching, scarcely able to believe this dream was coming true, begging him with the needy trajectory of her hips and the hands that found his shoulders and pushed. She'd never done this before. Never had a man...

Lower. Just the thought of it pushed her closer to the edge. Fever claimed her. She had to have him....

There. She exploded as his wet, open-mouthed kiss covered her, feeling better than anything she'd ever imagined. She was drowning then. Old, dark sensations took her completely. She'd never felt so wet. So adrift. And when the pad of his tongue settled momentarily, drenching her in warmth, she felt she'd die from the heat prickling every inch of her skin. Frustrated, she whimpered. "Please."

The word was magic. Better than the waters of Bliss. It made that maddening tongue move on her clitoris. As the tip circled her bud, she flooded. Hands, at his sides just moments ago, were everywhere at once. A thick finger thrust inside her, pushing her to the edge.

Wildly, she reached, desperate to close her hand over his stiffened length, wanting this uncanny pleasure to be shared. He turned, angling his legs so they were side by side, his mouth only leaving her once, to cry out in maddened agony as her hand found him. She stroked hard as her mouth descended, the kisses reckless with her own heat, unraveling sanity.

The Ariel Anderson who'd driven into Bliss only hours ago, wearing a new suit and feeling determined to change her reputation, flung back her head and shamelessly forgot herself. He'd held her at the brink too long, until she felt crazy. Frustrated craving replaced rational thought.

"Please," she begged once more. "Please. Make me come."

Another thick finger thrust inside her. His tongue went wild. And then she arched to the mouth drinking her in like a river, and as the dam burst, she let go of the last vestige of control.

6

"I TOLD YOU I RECOGNIZED that guy," whispered Jeb Pass. He was seated in front of the library's ancient microfiche machine, rolling the lever to advance the screen.

"Be quiet," said Marsh as he wrenched around, looking over his shoulder. "We don't want Chicken Giblets to come before we're finished."

They were lucky she'd let them into the library at all. Closing time was seven this evening, but the boys had explained they'd come earlier, only to find the library shut, and that they had to get in now, to complete a top-secret project on Bliss's history.

"You're lucky I'm here," Chicken Giblets had replied, as if she might have had reason to drive away in the two-room mobile trailer that served as the library. Once a week, on Saturdays, the trailer was driven to smaller neighboring towns by her assistant, a seventy-six-year-old man named Carl DeLyle who, unlike his boss, hadn't yet lost his license.

"It's not Saturday," Jeb had reminded her, wondering if she was starting to lose her mind as well as her vision.

"No, but Mr. DeLyle and I may have to use the vehicle. Who knows?" Her voice had dropped. "We might need to get out of town. As you may have heard," she added, "I'm the one who called the CDC. I think some-thing…well, that something funny might be happening in Bliss. Does your…" She paused. "*Top secret project*," she continued, using the boys' exact words, "involve that?"

Jeb considered. "We don't know yet, but possibly."

Now Jeb was wondering if Chicken Giblets was right. When they'd gone to the library the first time, he and Marsh had run into their schoolmate, Jay Jones. Un-believably industrious, Jay edited the student paper and traveled to Charleston for chess matches, and he was generally busy in the early evening, delivering newspa-pers. Instead, he'd been swimming in the spring with one of the summer visitors, a cute brunette, and even more disturbing, he hadn't seemed to care that he'd blown off his deliveries.

"What happened to him?" Marsh had said, unable to hide his shock.

Jeb had just shaken his head in dismay, feeling equally worried.

Not knowing what to do, Jeb and Marsh had taken over the paper route, only skipping delivery to the Teas-dale Terror House. Then, back in town, they'd grabbed a bite at Jack's Diner, and Michelle had sauntered over to sit in a booth with them during her break. When Marsh had gotten up to put some money into the juke-box, Michelle had asked Jeb to the movies. Stunned, he'd considered turning her down, if only because her change of attitude was so abrupt, and because the ru-mors about the spring had made him question her mo-tives. But then, he'd been waiting all summer for her to notice him, so he'd agreed to meet her at eight, which

meant that he and Marsh really had to wrap up this research project soon.

As it was, Jeb didn't have time to go home before
meeting Michelle. He'd have just enough time to duck
into Marsh's place, across from the theater, take a
shower and borrow fresh jeans. Which he'd better, he
thought now. He could swear Michelle had blown him
an air kiss through the window of Jack's when they'd
left, so he wanted to look his best. If he was lucky,
maybe Marsh's dad would even have some cologne.

Now Jeb scrolled upward. "I'm sure it's him."

"The Core Coal Company," Marsh whispered, rat-
tling off the names in the text under a picture, then shaking his head as he read the last. "Angus Lyons."

"I'm pretty sure," Jeb repeated.

"He looks different now," said Marsh.

"He's older. And he's got a beard and long white hair."

Both boys paused, silently reading the article that de-
tailed how the group had almost successfully bought up
Bliss's land by pretending they intended to develop
rather than strip-mine it, and how Eli Saltwell had uncovered the plot.

Marsh said, "Do you think he came back to buy
land again?"

"Dunno. Maybe he's connected to…"

"The fact that it might be happening again?" Marsh
finished.

Jeb nodded. "The recipe book's gone, and Sheriff
Underwood didn't even bother to question us, or Pappy,
even though Hammerhead's bandanna and paw prints
were found at the crime scene. And how could anyone
get into that safe, anyway? I heard whoever broke into

the Teasdale Terror House just opened it, as if they knew the combination."

"Maybe the witches did it themselves," suggested Marsh. "They're the only ones who know the combination. Anybody else would have to blow the safe up. Or like the last attempt, try to drag the safe off the property and open it elsewhere."

Jeb frowned. "But why would the witches do that?"

"A publicity stunt, maybe," Marsh offered. "To drum up more business for Terror House."

"They had a full house all summer," argued Jeb. "And now, that guy from the CDC is up there." Everybody had been talking about him in Jack's Diner. "Sheriff Underwood says he's checking the water for a virus that could have caused…"

Marsh swallowed hard and glanced toward the six-pack of bottled water he and Jeb had just bought at the Superette. Judging from the empty shelf, there were other people in town who'd had the same idea. "If there is anything to the rumors," Marsh said, "we'd better make sure we don't get infected."

Both boys had shared fantasies of saving the town, on the off chance that everyone became infected. "Ariel's back in town, too," said Jeb nervously. "And that usually spells trouble."

"I heard one of your granddad's friends was watching birds by Panty Point," said Marsh. "And he saw Ariel and the sheriff swimming. Now Joanie Underwood's mad and not talking to her husband."

"They never talk anyway," said Jeb. "Mom told me that Mrs. Underwood's wanted a divorce ever since their third baby was born. And she was always jealous of Ariel."

Marsh blew out a long sigh, as if to say the talk of the town would be too much for anyone to fully process. "But how did Hammerhead get all the way up to Terror House? You know how lazy he is."

"I could never even teach him how to fetch," Jeb said.

"Boys?" Giblets's voice trailed down the tiny hallway just as Jeb dropped a quarter into a slot to get a printout of the article. "How are you coming along in there?"

"Almost done," they called in unison.

But Jeb was sure things had only just begun.

A BONFIRE BLAZED in a concrete pit made especially for the purpose, and Rex glanced toward the kids who were enjoying it, roasting marshmallows. "Nice," he murmured, slipping a hand around Ariel's back and urging her closer on the picnic bench. The buffet meal served in the tearoom had been the best he'd ever eaten, even better than some of his own mother's specialty menus, which was saying something. Complete with roasted lamb, rhubarb, stewed tomatoes, okra and fresh corn, the dinner was topped only by the conversation. The guests had shared their life experiences, and they'd shown the usual interest in the Centers for Disease Control and Rex's world travels. They'd questioned Ariel, too, about her work in TV production.

Not that either of them had garnered more attention than the witches. Ebola, hantavirus and reporting human-interest stories had taken a back seat to the three solemn women dressed in black, carrying brooms and canes and telling tall tales of stolen books of recipes chock-full of killing poisons and love teas. But Rex had been pleasantly surprised to discover he fit in, and that Ariel's relatives had taken a shine to him.

Most times, he was put off by crowds. Analytical and scientific by nature, he was a reader, and he'd been an only child of older parents. Maybe that was why he'd hit it off so well with Gran and Great-gran, he thought now, as well as Ariel's mother.

"Quit," Ariel murmured, reacting to the way he was nuzzling her ear and scooting nearer on the bench.

"You don't really want me to stop," he whispered back. They were both waiting until they could sneak away and get into bed. Turning toward her, he swung a leg over the bench, then pulled her between his legs, drawing a satisfied breath when the pressure of her back hit the fly of his shorts.

"Listen," she said.

"You want to know what Matilda looked like?" Gran was asking the group of kids who were roasting marshmallows. Those less hungry stood off to the side, delighting themselves by holding sparklers, or playing badminton near the house under a spotlight. Traces of red light arced in the dark, and all the trees and bushes winked with fireflies.

"Yes," said a young girl. "Was Matilda pretty?"

"I imagine she was." Gran laughed. "Seeing as she was my relative."

Both children and parents giggled, but Gran wasn't perturbed. "Why..." She looked toward her granddaughter and Rex. "I do believe she looked nearly identical to Ariel, with long blond hair and blue eyes."

"Sounds good to me," Rex whispered, wanting to drag her back upstairs. He'd be gone tomorrow, so tonight was his only chance to explore every inch of her. He tightened his arm around her waist, still barely believing the sex they'd shared on the floor before dinner, or what the night before them promised. It was a good thing he was leaving in the morning, he decided. The chemistry between him and this woman was too strong. He'd lose his head over her, and since he'd just broken an engagement, he wanted to enjoy unattached sex for a while.

Janet really wasn't entirely out of his system. When he'd seen Ariel in that pink, feminine suit, he'd definitely wanted to take her down a peg. And then, when he'd heard Studs Underwood talking about their past, he'd felt…

Jealous. There was no reason for it. Rex tried to remind himself that he didn't even really know her, but then, rationality never had stopped a man's emotions. At the dock, maybe he'd been reminded of Janet, too, since it had turned out that Ariel, like Janet, had a more adventurous past. The impression was furthered when he'd ridden up Mountain Drive in Studs's Land Rover because the sheriff had talked nonstop about what a wild woman Ariel had been.

Not that Rex trusted Studs. Rex had always been a good judge of character, and something about the guy didn't add up. Beginning with his name, Rex thought now. The sheriff was hardly a stud. Balding on top and sporting unattractive stubble on his broad chin, he looked like he carried a chip on his shoulder, felt people owed him something.

Now Rex's eyes meshed with Ariel's, and he smiled. He'd definitely broken his own law upstairs, the one he'd written after Janet, telling himself not to get involved. Of course, his and Ariel's affair would only last for tonight. No longer. Pushing aside the thoughts, he forced himself to refocus his attention on Gran's story.

"…now about Running Deer. That was the name of

Matilda's escort," Gran was saying. "He was a big man. Taller than a house, and it was said he could fell ten men with one swoop of his tomahawk."

"Could he really?" one young boy asked.

"Oh, probably not," admitted Gran. "That might have been an exaggeration. Why, you know how people like to tell tall tales! But he was tough enough to get Matilda all the way over the mountain and then Matilda built the house where you're staying."

"Did Matilda and Running Deer fall in love?" asked a girl.

"An excellent question," said Gran, as she smoothed down the front of her black dress. "And many have thought so, although we don't know. All we have left of Matilda is the book of recipes, which has now been stolen, and the house she built."

"And are stories about the water true?"

Gran raised a brow. "Which stories?"

"Does it have magical properties?" asked an older woman, half in jest, as if to say she hadn't believed what she'd heard.

"Seems like it to me," Rex whispered.

After they'd made love, they'd separated long enough to change—her into another light, airy sundress, and him, into a pair of shorts and a button-down blue shirt. Now he dipped his chin, planting a kiss on a bare shoulder. His thumb followed, rubbing circles on the spot his mouth had vacated, warming her skin, drawing a promise that he meant to make good on soon.

"You've been drinking bottled water," she said.

"The pool," he reminded.

"You told me chlorine would probably kill a bug."

"Possibly, but who knows?"

"Well, let's not start widespread panic," she said.

"Panic?"

"Don't you watch movies about the CDC?"

"Some." He smiled. "What say we go upstairs and quarantine you?"

"You don't seem to be taking the threat too seriously."

"Judging by my last girlfriend," he admitted, "being infected by love could be quite dangerous. I'd say it's right up there with every other contagious disease."

Her shoulders shook with merriment. He liked hearing her laugh; the sound was as full as her voice and sent a thrill through him. "That bad, huh?"

He nodded.

"Were you madly in love?"

"Almost married her."

Turning to face him, she assessed him for a long moment. He found himself starting to feel strangely flinty. "Why so surprised?"

She shrugged. "You just didn't seem like the type of guy to…"

"Settle down?" Suddenly, his lips stretched into another smile. "I guess our own…" he considered carefully before he said the word "…*relationship* isn't following the usual pattern."

"A coffee date, then dinner, then a background check, then sex?" she guessed.

"You do background checks?"

She shook her head, her eyes dancing. "Not usually. But for you…"

"If you're going to hire a detective, you'd better hurry, since it's almost the bewitching hour."

Her expression soured. "Besides, the only lawman around is Studs." As if she didn't want to pursue that conversation, she said, "The dinner-movie thing. Is that what you did with…"

"Janet," he offered, surprised to find he didn't mind talking about her. Maybe there really was something buggy in the water because he wound up saying, "Yeah, until I found her getting it on with the chef right before our wedding."

"Ouch."

He was glad she hadn't offered saccharine sympathy. "I'm over it."

Her cheeks puffed, as if she were fighting a grin, and he could see her skin color, even in the dark. "Upstairs you didn't seem to be carrying a torch."

"And as you pointed out, I'm probably not even affected by the local water," he promised. "Clean as a whistle. Free of the love disease."

"Isn't that how you fight viruses, anyway?" she asked, placing her hands on his upper thighs. As she slid them down toward his knees, he felt a pull at his groin. He sucked in a breath, drawing it through clenched teeth as her hands ever so slowly continued moving over his skin.

At the touch, he'd lost all thought. "Hmm?"

"Don't you fight viruses by injecting a small dose of the disease itself?"

"Ah. True." He squeezed her thighs with his, sandwiching her in the crook of his legs. God, she felt good. He arched, just slightly, pressing his groin to her back, hoping for relief from the pleasure that had started to build, knowing he needed to get her back upstairs soon. When his eyes captured hers, they held, sparking. "I think little doses of sex might work for me," he murmured against her neck.

He was prepared. Before dinner, he'd driven into town and bought condoms, a trip that hadn't gone unnoticed. First, the size of his vehicle called attention to him, as did the nature of his purchase.

"Staying up at the Teasdale-Anderson place, huh?" the pharmacist had asked dryly.

"Sure am," he'd replied.

Only when he'd returned to the parking lot had he made the connection between the comment and his purchase. With a sinking feeling, he'd wondered about Ariel's reputation again. Not that he'd ever believed in proverbial bad girls, per se. In fact, he'd always thought it a shame when people couldn't admit that women had healthy sex drives, just the same as men. Nonetheless, he hated to think of such a beautiful woman growing up in the face of such ugly talk, especially in a town this small, and he didn't want to add to the situation. From what she'd said upstairs, and how she'd reacted, she was clearly sensitive about the issue.

Resting his chin on the top of her head, he marveled at how she fit against him. "Are you sure you're not infected?" she whispered.

"We'll know in the morning."

He'd collected countless water samples, and now each was in the cooker, the CDC's nickname for the tumblers in the mobile lab. They grew viruses and bacteria at advanced rates, so if any trace of Romeo really was here, he'd probably see something in the morning, when he observed the samples under a microscope. Of course, if something besides Ariel was clouding his judgement...

"I really don't think there's anything to worry about," he said, stating his earlier opinion.

"I hope not. I mean, even if it was in the water, and isn't harmful in any long-term way, it would still interfere with my story."

He brushed back a strand of hair that had blown free from a ponytail. Just like today, her hair was drawn tightly back, fixed by a clasp, and while that did accentuate her features—the wide-set eyes, smooth skin, and a small cherry mouth—he'd liked seeing it down, the impossibly long straight strands flying like silk over her shoulders. "The story's important to you?" he prompted, though he'd heard even more about the project at dinner.

Despite the low firelight, he could see the moment her eyes turned veiled. "Yeah," she said simply, her voice catching.

Then she quickly averted her gaze and he felt his heart skip a beat. He'd seen those old wounds again, ghosting in the irises of her eyes. They were so clear and crystal, but just like the springwaters, they seemed to hold secrets, and they were too expressive, too revealing. She wasn't a person who could always hide her emotions.

"Hard to imagine the local kids calling this place Terror House," he couldn't help but say, looking away from her and studying the house, keeping his voice low, since her grandmother continued to entertain guests.

No place could have looked less menacing. From this angle under the moonlight the dark, fresh white paint of the house gleamed, and the lemon-and-mint gingerbread trim made the house look like something decorated at Christmastime that any kid would want to eat. The grounds were extensive; they sprawled all over the mountain, in fact. And there were bike trails, as well as a pool, tennis courts and a barn full of horses.

"Now it looks inviting, but the winters are different," she said, as if reading his mind, wistfulness in her voice. "Desolate. We close the third floor, which is where most of the guests are staying, and even a wing of the second floor. The landscapers don't come back until spring. And because we're in the mountains, we get a lot of snow. The courts are covered, and the pool's under a tarp. Sometimes, weeks go by and you can't get off the hill."

He frowned. "What about school, when you were a kid?"

"Oh," she said. "I was always happy not to go."

"That bad, huh?" he said, echoing her earlier words.

"Worse." She shrugged. "Sometimes, depending on the ice, we'd walk down the mountain steps to the dock, and someone would take me over in the outboard. I'd catch the school bus in front of Jack's Diner."

He shook his head. "It's hard to believe the place is this transformed in the summer."

She eyed him. "Didn't you see *The Shining?*"

"You can't compare your bed-and-breakfast to that closed-down hotel."

"Sure can. Remember the opening…when Jack Nicholson and Shelley Duvall drive up the long, endless, snowy driveway, and the whole place is blanketed in snow?"

"You don't have any ghosts, do you?"

"No, but they say there's a graveyard in the woods where the Teasdale-Anderson women have buried bodies of all the men they've killed."

His eyes widened. "That's a hard one to live with. Uh…should I watch my back?"

She laughed, and the movement jarred him, sending tiny ripples from her back to the aching space between his legs. The vibration hummed like a lulling current. "I promise not to kill you tonight," she said. "But I admit, I didn't get many dates."

"You don't sound crushed." But judging by her exchange with the sheriff, maybe she had been. "Was the sheriff…"

"The only one to care for me?"

Now she looked amused, but he nodded.

She shrugged. "He wished." Craning her head, she settled her eyes on his once more, and she looked particularly beautiful in the firelight, with shadows dancing across her cheeks like fairy wings; the depth of feeling in her eyes stirred him like a fire.

There was such a hot core in this woman. "You do look worthy of Matilda Teasdale," he couldn't help but say.

"How so?"

His eyes twinkled. "Like you might have a line on some dangerous brews. Stuff that could drive any usually reasonable guy insane."

"Are you usually reasonable?"

"Not anymore."

"He made up all those stories," she said simply. "Every thing you heard. He's been doing it for years."

He was surprised to feel the gentleness of his own hand when it smoothed her hair once more. It was a silly thing, but he liked the shape of her head, how it felt beneath his fingers, which molded to it perfectly. Probably, he should have guessed. His throat tightened as he thought of her upstairs, prancing around him naked, furious and wanting to taunt him, and all in payback for how an ass like Studs Underwood had made her feel. "Want to tell me about it?"

"I just did."

He supposed she had. But he wanted...more details. Hell, maybe he wanted to get riled, so he could head down the hill, find the sheriff, and punch him. So the jerk had spread stories all over town and everyone had believed them, even though none were true. He suddenly felt he'd happily harm anyone who bothered Ariel.

"Who'd you hang out with?"

"Myself, myself and myself." Abruptly, she laughed, but he could hear the pain. "And the witches."

"You seem to get along with your folks."

"There are some glitches, as in all family relationships, I guess. But we do all right."

"What about your dad?"

There was a long silence, protracted enough that he was sorry he'd asked. She stared into the fire, then glanced over her shoulder once more. Everything around them seemed to disappear. He might well have just gotten punch-drunk on a gallon of the local water.

"He left," she finally said. "And Mom and I never really talk about it. It just didn't work out between them. You know, I can think of plenty of other things I'd rather do on your only night in town than talk about all this."

He was game. "Such as?"

She rolled her eyes in answer.

"Then we'd better get out of here."

She smiled. "What say we live dangerously and take a dip in the spring."

"Not afraid of infection?"

"Your samples are already in."

"If I get love-struck, I might never go home." Gliding his hands over the backs of hers, he dropped his fingers between hers, then rose, pulling her up with him.

"Why do I feel like a guinea pig?" she asked.

"Because I'm a born scientist. I need to explore every inch of my subjects." Snaking his hands around her waist, he smoothed her dress down, feeling the warmth of her skin beneath, the soft curve of her belly. "If Romeo's in the water," he promised, nuzzling his face against her neck as they began to walk toward the stone steps carved into the mountain, "the outcome could be very dangerous."

"That's my hope," she said. "And because you've already gathered all your samples, and the rumors about the bug seem to show that it only stays in the bloodstream for a week, things could work out perfectly…."

Rex knew he was acting uncharacteristically, but surely that was only because she was so gorgeous. "A week of sexual bliss," he murmured.

"Yes," she whispered simply.

7

"C'MON," REX CALLED from the opposite end of the dock, "don't tell me you're going to chicken out and not get wet."

Oh, she was wet, all right. She'd already walked to the dock's end, and now she turned from the water and peered through the darkness. She was just able to make out the shore and the outline of his body as he took off his shirt and tied the sleeves around a tree branch. He kicked off his shoes. Because being here with a man had been something about which she'd always dreamed, her throat tightened as he slowly came toward her.

"It looks nippy," she called.

"Dipped in a toe yet?"

She shook her head. "Not yet. But I grew up here, so I can tell you that the water's hot on top, cold in the middle, and then as warm as fire."

"Then let's stay near the surface then."

Nodding, she glanced upward, toward the house. She loved this place, mostly because of the fun she'd had with guests during the summers, and she'd always known that other kids in town would have loved nights like tonight, if she'd given them more of a chance. But she hadn't. And they hadn't tried to befriend her, so she'd never had a boyfriend in Bliss, no more than she'd tried to defend herself against the rumors Studs had started.

Maybe it had been stupid not to. But then, that was the road untraveled, so she'd never know. Even if she'd told her side of the story, no one in town would have believed her, she'd figured, both then and now. Besides, in addition to coming from a long line of tight-lipped women who wrapped secrets around themselves like well-worn shawls, Studs's accusations had hit a deep nerve that had made Ariel feel she'd be damned to grace him with a response.

Still, she'd suffered because of that decision. Sure, she felt she'd never want to know people who didn't give her the benefit of the doubt, but eleven years after leaving Bliss, she still felt shell-shocked whenever she returned. Had she really lived through high school with so few friends while Studs had tortured her?

Old habits had died hard. She hadn't exactly jumped into the social scene after she'd moved out of state, either. Her growth had been slow and hard-won. She'd started with small dips of her toes into the waters of the Pittsburgh social scene, meeting people for drinks after work, then joining clubs and accepting coffee dates. She'd met people through a barn, where she rode, and had even taken up swing dancing. Success at work had built her confidence, and occasionally, she'd felt a backlash of anger, as she'd realized how easily people in the new town had opened up to her, and therefore, how senselessly she'd been hurt in Bliss.

Maybe if she were growing up in Bliss today, things would have been different, she supposed, still watching Rex approach. In the past, Bliss had been even smaller.

More provincial, if possible. It had grown in population since Ariel's day—not much, but some—and nowadays people were influenced by the open-minded ideas touted on TV, by people such as Dr. Phil and Oprah. Maybe now somebody would have guessed at the truth of her innocence.

Anyway, as far as she was concerned, history was vindicating her, as it often did those who suffered silently. All grown up, Studs Underwood definitely resembled the pig he really was. On another level, Ariel hadn't totally minded her lot, anyway, if the truth be told. She'd learned to love solitary pursuits, which had led to a promising career. Growing up, her job around the house had been to care for the horses, which she'd loved, and during the winters, when the guests weren't there, she'd ride all day. One by one, she'd taken the horses deep into the woods, sometimes pretending she was Matilda, crossing the mountains for the first time with an amorous Cherokee medicine man by her side.

"Deep thoughts?" Rex queried. As he stopped in front of her, he slipped his arms easily around her waist, and her arms rose to wreath his neck. She felt her backside warm to the touch as he dipped his hands lower.

She smiled into his eyes. "Can't shake them."

"Then don't try."

She liked that, too…that he was accepting of moods, not trying to shake her out of them, the way some men would. He was taller than her, by at least half a foot, and while she sometimes had resented her petite stature, probably because aspects of her life in Bliss had made her feel so powerless, she didn't mind it now.

Instead, hovering in his shadow only made her feel

more feminine. His skin felt nearly hot, and as she touched his neck, she reached on tiptoe, brushing her lips to his chin. Slowly, she let her thumbs explore the shells of his ears as she feathered kisses on his neck, lightly pinching the lobes with her teeth before licking a trail to his collarbone. She reveled in the smoothness of his skin and the feeling of the strong muscles that rippled like a breeze.

Turning her cheek then, she simply lay it against his chest, feeling warmth seep onto her cheek, and she sighed, enjoying his closeness. He hauled her all the way into his embrace, and after a silent moment, he began to sway, slightly rocking her. As she drew a deep breath, something edgy and male rode to her lungs, piggybacking on pine and apples—and maybe even stardust. The pads of his bare feet shifted on the silvered wood beneath them, seemingly in tandem with a whir of crickets, coming from berried thickets by the bank.

She didn't know how long they stood there, simply swaying, and if the truth be told, she hardly cared. It could have been minutes, or hours, but when she finally felt his fingers find her chin and lift her mouth for a kiss, something had changed. No one had ever held her like this, no more than anyone had kissed her like this.

No, no one would ever kiss her like this again, she thought; this was a one-time event. A one-of-a-kind kiss. A fleeting moment of luck, never to be relived. He wasn't hungry, like before. Nor hurried. His mouth hovered, the breath nothing more than a teasing flicker of shivery warmth. His lips brushed hers—once, twice, thrice—barely touching for an eternity, before firm lips offered increasing pressure that threatened to do her in.

Yes, it felt like nothing, yet the kiss brought more than mere arousal...even more than the explosive response he'd wrenched from her upstairs.

His lips parted farther, urging hers open, and his tongue darted, seeking hers. He was making more than just her body ache. Her heart was tugging as he probed farther. What he sought was as timely, old and mysterious as the Teasdale house itself, and he was patient in the pursuit, deftly rolling his tongue, then flickering languorously.

Memories unleashed in a stream of images that seemed, however absurdly, to have been solicited by that sweet probing, and by the hands that dropped over her buttocks, cupping her flesh, squeezing as he moved her against him. His upper body drew back, just enough so their lips barely touched once more, and now, her moan was caught in the open-mouthed kiss; it hovered unheard in a realm of shared fire that jetted between them, and she felt sensations building, turning edgy, wanting...release.

How many times had she stood on this dock, imagining she was Matilda? Or that she was about to be ravished by Running Deer? This was so much better than any lonely, teenage fantasy. Arching, she sought the erection pressuring the fly of his shorts. He was so big there, already hard for her. Yes, he wanted her, and she could use him for any pleasure she wished.

He deepened the kiss once more, and gasping, she fought the impulse to turn away; the deeper contact with the hard ridge of him suddenly seeming too intense. She could love this man, she thought, marveling at that....

Somehow, she'd rounded a corner—driven into Bliss

and then everything had changed. Her feelings for him had come suddenly, arriving with the force of a premonition. "I think I might need one of Matilda's teas to calm my nerves," she whispered against his lips.

"I'd rather drink an aphrodisiac."

She felt she already had. "That's what her teas are."

"Then pour me a drink."

"Do you really need an aphrodisiac?"

"No," he whispered. Then adamantly he added, "God no. Ariel…" He leaned away a moment, looking into her eyes. As if at a loss for words, he murmured, "You feel so good."

Maybe that's why she felt relieved that he'd be leaving in the morning. She'd wanted something like this to happen for so long, true. What woman wouldn't? He was a dream man, the perfect lover, and he'd come out of nowhere, into her life….

But she knew better than to get attached. Instead, she'd be everything she'd always wanted to be with a man. Brazen. Flirtatious. Serious… Anything. He'd proven himself to be so easy to be with, so nonjudgmental. Almost instinctively, he'd seemed to grasp how she felt about her past. With a few simple words, she'd been able to communicate how life had been for her, and he seemed to want to show her what she'd craved during her loneliest years….

He kissed her again, long and hard, then leaned back, breaking the kiss, keeping his hands cupped possessively on her behind. He stroked. "C'mon," he said huskily, "get in the water with me, Ariel."

She considered, since the heat coursing between their bodies was arguing for simply turning around, heading to the house and to her bedroom. Or his. But she nodded.

"I don't want to get my dress wet," she managed to say, trying not to notice the tingling spreading through her. She glanced toward the house. "And I hope no one comes down."

"People looked tired," he said, tracing his hands down her arms, catching her fingertips and bringing them to his chest. Leaning, he kissed the tips, one by one, and she had a fantasy of heading for the shore. She could almost feel the dark, damp earth beneath her, the softness of it on her backside as he plunged deep inside her.

But the condoms were upstairs.

"Here," he murmured, sounding equally affected. Leaning deftly, he caught the hem of her dress, lifted it and brought the fabric over her head. She shuddered as cooler night air hit her exposed chest, the already tight buds yearning for the salve of his mouth.

"You're beautiful, Ariel."

It seemed stupid to say it, but she did, anyway. "You, too."

He didn't even smile. It was too magical out here to make light of such a moment. He was facing bright stars scattered across the jet sky and a full glowing moon, the pale dress in his dark hand seemed to catch light, refracting it, and reflecting beams back to his face. The air seemed strangely, impossibly moist. The night was so clear and yet dense, too, as if shrouded in a fog. Strange, she thought again. Uncanny.

She barely recognized her voice when she finally spoke. "Just wrap my dress around the dock post. I'll wear panties."

"Don't," he whispered.

Her throat tightened once more as she watched him take off his shorts. They dropped to the deck with his briefs, and as he stepped toward her again, she exhaled on a soft whish, trying to steady the mad hammer of her heart. A second later, his hands were on her waist again, circling it, drawing her closer, and she melted when she felt the engorging length of him pressing the panty silk. He brought his head lower. She thrust her fingers upward, drawing his head into cleavage.

Something crashed inside her—jumbled and fused—as she felt the lick of his tongue and heard him groan with need. He hadn't shaved since morning, and stubble roughened her skin, shooting awareness through her, making desire darkly spin in her veins. She remembered other burns he'd marked her with today…burns of his suckling mouth on her neck… burns on her back from the carpet where she'd lifted her hips to take more of his intimate kiss. But, she longed to feel what she hadn't then—his hard, steely length pushing her higher and higher until she tumbled over the highest edge into unknown depths of ecstasy.

Yes…the fall. That's what she wanted, so she gasped as big hands slid upward, lifting her breasts from beneath. She was full and wanting, more than his hands could accommodate, and she'd couldn't believe the shivery feeling when he licked his lips, then locked them—hot, wet, tight—over a nipple. Palpitations poured through her, and the flinch of his erection against her belly made her mutter something senseless.

This was bliss. Pure, unmitigated bliss. She flung back her neck, forgetting her surroundings as he kneaded her, the strong, slender fingers closing. Feathery kisses nibbled at the stiffened tips, and her fingers cupped his head, urging him closer still.

"Beautiful," he pronounced once more, leaning to look into eyes she'd half shut. He looked his fill, even as his hands found her again, using a thumb to circle a wet, glistening nipple.

"Kiss me...."

Love burst in her heart as he did as she wanted, his lips closing tightly—so impossibly tightly—and he suckled deeply. Only when he'd slaked his thirst, and she was teetering on the edge, did his eyes find hers again.

"C'mon," he managed to say, his breath labored.

But she needed...

He grabbed her hand. "Let's swim."

Following him to the water, she sat on the dock and watched as he lowered himself, not stopping until his shoulders were submerged. "It's not deep," she said, surprised to hear the normal sound of her voice. After how he'd just touched her, she'd have expected it to come out jittery.

"My toes feel the bottom."

"It drops off about ten feet out."

Lifting her hips, she slipped off her panties, then tossed them toward his shorts. His eyes were on her, just slits of midnight-blue that glinted with starlight as he trailed the trimmed tuft of blond hair. His eyes settled, and as she gripped the side of the dock, she could hear his breath catch. Gripping her thighs, he parted them as he had earlier in the day. He leaned and nuzzled her, kissing her once as his hands dipped beneath the water, curling around her calves.

He smiled up at her, then slid his fingers down to her feet and cupped the insteps, massaging. Placing her hands on his shoulders, her eyes traced the water lapping his neck, settling where wet tips of his hair cleaved to skin. She slipped into the water, shuddering against him as their water-slick bodies rubbed.

His feet had gained purchase and her legs wrapped around his waist. She was loving this, so much so that she said it out loud. "I like being…"

"Hmm?"

"Naked like this."

He shot her a playful look, his eyes sparkling with awareness. "Uh…yeah." As if to say, Duh.

"I mean, playing but not making love," she clarified.

Heat was in his eyes. "This *is* making love, Ariel."

She supposed it was. Generally, she thought of the act of sex, itself. His eyes were on her face, assessing, as if he were registering that she'd never been this free with anyone. Oh, she'd had boyfriends. But it had never been…like this.

"Ready?" he asked.

"For?"

He bounced her lightly, his hands cupping her bottom, his smile and teasing lift of brows preparing her for what was to come. She took a deep breath, trying not to laugh—but then she laughed, anyway—as he plunged into the water, submerging them.

As he brought them both back up with a splash, he flung back his head. The mouth that immediately found hers was cool, and right after she opened for the quick meshing of tongues, she heard him say, "Let's go deeper."

She was still tasting the kiss and feeling the rumble

of his voice. It made his chest vibrate, and she knew he wasn't only talking about going deeper into the water. He was talking about going deeper, into each other. "Okay," she whispered.

He was like a drug, drawing her into some delicious underworld of sensation as he began walking farther into the spring. Looping her hands around his neck, she loosened her legs around his back, so her feet massaged his thighs. Like the water, he seemed to call her into depths she'd never dreamed of exploring....

"They say the source of the spring is under the mountain," she found herself saying, when the water deepened and they broke apart to swim. He was a good swimmer, she realized, watching the smooth, easy glide of his body, how the powerful muscles of rounded shoulders rolled as he moved. "Swim a lot?" she asked.

"Most days in the gym. At least when I'm in the country. Rarely outside. It's always a treat." He was a few feet away. "How deep does it go?"

How deep will we go, Ariel? She shook her head, scissoring her legs and pushing her arms outward in a wide circle, feeling an ache in her muscles. "No one knows. People have gone diving beneath the mountain, but no one's ever really found the mouth of the spring."

"Must be deep then."

She couldn't help but grin. "Like my mind."

"I wouldn't argue with you there."

"You don't know me."

"Yet," he promised.

Suddenly swinging her arm in a wide arc and catching water in a cupped hand, she didn't make an honest effort to splash him, but then, Rex wasn't nearly so kind. He sent a wave her way, and just as she quickly swam toward him, he neatly ducked, dovetailing as easily as a dolphin.

"Where did you go?" she muttered.

He disappeared for a good long while…long enough that she started to worry. She glanced around, treading water in circles, looking toward shore, wondering if he'd swum away.

A thrill of anticipation zipped through her. He was right beneath her, tickling her feet! Or at least she hoped it was him. She tried to swat beneath her, waving a hand in the water, but once more, something slimy—most probably his wet fingers—ghosted an instep.

"Is that you?" she asked, giggling, tucking her feet toward her belly, trying to escape. Not that there was much else in the water but him. Snakes in Bliss were usually of the land variety, rattlers and copperheads. All at once, he surfaced, blowing out whatever was left of his breath, bringing enough water with him that he could have been a whale. His shoulders were shaking with laughter.

"You scared me!"

He didn't exactly sound sincere. "Sorry."

"What?" she asked rhetorically. "Can you hold your breath forever?"

"Almost."

"Bet I can hold mine longer."

"Competitive, are you?"

"Only when I know I'll win."

She found his hand, then realized they could swim together, with one set of hands loosely linked, and their free hands plowing through the water. Feeling like a wild, naked animal in the moonlight, she could barely believe the beauty of how it felt to swim with him. The water was as she'd always remembered it, warm on the surface, colder as they moved from the dock, then warm once more, as they dove down... down...down....

It was pitch dark now. The light of the moon was lost, and there was only him, a man whose name she hadn't even known just hours ago. They played and frolicked, swimming over and around each other. Ducking and diving, they twined arms and legs like seaweed, grew into one strand, then released again.

And then they were suddenly kicking, their feet moving as fast as flippers, holding hands and heading for the surface...the far-off stars and moon and air. She felt her lungs would explode; then they broke the glassy surface, gasping for breath.

"It feels weird down there," he managed to say, jerking his head to flip back his hair and sending an arc of water spray behind him.

She treaded water. "Hot."

"You're right. You can feel the temperature change."

"Nice, huh?"

"Very."

"I loved everything about Bliss," she found herself saying. She paused, then added, "Except the people."

He looked around, taking in the lush green shorelines. Far off, through the trees, tiny white lights winked through the trees, and far up the mountain was the impressive edifice of Matilda Teasdale's legacy. A rare, perfect full moon shone down at them and the stars were glittering. Dark waters eddied by their faces, lapping softly, kissing skin. "It's one of the prettiest places I've ever seen," he admitted.

"Since you're a world traveler, that's saying something."

"Yeah," he said, his voice lowering, catching as he took in her face. "Yeah, it is."

This time, the beauty was her, not the place.

Being with him was definitely dangerous, she thought. More than one day of this kind of treatment and she was sure her heart would be lost forever. Tomorrow when they parted, she thought, she'd play it cool. She wouldn't even suggest they exchange addresses, or try to keep in touch. After all, he was in Atlanta, and only when he wasn't traveling abroad; she was in Pittsburgh. Fate had brought them together only for a night, to swim together in the wilds of West Virginia, under the blanketing trees and stars. She had to let this be exactly what it was meant to be—a fantasy.

Reaching, he swam closer and grasped her hand. "Take a deep breath. Let's go down again."

She nodded, then felt a jolt when his hand tightened over hers, fitting like a glove. Their eyes met. Simultaneously, they drew in the moist night air, filling their lungs, and then they plunged. This time, as the cold mid-waters gave way to more intense heat, she felt them stoking the darker flames inside her, instead of quenching them.

A wake fluttered past, a ripple as his body glided next to hers. Surely, he felt the heat of the spring now, how it entered the very bloodstream. Way down, deep in the waters, was magic at its best. Here, it could never matter whether Matilda had really traveled to Bliss after having heard about the spring's special properties, or whether she'd wanted to harness its powers for teas, no more than Ariel cared if the love bug actually existed, returning periodically, compelling everyone in Bliss to stop their usual routines.

No, all that mattered was the sensation. Waters warmed her from the inside out. Even if a hundred Studs Underwoods had tortured her, instead of just one, Ariel still would have loved this spring, just as she loved the land in the most desolate winters, when the kids in town had huddled together, terrifying themselves with tall tales, while she—and only she—had had the freedom of galloping on horseback through woods rumored to hold gravesites…riding hard with her head down while cold air had knifed her lungs and hooves had kicked up snow powder.

Freedom.

That's what Ariel had known. It was the hidden silver lining in the cloud of the way the other kids had treated her. Whatever fury she'd once felt had been soothed by these waters so many times, and as water around any grain of sand, they'd finally turned out a beautiful pearl. Tonight, the man beside her was cracking open her shell, finding the part inside that glowed.

One night, she thought once more. She'd had so many fantasies in this town. Now, she had plenty to fulfill with him—and only a few hours left in which to do it. Already, earlier today, he'd done what no man had before. Heat gushed through her at the recollection of his mouth fixed on the most intimate part of her.

And now, as they turned to swim toward the surface again, she intended to find at least one thing Rex Houston would enjoy, something extra special that she could do in return.

8

"YOUR ROOM OR MINE?" he asked. She was backlit, her face in shadow, and as he took in how the dim, dancing light played on her skin, his body felt strangely invigorated from swimming, even though it had been a long day, full of unexpected twists. Yet he felt drained, too. Had he really traveled from out of state, driven from Charleston to Bliss, then met Ariel? It seemed as if his last conversation with Jessica had occurred a thousand years ago, instead of just this morning.

As if reading his mind, Ariel stepped to the threshold between their rooms, whispering, "You looked tired."

"Not *that* tired," he said, hoping she hadn't decided to go to bed alone, not that he really thought she would. Nor would he let her, he realized. Not without a fight. She was his tonight.

"You're dirty, too."

Noting the white nightie in her hand, he said, "I don't think you'll need that."

"Thought you might like to see me in it."

He shook his head and simply said, "Naked." A streak of mud trekked across his bare chest, and as she dropped the nightie and stepped forward and traced it, the slow rake of her fingernail raised goose bumps.

"You don't look much cleaner," he managed to say, his chest feeling suddenly tight.

"No?"

Because she looked more beautiful than anything he'd ever seen, he said nothing. Her hair was pulled back, exposing her clear face; stray strands loosened from the band fell against her neck. Something in her expression—he wasn't quite sure what—made her look younger than she probably was. She was strong, but carried a lot of vulnerability, and he liked that. He wasn't sure why. Maybe because he hated simple people. And he liked challenges. Besides, the older he got, the more people seemed to shut off and tune out. Building a life—working and raising kids required too much focus to stay in touch with emotion. He'd lost some friends that way. He wanted to keep things fresh in his own life, always to feel alive.

"How old are you?" he asked.

Her lips twitched playfully as she considered. "Think I might be jailbait?"

He laughed. His hands found her shoulders, and now both thumbs slowly stroked her upper chest. After a moment he dropped his hands. "Tell me."

"Twenty-nine. You?"

"Thirty-two."

"Young for a doctor. Isn't it?"

He shrugged. "Not really. But I graduated high school early. College, too."

She looked impressed. "You must be smart."

He laughed. "Very. But for me, it wasn't what it's cracked up to be."

She leaned against the doorjamb, cocking her head as if to better look at him. "No?"

"All the stupid guys got the girls."

"What?" she asked rhetorically, chuckling. "Did you start analyzing theorems on dates?"

"I might have tried to explain pheromones," he admitted. "Or explained how velocity related to my model cars."

She didn't look convinced. "You're, uh…"

"What?" he prompted.

She settled on saying, "Pretty hot."

"Glad you think so."

"If you weren't," she added, "I'd have settled for smart."

"Good," he murmured. She was barefoot, and mud from the bank had splashed her ankles and calves. The sundress, dampened by springwater, clung limply to her body. In the long silence that fell, he was surprised to find he wasn't uncomfortable. Janet had been a chatterbox, filling every emptiness between them, as if space was hers to wrap neatly, package and dispense. She hadn't cared what she talked about, either—usually clothes shopping, books and movies. Not so Ariel. She was entirely at ease with pauses and wordless moments.

He could smell the heady scent of her. It was a palpable thing between them, like a sinuous cat stretching, arching its back. His familiar, he thought, feeling the pull of his groin again.

She was eyeing him. "Hmm?"

He shrugged, not sure how to put what he was feeling into words. He was a reader, but if the truth be told, he was more at ease with slides and tumblers than feelings. Earlier, the spring's current had felt strong and forbidding. Even now, he felt the urge to dive again, to swim toward all that mysterious heat and maybe discover what no man ever had—the source. "The spring…"

She smiled. "It has its magic."

He lifted a brow lazily. "I'm a scientist, remember?"

"You don't believe in things that can't be explained?"

"Not usually."

"Maybe it's time you start."

"Maybe so," he murmured, stretching to push aside a fallen lock of hair and touch her cheek. "No one was around when we came in," he commented, glad they hadn't seen anyone. He wanted her all to himself. Besides, the swim had left him feeling oddly raw, too open emotionally, and he wasn't used to it, no more than he knew how to communicate the rare feelings.

She said, "They go to bed early."

"The guests?"

"And my folks. They get up and start cooking at the crack of dawn. Though I didn't see Mom's car in the lot, come to think of it." She paused, then, as an afterthought, added, "And that's strange. Usually, Mom doesn't go out at night."

"A homebody?"

"All we witches are."

He laughed once more. "I'd be more scared if you'd really been able to show me the graves in the woods where you keep all your ex-boyfriends."

"Husbands, too," she reminded.

As her bare shoulders lifted, shaking with merriment, her skin hit the light, just so—and he was struck once more by her quiet beauty. Reaching, he cupped a shoulder, slowly rubbing a thumb along the collarbone again, then into a hollow, somehow amazed at the feel of the skin. He'd completely lost track of what she was saying.

"...When I visit, I do as much work as they'll let me

do—cooking, cleaning and entertaining guests," she continued. "But they like for me to relax and enjoy myself."

He pulled his gaze from her; he'd been staring as if mesmerized. He forced himself to refocus his eyes on hers—the neat tufts of blond eyebrows and spiked light brown lashes. "They want you to act like you're a guest?"

She nodded.

"Nice of them."

"It is."

"Do you think they'll…"

"Think we're together?"

They'd been pretty obvious about their attraction at the bonfire. "Would that be a problem?"

"Honestly?" she asked with an impish smile that brightened her eyes and dazzled him. "I don't really know. But I guess not. They seemed to like you." She shrugged, still smiling. "I locked my door."

"Good." He hated to think about the possible scene if anyone had walked in on them earlier, rolling around on the floor. Even now, the musky sweet scent was entering his bloodstream, and he knew he'd remember it forever.

"Maybe we shouldn't have stopped at the barn," she said. "It's late now."

But he'd enjoyed watching her. "You like the horses," he said simply. They'd recognized her immediately and had come to nuzzle her hand. He didn't ride, and she'd said she was sorry he wouldn't be staying longer, since the horses were used to inexperienced riders, which many of the guests were, and she would have taken him.

His first thought had been that he might change his mind and stay. Easily, he could imagine her in the saddle, hunched down, her hands in the mane, her thighs squeezing the flanks. But then, once he checked the water samples in the morning, he knew he ought to take off. He liked the idea Ariel seemed to have warmed to—of the two of them spending the next few hours getting hot and heavy, really letting themselves go.

"Too bad we didn't find anything in the root cellar," he said now. He'd suggested they stop there, on the way back from the barn, just to check things out.

"We're not detectives," she pointed out.

"I do trace viruses around the globe."

Her eyes widened, as if to say she hadn't quite seen it that way before. "True."

Not that he'd found anything new. "It bothers me that the sheriff didn't check more thoroughly. Or question people yet," he mused. "Wonder why?"

She shook her head. "His issues with me probably have something to do with it. I just hope the book's recovered."

"Me, too." The conversations he'd had over dinner had clarified how important it was to the women of the house. Without it, Great-gran said she didn't trust herself to concoct specialty teas for the Harvest Festival, although Ariel's mother and grandmother had assured her they could make do, if necessary.

When he spoke again, the words were barely audible, touched with desire. "I like the way you're looking at me, Ariel."

Awareness sharpened in her eyes. "How's that?"

"Like you want to screw my brains out."

"How indelicate," she teased.

His eyes lasered into hers. "Exactly."

The humor that had sparkled in her eyes faltered and was replaced by something less easy to interpret, vulnerability maybe. Uncertainty, he decided. Her voice lowered, catching. "As dirty as we are…let's run a bath."

"Now, why didn't I think of that?"

"The spring," she assured. "It loosens synapses."

"So, I take it that we're in my room?"

"It's cooler in here. I left my windows open. I usually do, and keep my doors shut, so cooler air from the rest of the house doesn't escape."

"Then c'mon in."

Turning, he headed for the bath, lifting some condoms from the bedside table as he moved, feeling eyes on his back that were every bit as warm as the water had been outside. He didn't wait for her, but let her take her time, and as he dimmed the lights in the bathroom and flicked a radio on a shelf to On, he heard his door shut. Good. He'd left it open, anxious to open the other door between their rooms, since she'd gone for a change of clothes, but the last thing he wanted now was intruders. Jazz played softly as he twisted the faucet and tested the water.

He glanced at the mirrored wall, and then, noticing a basket between the two sinks behind him, he found a bottle of bath foam and squirted some into the tub. In the mirror, he could see Ariel enter.

Turning to face him, she leaned against the cabinet and raised an eyebrow. "Hmm?"

"More suds than I expected."

Not that he really gave a damn. They were alone now. Alone, somewhere other than in a public place, and that meant they could get naked again. He stepped closer, and as he lowered his head to taste her spicy mouth, his hands found her, and his mind exploded with questions he knew better than to ask. Was she as affected as him? Had she been as blown away by how they'd swum together?

He leaned away from her, just enough so he could urge the dress over her head. Her chest was as pale as his was dark, her breasts heavy. Running his fingers beneath them, he tested, teasing her by feeling their weight. The buds tightened, growing rosier. Spreading his fingers wide, he trailed them down her belly, then turning his hand at the last moment to arrow his fingers into her crotch, cupping her mound.

"You're wet," he whispered hoarsely.

"The spring," she whispered. "We didn't have a towel."

"It's you, baby," he whispered back.

"That, too." Her voice was edgy with need as she arched for the hand that warmed her. "You're making me wetter."

"Wait till I'm inside you." His labored pant turned harsher when he slipped a hand under the waistband, over impossibly soft curls. He lightly tugged, soliciting a fluttering breath from between her lips. It beat by his ears as delicately as wings, and when he used a finger to part her, the shakiness he sensed in her thighs drove his excitement, taking it up another notch.

"You're so easy," he muttered, heat pouring through his veins, pooling in his belly. He pushed a thick finger inside, intending to ready her further, but the slick heat that greeted him told him there was no need. Backing against the cabinet, she opened wider, parting farther, giving him full access.

She whispered, "Easy?"

"To arouse," he murmured. He pressed his lips deep against her neck, nuzzling. A second finger joined the

first. He held them rigid, pushing her open wider…
parting her until she uttered a wistful, pliant sound.

As he twisted his hand, hers came between them, fumbling to unbutton his shorts, making him wince as she wrenched the zipper over his hard-on. When the fly was open, she moved her fingers over the ridge. His flesh was painfully aroused, but he might have survived if she hadn't squeezed, closing her fingers around his length—then hard—and he exhaled a curse, thinking he'd die from this.

Her mouth finding his sent him soaring. She kissed him the way he was used to kissing women—without apologies, taking what she wanted, her tongue asking his to fight like a sword. "Not always easy," she countered wetly against his lips, the words sounding strangely jumbled and senseless. He didn't know whether it was the kiss or words that sent blood to his groin. Whichever it was, the sweet, slow ache filled her hand.

He wanted her mouth around him again, just as he needed to hear her voice. "Say you're hot for me."

"You want to hear me say it?"

"Even if it isn't true."

"You can feel how true it is."

He moaned. He wanted to screw her all night long. Maybe it was the call of something he'd felt in the spring, but he wanted—no, needed—to drive himself so deep she'd scream with pleasure, then beg for more.

He probed her mouth, forcing open her lips, offering his tongue in tandem with his stroking hands. He was bursting and felt heat exploding in her. Fever had hit her skin and the sheen of glistening perspiration as he pushed the love-slickened fingers deeper; soon she'd have more of him. If he lasted.

"Yes…" Her voice was jagged. She was starting to shake, her thighs quivering, her hips breaking rhythm, her excitement climbing beyond her control. He pushed his fingers all the way up…all the way in. Her hand left him and she reached behind herself, clutching the cabinet's edge.

"Not like this," she whispered, her voice shaking.

But she couldn't stop. She was going to come. Leaning back a fraction, he watched her as he ever so slowly thrust farther inside. He felt her close around his fingers. "Tight," he whispered, sweat prickling his skin, tickling his nape. Probing her inner ridges, he paused when he was buried deep, then he moved his hand in slow circles, twisting his wrist, forcing her to feel every tantalizing, torturous gesture.

Licking lips that had gone dry, he watched her gasp as he strummed her, using his whole hand until it was drenched with her passion. She was still stroking him, too, and her hand slackened on his penis as she emitted a hungry groan.

"Yeah," he whispered. "That's right." She was straining now, trying to come…

He wanted to hear her voice again—that sound of wild, dark lust meant to be spent in forbidden places, so he asked, "Do you want me inside you, Ariel?" Then he withdrew his fingers, intentionally taunting her, loving the need he'd left in her dazed eyes.

Knowing she was right on the edge, he took a condom from the counter, ripped open the foil and then he glanced around, blowing out a shaky breath when she said, "The water!"

It had almost overflowed. "Damn," he muttered.

Just as she stepped past him to the bath, he realized he'd almost forgotten the mirrored wall. Now he took in her back—the slender shoulders, nip of waist, rounded backside and endless legs. From the front, he could see her reach behind herself, pull the band from her hair and toss it aside. Her breasts swayed in tandem with her hips as she took the step into the water, ducked and was submerged into a tub big enough that she could go all the way under. When she came up, her hair was slicked back against her head. He followed her, reaching for her as soon as he hit the water. As he seated himself on a hot-bed step, he hauled her near. Her legs stretched around him, and as his stiffened length glided beneath her, he released a strangled male sound. Then his hungry mouth slammed down on hers again.

The water had gotten hotter than he'd intended. But it was no match for him. They'd been teasing each other all night, and now she was his. Panting, he said, "God, you are a witch." Then, thinking of the water's heat, he asked, "Too hot for you?"

She looked as if she wouldn't care if she'd just landed in the fiery reaches of hell. "I was already boiling."

Reaching, she pushed a control and started the Jacuzzi jets. Hot currents surrounded him in tandem with arms that wreathed his neck, and suds frothed. He urged her onto his lap, feeling desperate.

As she eased slowly over him, thought eluded him. Far off, music played, but only the hitch of her breath mattered. How could any man take such softness? Air. Suds. Feathers. And yet she was burning. She was water and fire, gripping him with her lower body, down...and down....

"What the hell's happening," he gasped, fingers tightening on her backside as she hit bottom. She was holding back, the way a man might, and the strain was killing them. She withdrew slowly, and he wondered if she'd been trained in some special torture chamber. "Witch," he murmured thickly against her neck.

A splayed hand drove hard into his hair, her soap-slick breasts flattened against his chest. Fire spun through him, and suddenly, everything was too hot. Finding her mouth again, he savaged it, his lips covering hers, devouring...until she was kissing him back. Lost, he thought. Raw. Desperate.

"Now," he said softly. Grasping her, he pulled her down, hard. "Ride me," he rasped. He thought of her with the horses...her hair streaming behind her, her thighs flexing against flanks. "Ride," he whispered again, slamming his eyes shut. "Fast, Ariel."

She clung, her quivering lips locking to his, then her hips bucked and he gasped. The release came quick, in a sudden twisting like a clenched fist. "Bliss," he whispered simply.

9

ARIEL PRESSED A FINGER to Rex's lips, lightly tracing the contours with a fingernail. "Lie back."

When he reclined on his bed, as she'd asked, she smiled, angling her body next to his before propping an elbow on a pillow, so she could better study the man who'd satisfied her beyond her wildest expectations. Sighing, she glanced over her shoulder, toward where floor-length curtains were drawn away from the picture window, exposing the night sky.

Directly beneath his room was the tearoom proper, which was built on an outcropping, and so they seemed to be in a planetarium right now, thrust into the glittering world of moon and stars. This view was what she loved most about the adjoined rooms. Despite the closed windows in his, and the fact they were above the tree line, she could still hear night sounds—hoot owls and crickets, and an August breeze that stirred leaves of the underbrush. Just enough light shone into the room that she could make out shapes of furniture inside, a long dresser, an armoire and the duffel he'd decided not to unpack. Eyeing it for a moment, she tried to ignore a tug of wistful regret…an unbidden fantasy that something would happen and he'd stay, at least for one more day.

Her gaze returned to his face, and now she listened to sounds that were nearer, the rustling of sheets as their feet glided over each other, the rise and fall of his breath. He was watching her, his eyes just midnight slits in the dark. Darkness inside darkness, she thought now, returning the gaze. Strangely, she did feel like that—as if something mysterious were unfolding between them. It was like a hand in a glove, or the first layers of an onion being peeled back before she made dinner, or veils blowing in a breeze. Always more to be revealed. Flavors to be discovered. Lifting a hand, he brushed a drying lock of her hair, pushing it from her temple.

For a long moment, she continued to survey him. His hair was drying, too, and she raked splayed fingers into it, then brought her face closer, studying the overly long, light blond strands that were, for all their thickness, as flaxen as a spider's web, one spun, she decided, for the express purpose of enmeshing her.

There was an incongruity in his looks that had captivated her from the first, she realized, leaning away. His boyish hair was cut in flat-edged hanks, as if both he and the barber had been in a hurry, and he had shockingly blue eyes, as well as an easy smile. Altogether, the kind of good looks she didn't associate with medical doctors or scientists.

When she cracked a smile, she saw an answering crinkle in his eyes. "Hmm?" he hummed as his hand slowly moved down her back, finally settling on her backside, then rubbing lazy circles.

Heat from the touch suffused her limbs. "You look like a surfer dude."

His soft chuckle hit the air. "You think?"

"Yeah. Aren't guys like you supposed to wear pocket protectors and lab coats?"

"Not when I'm naked," he said.

A breast was pressed to his chest, and when he spoke, she could feel rumbling vibrations that made a nipple tug, tightening. Binds seemed to circle her chest then, stealing her breath, and she swallowed hard. After what had just happened in the bathtub, she'd have thought herself finished for the night, but now, she wanted more. There was no denying it.

Tomorrow, he'd be gone. So, all she had was tonight. Tomorrow, she'd share the continental breakfast with him in the tearoom, then maybe make love a final time before she kissed him goodbye. Then she'd be able to sleep.

"A surfer dude?" he murmured, looking amused.

She nodded. "Blond," she explained.

"Muscular," she continued after a moment, now sensing the lift of his hips as he stretched.

"And your hair's kind of long," she added, the distraction of conversation offering her mind a secondary focus, since a flood of sensation was rushing through her. Definitely lawless, she thought. Primitive.

Lifting one of her legs, she scissored it over his, noting how smooth her skin felt when teased by the coarser, rougher hairs of his thighs. As she brought her knee upward, almost to his groin, the hand on her backside roamed again, running freely, cupping under a cheek, a finger exploring the crevice near her thigh.

"Hmm." His voice was thick with sex, almost lost in the whisper of their joined breath. "You were saying you thought cute blondes lack brains?"

"Until earlier today when I met you."

"Good answer."

He was playing with her in earnest now, just as she was playing with him, distracting herself with gliding her hands over the solid muscles of his chest. She shifted, raising her knee higher, sliding it over both his legs.

A hand swiftly caught her leg and hooked beneath the bend in it, urging it higher still, over his groin. He groaned as the hard knob of her knee, then the softer, smoother flesh of her inner thigh covered the most intimate part of him, and her pulse jagged when she felt his lightning-quick reaction—the flexing of his erection, its burning as blood raced through his limbs, filling and engorging where she'd crushed him.

"Dumb blondes," she murmured, the halfhearted attempt at silly conversation now seeming like exactly that—silliness.

"That's the stereotype. Isn't it?"

"You're one of a kind," she whispered.

"You don't even know me."

"Maybe that's when it's easiest to know a person," she managed to say, her chest so tight that she wasn't sure she could catch her breath.

"Now, there's a paradox."

And it was. But she'd never have let herself go like this, not with a man she'd been dating. "Maybe it's easier to lose yourself with a stranger."

Probably. Because his thoughts were elsewhere. She could see that in the sleepy-looking pull of his heavy-lidded gaze, the parting of his lips. A spear of tongue appeared, licking at the luscious mouth she was hungry to feel on hers, and he seemed to sink farther back, burying his head more deeply into the ample pillows. He finally murmured, "It's kind of a double standard, isn't it?"

"Like all dumb blondes being women," she agreed.

As if coming to his senses, he blinked and rattled off names of smart blondes, ending with Helen Hunt.

"Hillary Clinton," she countered.

"Salon streaked," he argued back.

"Ah. So, you know your hairdos." Judging by his, she wouldn't have thought beauty techniques to be his strong point.

"The ex-fiancée," he explained, his long finger further exploring her now, moving downward until he'd found the slick heat of her opening. When he uttered a deep, rumbling sound, she knew he'd registered the flow of her juices, how hot she'd gotten. This was payback, she realized, because he was circling where she was so open for him…then fondling her clitoris, the tip of his finger barely flickering before vanishing once more.

"My ex talked a lot about clothes and hairdos," he said on a soft pant.

"Why don't you and I talk about something else?"

"This?" he suggested, rolling the pad of a finger over the bud of her clitoris once more. She cried out now, arching. Even as she ground her hips against him, she realized the movement had taken her away from, not closer to his touch, so she corrected, now seeking the hand that came from behind by lifting her backside and wordlessly guiding him.

Not that he gave her full satisfaction, even now.

"Some conversation," she muttered as frustration claimed her. Every new wave of heat brought no relief.

Finally, her eyes slammed shut, and she uttered a sense-less protest as he plunged his finger, coating it, using the heat of her own body to tantalize her.

Somehow, that didn't seem fair at all. It was as if her own body were working against her. With every bliss-ful stroke, he was only engendering new itches. Open-ing her eyes, she reached for his lips, pushed a thumb inside. His mouth closed tightly then, and he drew hard, sending a jolt of pure molten pleasure through her.

Suddenly, it was too much to take. With any other stranger, she might have felt embarrassed, or at least uncomfortably exposed, but with him, she felt only surges of burning passion clamoring to be squelched. She was climbing....

Their eyes met.

He was loving every minute of it, too.

Damn him, she thought, her mind hazing. She was dripping for him now, and his hardening length was still begging for attention, trapped by the softness of her thigh. "C'mon," she whispered huskily, knowing that, right now, he really could read her mind. He knew she wanted more. Need was twisting inside her, more de-manding as the magic of his fingers quickened.

But he wasn't going to quit teasing. "Dumb blonde," he whispered devilishly, as she withdrew her thumb.

She lifted a lock of his hair. "Natural?"

"Who cares? The main thing is that blondes have more fun."

"I'm blond, too," she reminded him, suddenly giv-ing up on what they were doing and simply rolling on top, straddling him.

She gasped as he grabbed her wrists just as quickly,

swiftly wrenching his powerful upper body, bringing her beneath him, sandwiching her between him and the mattress. Her head sank into the pillow, landing exactly where his had been. His entire weight covered her, so warm and delicious, and as he stretched her arms wide, everything inside her started trembling. Her legs were trapped. Parted. His lay on top, and because he held her arms so wide apart, she felt dangerously open to him.

His palms flattened on hers; the sheet felt as cold as ice on the backs of her hands, by comparison. Curling his fingers, he twined them with hers and squeezed. Then his mouth descended, greedy and wet, deeper and more molten as his chest settled more heavily on hers, crushing her breasts against the hard wall of his chest. Her arms strained to circle his neck, but they were held captive beneath hands that gripped her like steel. All her breath was in the kiss, and she was at his mercy because everything inside her needed him.

Not that he'd ever soothe the sensations he'd built. Maybe he'd only kiss her, his tongue driving into the farthest recesses of her mouth like this, until she hung like a star in the sky, begging to burn and fall....

Yes, a falling star, she thought. She was bursting, shooting in a ball of fire through the night. She tried to lift her hands—desperate for them to be in his hair now, or roving over his back, or raking across his buttocks, or dragging along the backs of his thighs or fisting around his erection....

Anywhere but here, imprisoned beneath him. But there was no movement, just his searing, relentless tongue probing hers. And when he finally broke the kiss, she released a high whine against his mouth, a strange sound that seemed to come from outside herself.

His answer was a shaky breath as he brought his cheek to hers. Everything seemed so quiet. Only their quickened breaths sounded in the dark silence.

This was so intimate. Too intimate. Not just about sex, after all, she thought as her pulse raced. Maybe nothing could be about sex, alone...just sex, pure and simple. She realized that now. She'd been crazy to think she could share this deeply, really believe it didn't matter, and then walk away.

But she would, of course. In the morning. Right now, all she knew was that she'd never experienced so much excitement, nor emotion. She didn't understand it, either. They'd done nothing people associated with wild sex, after all. There had been no toys. No exotic poses she'd seen in magazines and movies, nor aphrodisiacs, unless there really was a bug in the water.

This was just good old down-home lovemaking, really. At least, so far. And in truth, he'd only been inside her once. And yet, she felt they'd shared so much more. They were...

Lovers now. His breath was fluttering on her neck, and she wanted that rough stubble elsewhere, dragging burns over every inch of her pale, sensitive skin. Instead, his hands loosened in hers, trailed to her wrists, then fisted around them. She knew he could feel her pulse pounding against his palms, but he didn't let go, only tightened his grip possessively.

"Let me up," she whispered shakily.

He murmured in her ear, "Never." And then damp

sensation swirled through her, since his tongue followed where his voice had been—nibbling her earlobe, then plunging inside. God, she ached. Truly, he was burning against her belly and she needed him lower…inside….

"For a condom," she whispered.

His hands loosened their hold. "I'll get one."

"I'll go."

Right before he rolled away, his mouth found hers again. She let him kiss her, too. For a good long while.

Let *him* kiss *her.*

She didn't kiss back, but only submitted. And then his heat and weight were gone. Completely dazed, she rose, feeling like an amnesiac awakening from a dream. What on earth was the man doing to her?

…The condom. She remembered that was the whole point of her getting up. As she went over to the dresser, she felt his eyes following her through the darkness. A lump lodged in her throat. The way he'd crushed her against the mattress had really made her feel totally…

At his mercy?

And it had been so sexy. Simple, but even more arousing than bathing together. She'd been with men, had orgasms with them. But she'd never felt this kind of power. And she wanted…

To possess him, too. Maybe even to torture him. Just a little. To make him plead for what he wanted. Yes, she wanted to see Rex Houston come apart at the seams, until he was shattering and writhing, totally dependent on her for a release he was sure would never come. Maybe she'd keep him where he'd kept her most of the night—suspended in space, reaching and reaching, but never…

As she lifted a foil packet, she was seized by the idea

that she wanted to tie him up. Finding scarves only took a minute. She used to wear them all the time. And when she returned to bed from her room, she was greeted by a husky chuckle. "What do you think you're…"

She didn't give him a chance to finish. Already, she'd caught a wrist and bound it to a bedpost. Circling the mattress, she lifted his other hand, kissed it, then quickly twirled silk around it. Somehow, she was surprised he let her do it. Especially when she didn't stop at his hands, but secured his ankles as well. Her knots were tight, too. From living beside the spring all her life, she'd learned about boats, and when a woman knew about boats, she also knew about boating knots.

"I'm getting ready to torture you," she whispered now.

He was breathing hard, and his gaze had turned sharp and assessing, following her every movement. His fingers suddenly fisted and his darkly tanned arms strained, delineating muscles and making veins pop as he tested the bonds. Only now realizing that she'd been in earnest, a protesting sound came from between his lips.

Not that he meant it. "Well, come on then," he muttered thickly, daring her.

She had to chuckle at that. After all, she, not he, had the upper hand. "Torture," she whispered again, speaking each syllable succinctly. "That means that we don't do what you want, Rex."

His head was tilted back taking in the one remaining scarf in her hand. It was long, narrow and very bright red. "Really?" he said.

She nodded. "Really."

"What do we do then, Ariel?"

"Whatever Ariel wants."

He was thoroughly excited. His hips, straining. He could barely move, but he tried, and his legs spread just a fraction wider. His chin raised another notch, and his head moved from side to side on the pillow.

Standing at the foot of the bed, she looped the scarf around her neck and touched her breasts, lifting them for his eyes, gently squeezing, until his sudden intake of breath made her consider letting him watch her bring herself to climax. And why not? She could do absolutely anything...*anything* at all with this man tonight.

But she wanted to touch him. Capturing his feet in her hands, she massaged slowly and deeply, cupping her fingers tightly around the insteps, rubbing thumbs into the hollows, crunching fingers around his toes—all of which seemed to have an incredible effect on the man, but not nearly so much as when she leaned and drew a big toe between her lips and nibbled.

Sex charged the air then. Her hands rose, burning on his calves, her tongue languorously eating up every inch of him. Loose, ropelike circles of kisses looped, climbing his sensitized flesh, drawing guttural cries. Unbroken, the liquid trail hit his inner thighs, and his arms jerked, pulling the bonds taut, stretching them to breaking. His hips lifted then, as if in hopeless supplication...begging.

She was stunned by the tight muscles of his thighs as she slaked her thirst on the flesh there. Her hands molded his waist, her tongue bathing his lower belly, but circumventing where he most ached, toying instead with his navel, plundering wetly, then blowing the spot.

"Ariel," he muttered harshly. "C'mon. That's enough."

She didn't want to do anything nonconsensual, of

course. But when she glanced up into those glazed eyes, it didn't look like enough to her. No, she decided, not nearly enough. "In just a minute," she assured.

"Dammit," he whispered hoarsely, his arms yanking, the scarves threatening to snap, even as his movements tightened her knots.

"What would you do to me if I let you loose?"

He was too frustrated to answer. But his eyes said he'd be on her like a wild animal. So, she supposed she could at least touch him there, just once. "Here," she whispered, trailing a silk end of the remaining scarf over his legs.

At the softness of the touch, she thought he'd come undone. He went into spasms, his hips twisting as she masterfully twirled the watery fabric around his aroused length. Ever so slowly, she wrapped him like a present.

"Let me go," he whispered.

"Should we tie a bow?" she asked innocently.

She tugged the scarf's ends, as if to tie another knot, but only so he felt the pressure. "All right," she whispered back, only pretending to understand. "I'll let you go." But she only removed the scarf. Leaning, she blew air kisses on his skin, until her mouth suddenly lowered, searing the flesh of his belly, then slowly working more magic from his navel up...up...

Gasping, he jerked his arms harder. This time, one broke free and he caught her upper arm with his hand. Fingers sank into her flesh as he hauled her on top of himself. His lips covered hers completely, his tongue seemingly mad for hers as he wrenched away from the one bond from which he'd managed to free himself.

He was rolling toward her, wanting her beneath him,

but she, herself, was about to shatter. Rustling hands over the covers, she fumbled for the condom, now lost somewhere in the sheets. Dammit, she had to find it. Relief flooded her when she did. More, when she slit the packet and studied the contents for a moment. She'd never done this before, but instinct took over and she smoothed the latex over him, then rolled it downward.

Just touching him there sent him reeling. She could tell he was about to explode. So was she. She'd been so lost, concentrating on teasing him, that she hadn't even realized she was so far gone!

As she straddled him, everything else vanished. She needed him now. And she wasted no time, but sank onto him, moving fast, as his freed arm wrapped tightly around her back, clutching her to his chest. Gasping, she felt long-awaited relief claiming her. He was so hard, like steel. And so unbelievably hot. He split her, opening her completely, burning. Each inch promised the release she'd craved. It would come now; it had to.

He was an ocean, the pleasure endless, and she was lost to his currents. She rode them, then plunged, her hips shaking, thrusting. The world no longer existed. This wasn't the house in which she'd grown up. Not the town she both loved and hated. There was no missing recipe book of mysterious teas that could kill a man, or make him love you, no more than she was to film a Harvest Festival. She had no job to do in a town called Bliss, and she'd never needed to prove herself to anyone.

Certainly, not to Rex Houston. She was wrapped so tightly in his arms that she didn't know where she ended and he began...could only ride the waves, swept by the currents.

Suddenly, the dam burst; the wall crashed down. The crest was overwhelming. She didn't even know this man, but tears welled in her eyes as she crumbled, the spasms shaking more than just her body. He'd reached something raw. So deep she'd never even known it was there....

A moment passed before she realized he'd come, too. And as he had, he'd broken his bonds. All but one of his feet had come free. A leg circled her, and like his arms, it drew her closer. They were still breathing hard, their bodies drenched with heat and sweat. "Ariel," he muttered simply, his voice hoarse with emotion. "C'mere."

Already, she was as close as she could get, but her arms clung more tightly around his neck; his arms wrapped around her back, and they shuddered together in the embrace. Her face buried in his neck, and one of his hands rose, cradling her head gently.

Her last thought was that nothing could ruin such bountiful perfection.

10

"You bitch."

Startled, Ariel blinked, her eyes fluttering open. Had someone just called her a bitch? Her first thought was of Rex, but she realized he was beneath her, fast asleep. She was sprawled on top of him and he was starting to stir now....

It wouldn't be one of her relatives. She'd never heard them curse. As she rolled away from him, she realized the room was freezing. The air conditioner had run all night. Because they'd been making love, she and Rex hadn't noticed the artic chill. Which was why they'd covered up in a duvet and a blanket.

She glanced toward his face, registering that it was covered by a pillow, just as somebody grasped the covers and yanked, sweeping them away. The room was freezing! Chill bumps rose on her skin and she gasped when a female voice shrieked, "Get up, you son of a bitch!"

"Joanie?" she managed to say. Why was Joanie Underwood here? She looked fit to kill, too. Everything about her was cut out in sharp angles. She was wearing a boxy Chinese-style jacket over jeans and her black hair hung to her shoulders in a razor-cut bob.

"Get up, Howard," she commanded.

Joanie Underwood was the only person in Bliss who called Studs by his real name. Under other circumstances, hearing her do so would have been funny, since Studs really had grown up to look more like a Howard than a Studs, after all. As it was, though, Ariel could only stare. "Joanie," she said simply, in protest.

Rex was pushing the pillow away, struggling to sit, but he'd just discovered one ankle was still tied to the bedpost. One look at the bed left little to the imagination. Judging from the murderous trek of her gaze, Joanie had become a lot less interested in whatever man she'd uncovered than in the trail of clothes on the floor and the silk scarves littering the bed. Even the fitted sheet had come untucked, its elastic underside now visible atop a corner of the mattress. Ariel scrambled, grabbing a handful of the bedspread and pulling it toward her chest. By the time she'd wrapped it around herself and tossed a sheet toward Rex, Joanie's gaze had returned to them.

"Who are you?" she demanded of Rex, clearly surprised to find a man other than her husband in bed with Ariel.

Rex's voice was thick with sex and sleep. "I could ask the same of you, lady."

"And to think I thought you might have changed," Joanie said, staring at Ariel. "I even waved at you as I was leaving the hardware store!" She looked at Rex. "You must be one of her out-of-town friends."

What right did Joanie have to barge in like this, much less to ask who Rex was? It didn't help that the door between the rooms was open—Ariel had made a trip there in the night to get the scarves. And since her closet door was open, Joanie was getting a view of the wild outfits strewn about.

"How did you get in here?" Ariel snapped.

"The door," Joanie retorted.

Hadn't she locked it? Or, no…that's right. Ariel had locked her own, but only shut Rex's. She'd been so excited, watching him head for the bathroom, that she hadn't been thinking clearly. Damn. How could any of this be happening? Yesterday, she'd been so focused on what she needed to do here. Now, her plans were ruined. Joanie would tell everyone in town she'd come here looking for Studs and found Ariel in bed with Rex, whom others would identify, soon enough, as being from the CDC.

"Didn't anyone ever teach you to knock?" Ariel ground out, deciding Joanie hadn't changed a bit from the years she and her cheerleader girlfriends had shut Ariel out. If the truth be told, they'd done so long before Studs had ever started messing with her. Ariel had never known why, except that she'd had to carry the legacy of her husband-less relatives, not to mention Matilda.

Rex had covered his lap and he was reaching toward the foot of the bed, trying to unknot his ankle. He looked luscious, too, and she suddenly hated him for it. If he hadn't been so good-looking, she'd never have given in to temptation, wound up in bed with him, nor been confronted by Joanie this morning. She'd have been found alone in bed, and Joanie would have had no new gossip to spread around Bliss. Even worse, this time the gossip was true. Ariel really had picked up a stranger.

She glanced at him. His shoulders and chest were the color of dark chestnuts shining under sunlight, and a tangle of hair she knew to be as soft as spring rain ran between his pectorals like a blond river. Darker blond whiskers roughened his strong jaw, making him look rangy and dangerous.

Joanie had planted her manicured hands furiously on her hips, stabbing her own skin with the squarish opal-colored nails. Her lips were pursed tightly, while the nostrils of her straight nose flared as if she'd smelled something foul.

"I should have known," she muttered, shifting her gaze to Ariel. "It's not even him." The woman was shaking with rage, from head to foot, and the controlled sound of her voice was probably the most frightening thing about her, since she was hovering on the edge of violence. Ariel could only pray her relatives or a guest didn't hear her.

"Keep your voice down," Ariel urged.

"Where is he?" Joanie demanded, looking around, clearly not intending to go anywhere.

"What?" Ariel managed to say, annoyance coursing through her as she followed the other woman's gaze. Joanie was looking around, as if she expected to see her husband come from the bathroom or leap out of the armoire.

As Ariel forced herself to get up, she said, "Do you really think I'm entertaining two men up here?"

"I know damn well you are," Joanie charged, her flashing eyes piercing Ariel's. "So does everybody in Bliss. The news of how you were skinny-dipping with him yesterday at Panty Point is all over town. He went back to his office dripping wet."

Ariel knew defending herself was useless, but she decided to try for once. "He wouldn't leave me alone, and I pushed him into the spring."

Joanie rolled her eyes. "We all know what you are."

What you are. The words reverberated, feeling like slices of a knife. "He's not here," she ground out. "He's never been here."

She wouldn't have let Studs Underwood in the door, unless it was to question suspects about the missing recipe book, and he hadn't even done that. Otherwise, she wouldn't have let his boot heel defile the floor of the place she called home. More than anything, she'd never wanted her relatives to know the extent to which she'd been ostracized. And yet, even though that had been her choice, she'd resented their lack of intervention, too. Because deep down, she guessed she really hadn't thought they would know how to help. They were so naive. So schoolmarmish.

The few incidents she'd mentioned, they'd pushed aside, as if to say they were inconsequential. Besides, they'd always thought her so perfect. They couldn't imagine anyone mistreating the girl they loved so much. They'd just thought her a loner, the same as them, and had assumed she'd loved her chosen freedoms—the hours of riding and drawing. And, well, of course she had.

And anyway, what would they have been able to do? Sell Matilda's house, pack up and leave their home of so many generations, just to get her out of Bliss? Fat chance.

Joanie was glaring at her. "When did he leave?"

"He was never here."

"Did he say where he was going?"

"He wasn't here," Ariel repeated.

"We both know he was."

There was something lethal in Rex's voice that got Joanie's attention. "You're the sheriff's wife. Is that right?"

She drew herself up to full height. "I am."

"Your husband's not here. He hasn't been here. He's never going to be here." He eyed Joanie a long moment, then added, "If he lays a hand on Ariel, I'd probably kill him. Now, get out, lady. You're ruining my morning."

"Oh," Joanie said lightly. "I can see that. It looks as if you two have been having a grand old time. Just the kind Ariel has always shown the boys."

Thankfully, Rex heeded Ariel's warning glance. She wouldn't have a man defending her. She didn't need that. Still, when Joanie leaned and lifted the scarf that had been tied to his ankle, it was tempting to give Rex the go-ahead.

Staring down at the scarf, Joanie rubbed it between her fingers and thumb, then she let it drop as if it were something dirty. With that one gesture, she seemed to sully everything Ariel had shared with Rex the night before, but Ariel continued to bite her tongue, knowing that what the other woman wanted most was for Ariel to become hurt and defensive.

Slowly turning, she sent Ariel a pointed parting glance over her shoulder, as if to say the scarf had said it all.

Ariel felt emptied out inside, and worse, when her eyes trailed Joanie's retreating form to the door, she saw Great-gran, Gran and her mom huddled in the door-way, standing so close together that they might have been one person, all wearing white aprons over unchar-acteristically bright floral-print dresses. Before Ariel could contemplate that, they separated, just long enough to let Joanie pass, then huddled back together like a foot-ball team after a particularly difficult play.

"We heard a ruckus," Gran said weakly when Joanie was gone, her hair in disarray, as if she'd come running fast. She was pressing one hand to her heart worriedly and, in the other, she held a wooden spoon splattered with pancake batter.

Great-gran nodded, and Ariel's heart wrenched. She was the spitting image of Gran, a petite woman with wrinkled skin and a ramrod-straight posture, except that with greater age, she'd shrunk, becoming even shorter. She was wielding a spatula. Probably, they were still cooking breakfast. She'd grabbed a broom for good measure. "Why, Ariel, we thought maybe some of the guests were having a fight," she offered, her china-blue eyes widening as they focused past Ariel's shoulder.

"We thought some sort of domestic violence might be happening," added Gran with concern, speaking the phrase *domestic violence* as if she'd only known that to exist on other planets before today, certainly not in her home.

Ariel's mother's eyes were also fixed on the great beyond, and Ariel was hardly going to turn around. She just hoped Rex had pulled the covers over more of himself than the square of lap he'd covered for Joanie.

"Are you all right?" her mother asked.

She managed a nod, her eyes skating to a dot behind her mother's head, avoiding her gaze. The witches of Terror House had never been forthcoming with regard to personal relations, especially not when the questions involved intimate relations with men. And if they had been, Ariel suddenly fumed, then finding her sexual self would have been much easier. She'd have come into her own sooner in life and without so much unnecessary pain. Maybe, like Joanie, she'd have been married years ago and had kids. She wouldn't have felt so much career pressure, to succeed and prove herself. Oh, she wasn't given to blaming others. She believed in taking personal responsibility, and she always would. She even owned up to her worst choices. In, fact, she *especially* owned up to her mistakes. But in this one area...

All the fantasies she'd had twenty-four hours ago about dating her boss, Ryan, dislodged from her mind entirely. They seemed silly and juvenile compared to what she'd experienced with Rex last night and the complexities of her past in Bliss.

"Please," she suddenly muttered, speaking with uncharacteristic anger. "Can everybody just please leave?" When her relatives actually looked at Rex, as if she'd meant him, she clarified, "You."

Shock and hurt appeared on their faces, and suddenly, Ariel was seized by another bout of pique. She was tired of the lies and secrets she associated with this place. As far as she was concerned, everybody in Bliss except her needed to have their heads examined. She couldn't get back to Pittsburgh fast enough.

Yes, that's what she needed, a gritty steel town without illusions. Everybody lied here, whether it was Studs, who kept pretending she was in love with him, or the women she'd lived with all her life, or Joanie who had always lied to herself about the true nature of her husband's character.

"Of course we can leave," her mother said tightly. "We were just concerned. We overheard Joanie Underwood say something about you having affair with her husband, and..."

Ariel's lips parted. "You believed it?"

Great-gran wrung her hands. "Well, we didn't think so."

"But," Gran quickly said, "you're entitled to your secrets. We all are."

Spoken like a true widow of Bliss. Ariel supposed they were referring, too, to her secrets about the man who was still in bed. "Oh, yes," she couldn't help but say, teetering on the edge of reason. "We are entitled to them, aren't we?"

"Ariel," her mother said in warning.

Everyone knew what she'd meant. So, why not say it? The last fifteen minutes thoroughly encapsulated everything that was wrong with her life. Studs had attacked her yesterday, and last night had been everything she'd always dreamed of with a man....

Quickly, she pushed aside the thoughts. Because that sweet chapter had passed swiftly enough into history, hadn't it? The next thing she knew, Joanie Underwood, who'd snubbed her in school and had always called her names from the back of the school bus, was hulking over her and Rex, turning their lovemaking into something vile. Why had Ariel thought she could come back here and change anything?

Her eyes were still on her mother's. "I don't even know who my dad is," she muttered. "After all these years."

Her mother looked stunned. "I...didn't know you still wondered. You quit asking so long ago..."

She quit asking because no one would tell her anything and because sheer survival in high school had overtaken her energies. Was her mother joking? "He's my father," she said, her eyes challenging the woman she loved most in the world. "Of course I wanted to know."

"We can talk," her mother said levelly. "Any time."

Like always, it was as if years were stripped away whenever that stranger was referenced. Her mother's pain was obvious. It was one reason Ariel had never asked to divulge more. She also suspected that her own fantasies about the mystery man might sustain her better than whatever grim reality was there to be discovered. Whoever Ariel's father was, Samantha Anderson had loved him, and the man left her. Most of Ariel's life, that information had been enough. Who wanted to care about someone who abandoned those who loved him? Who wanted to chase after a phantom, like a fool?

"That's all," she managed to say, wondering at the ease of this...that she could simply sit down with her mother and a cup of tea, and hear all the real-life secrets of the widows of the house, including the identity of her father. "After all these years? Hmm. And maybe you can tell me whether you killed all the men you were supposed to have married," she muttered, angry at the world and wanting to hurt them all.

Her relatives stared back, stupefied. "Don't act as if you never heard the rumors that fly all over town," she said.

"We'd heard kids think we're witches," said Gran, mortified. "But now they're saying we killed some men...?"

Ariel was clutching a sheet around her and a naked man was in her bed. Definitely, this was not the time for any of this. "They call our house Terror House," she forced herself to say. "And the kids think we're witches. You're all widows, who buried their husbands in shallow graves on the mountain."

"Oh my God," her mother said.

Great-gran wasn't as put off by the idea. Ariel could swear she heard her mutter, "I wish that's what I'd done to him."

Gran suddenly gasped. "Oh, no!" she exclaimed. "Can you smell that? Something's burning in the kitchen!"

"The waffle iron!" her mother nearly shouted. "I left batter in it!"

Saved by the bell. Ariel smelled burning blueberries now, and as she watched her mother whirl, her stomach rumbled. "We'll talk whenever you're ready," her mother called over her shoulder. And then she was gone, with Gran speeding after her. Great-gran moved as fast, the broom she'd brought doubling as a cane.

At the last minute, she lifted it, using the handle to push shut the bedroom door, leaving a deafening silence. For a moment, Ariel simply stared, stunned at what had transpired. Suddenly, her life seemed as airy, light and insubstantial as the scarves strewn on the bed. Nothing more than a breeze might have blown it all away. Hours ago, she'd been driving into town, knowing exactly where she was headed and why....

She wasn't surprised to feel two warm hands settle on her bare shoulders, urging her to turn around. He hadn't brought the sheet with him, so he was butt-naked. Gorgeous, too. His eyes were intense and so blue that they almost looked violet in the streaming sunlight.

The cold light of day, she thought. Even with him in front of her, enticingly naked, her mind was still on the previous encounter. Not that speaking with her mother would bring any new answers into life. So what if she learned the man's name? He'd always been gone and he'd never been a part of her life. That was the important thing. She was grown now; she didn't need a father. She needed...

A partner. But this morning, Joanie had brought back all the old feelings.

"You'd better go," she said.

Surprise registered in Rex's eyes. "What?"

"You heard all that." She'd almost laid bare the past and had demanded some semblance of the truth from her flesh and blood. Now, that was a red-letter day. She really was so tired of lies. But how much should she tell Joanie about her husband? Wasn't a woman supposed to figure out for herself that her husband was a horse's behind? And even if she told the whole truth, would the woman believe her?

She eyed Rex. How much truth had really been in what they'd shared last night? "You said you had to head out early this morning." She glanced around, her gaze settling on a travel alarm. "They serve breakfast in about a half hour," she added. Whatever was left that was still fit to eat. And now, she thought, she didn't exactly feel like running downstairs to help finish making it. Everybody had been concerned, and she'd lost her temper. But then, they were closemouthed, and it had cost her....

So, maybe a part of her wasn't really sorry she'd just rocked the boat. She wasn't sorry they'd caught her in bed with a man, either. She was tired of pretending the sexual part of her life didn't exist at all.

He was still staring at her as if he'd never seen her before, and that, more anything, made her ache. Last night, he'd felt like what she'd read about in a new-age book, a soul mate. But who was she fooling? Her life in Bliss had always been full of lies and accusations.

Now she wanted to remember last night just as it had felt to her then. It could stay crystalized in her mind as one night that was absolutely perfect.

"Really," she murmured. "I'd better go change. We…" Her voice trailed off.

Wordlessly, he waited.

"…We can eat together before you go."

Turning, he went over to his duffel, pulled out a pair of jeans, thrust his arms into a shirt, which had been stacked in the duffel, still wrapped in the launderer's cardboard. She watched, half in awe, as he strode around the room, then into the bathroom and out again, using the wide arc of an arm to simply sweep the rest of his belongings from the tabletops into the duffel.

Apparently, that was how Rex Houston packed. She guessed working all over the world taught a man to travel lightly and pack in minutes. He paused by the bed and stared down at it, taking in one of the scarves, one other than that which Joanie had touched. She imagined he was considering taking it with him as a souvenir.

She didn't blame him. Suddenly, she wanted something of his, to remember him by. A picture, maybe. A shirt she could sleep in that held his scent. But he walked to the door and swung it open. "Don't worry about breakfast," he muttered as he crossed the threshold, tossing a last glance over his shoulder. "I'll pick mine up on the road."

And then he was gone.

11

"SHE'LL EAT BREAKFAST with me before I go," Rex muttered, repeating Ariel's words as he reached for a cell phone from the dashboard and dialed the CDC. As the phone rang, he climbed into the mobile lab, pulled the door shut, then stared through the windshield at the house. It was the wrong thing to do. Right now, he…hated her. Loved her, too. Or at least, he loved her as much as a man could love a woman he'd only known for a day.

Someone picked up. "Centers for Disease Control and Prevention. Atlanta."

"Jessica Williams please. Rex Houston calling."

"Sexy Rexy, huh?" The operator giggled. "It may take a while to get her on the line."

He sighed. "What's she doing? Her nails?"

"You're in a bad mood."

She didn't know the half of it. "Take your time. I've got all day," he said. The phone clicked and an instrumental version of "Love Me Tender" began to play. Right now, hearing it made his skin crawl and he could only hope Jessica would hurry.

He wanted to make sure she'd been busy, finding him a nice assignment at the far edge of the world, away from Bliss, West Virginia. There was no stopping the tide of emotions, although he knew they were out of proportion to the situation. Right now, it was taking everything he had not to go back inside and tell Ariel exactly what he thought of how she'd handled Joanie. Why had she put up with the woman at all? But then, what right did he have to confront Ariel…?

He was nothing to her, right? Nor she to him. Wham bam, thank you ma'am… She'd just made that clear. Yeah, this was just a one-night deal. A blissful daylong interlude where he'd forgotten reason and fallen into a realm of pure sensation, plummeting over the edge and flying through the night with her only to crash….

Well, maybe her accusers were right. Maybe Anderson women bewitched men, singing to them like the sirens of ancient Greece. Maybe they'd called men toward Terror House, after all, breaking them into tiny pieces against the rocky shore. Rex pushed aside the thoughts, not really believing them. But Ariel had definitely…captivated him. She was so like her name, which conjured airy, winged creatures with wands, dressed in filmy white gowns.

He sighed. Where were these thoughts coming from, anyway? They didn't belong to him. They were too poetic. But he felt strangely out of control and compelled to go back into the house and demand more from her than he had a right to.

Was this what he deserved? Wouldn't any man understand that you couldn't just scratch an itch? Everything came with a price, especially sex. Give him science any day, he thought. It was neat and rational. Easy to quantify. Nature always followed rules, regulations and laws the human heart could never hope to understand.

In less than a day, Ariel had gotten inside him like the worst kind of bug, and there was just no cure. Like her, he wanted to undo his past right now, in which case he never would have heard her name. Yeah, he could have lived his whole life without feeling the level of passion to which she'd introduced him. His throat constricted as his eyes flickered over the hill, down the mountainside, toward the dock.

The emotions weren't only about the sex. Maybe that was the worst thing. He liked her chutzpah. The loyalty she felt for her family, despite her anger at them. That she didn't rip apart a woman like Joanie, despite the fact that the woman deserved it. But Ariel was nice. Unfortunately, all her best qualities were the exact same ones Rex hated at the moment. His muscles tensed as he studied the front door. Inside, the guests whom he'd enjoyed meeting last night were crowding into the dainty tearoom, with its lace tablecloths and polished silver, serving themselves waffles made with fresh blueberries. Despite the fact that some had burned, the scent had assaulted his nostrils as he'd walked out the door.

Now his stomach rumbled. Was he really going to drive away from here without any promise for the future? Should he go back inside and talk to her? If reasoning didn't work, he knew he could savage her mouth. He could haul her close, making something wild ignite. Within minutes, she'd be opening the liquid cream of her thighs....

Thinking about loving her made explosions burst inside him. Without doubt, he could swirl down into the musky darkness of her scent and never come up for air again. Given the way she'd looked at him when he'd left, she wasn't finished with what they'd started, no more than he was.

Or was she? Maybe that was just his own desires talking. Right now, he didn't care much about the goals that had brought her to town. He wanted her to forget about the show she needed to tape, just as he wanted to forget the bug he'd been sent to find.

What most mattered to him now was how she'd slipped between his fingers. She'd sifted right through, like sand from the banks below.

Stepping between the seats, he tucked the cell under his chin, sandwiching it between his ear and shoulder. Lifting a lab coat from a shelf, he slipped it over his shirt, then he reached into the pocket protector for a pen. As he clicked the cap, he grabbed a clipboard and the thick folder Jessica had given him, then he headed for the white tumblers in the back.

"One thing's for certain," he muttered. "Romeo's not infecting this place." After all, Ariel had just ditched him cold. That was his proof. Too bad the lab carried the scent of her. He wondered how the smell could remain, since she'd only driven the vehicle a few moments the previous day; then he realized the scent was on his skin.

He still couldn't believe she'd driven away in the mobile lab yesterday, acting as if she owned a vehicle for which the government had paid millions. If he'd pointed out that criminal courts would prosecute her for theft, she'd only have told him that her tax dollars, not the government, had bought the vehicle. She'd have a point, too. And what better use for it than escaping Studs Underwood? From what Rex knew of the man and his wife, pushing either one into the spring was the least they deserved.

The phone clicked on again. "You still there, sexy Rexy?"

"Yep."

"I'm still trying to locate her. She's in the building."

"I'm still here."

As the music began to play again, he flicked the off buttons to the tumblers. The soft sloshing sound of the washers ceased. It would take the contents a good half hour to cool. Then he'd open the lids and see what was inside. By heart, he knew every bacterium and virus that would mushroom, blooming in the hot, dark confines. Shaking his head in mute frustration, he tried not to be too angry with Jessica for sending him here.

Oh, the place was beautiful, all right, hills covered with thick greenery and bright flowers; crystal waters peeking through trees. But within two hours, he'd be finished logging the results of all the water samples and he could drive away. By nightfall, he'd be kicking back on the balcony of his apartment, drinking a beer and trying to forget Ariel. By morning, with any luck, he'd be headed for someplace more hospitable, like the Ivory Coast.

Meanwhile, he unlatched a Formica tabletop attached to the vehicle's side and pulled it downward. Behind the makeshift table was a neatly hidden door, which he now opened. Voilà. A tray containing a mounted microscope slid out. Returning to a space next to the washing tumblers, he unfastened two seat belts that secured a chair to the wall, so it wouldn't roll along its built-in track while the lab was in motion. He rolled it in front of the tabletop.

There. Instant lab. And he was glad he was in it, too. Better than still in a room with Ariel clad in nothing but a bedspread, her skin reeking with the kind of sex that hooked right into him, begging him to drag her down to the floor and plunder. He shook his head. To get her off his mind, he'd need a trip to some truly compromised little backwater village, preferably one overrun by the kind of bug that could kill a man in under twenty-four hours. Rats infected with the bubonic plague would do. He needed the kind of rush that came with ripping a spacesuit in bio-level four while handling diseases that would eat a man alive if they touched his skin. Maybe that would keep his mind off her.

Shifting the phone to the other ear, he wished Jessica would pick up. He'd tell her there was no bug here. Then he'd remind her that she owed him one and say he was calling in the favor now. Sighing, he glanced at his watch. Only five minutes had passed. The washers had to cool for at least a half hour, minimum.

The phone clicked on. "Still looking."

"I'll try back," he said, seating himself. Ringing off, he tossed the cell next to the microscope and opened the briefing file he'd read on the plane. His eyes sharpened as he read the story once more. An under-equipped lab in South America had discovered what they'd called the love bug after extensively testing the inhabitants of a small village called Szuzi. Usually industrious, the natives hunted, fished and grew produce, mostly palms and yams. But out of the blue, they'd ceased to come to the common markets.

Fearing the worst, nearby villagers, with whom they'd traded regularly, had suspected a plague had wiped out Szuzi. Or that flooding had washed away the mud huts, as often happened, since Szuzi was located on an inlet fed by a hot spring. Judging from the photos in the file, it was paradise on earth. Like Bliss, he thought, glancing through the windshield again, taking in the stone stairs visible in the mountainside's sheer drop....

Then he turned his attention to the file again, wondering what had happened. Members of a research team had emerged after a week's work with tall tales of how uninhibited the natives had become, and they'd isolated a virus they felt to be responsible. The samples had been lost on the way out of the rain forest, and all that now remained were some badly drawn sketches. Given the prominence of some of the researchers, that seemed odd. Was it possible they'd fallen under Romeo's spell, as well...?

The phone's ringing drew him out of a deep reverie, and he checked his watch. More than a half hour had passed. Hell, where had he gone? The zone, he thought. That far-off place his mind escaped to when he was working. Or where he'd stored the memories of last night, which now seemed almost like a dream. He clicked the phone on, rose, and headed for the tumblers, opening the lid of the first. Within minutes, he'd have the proof that nothing viral had mushroomed in the heat. "Yeah," he muttered, suddenly realizing he hadn't yet said anything. "Houston speaking."

"I heard you called."

It was Jessica. "Just putting in a call to make sure you're booking my flight to somewhere more interesting."

"Demanding, are we?"

"For this," he said, "you owe me."

"Find anything?"

He could almost feel the old, smooth, silvered wood of the dock beneath his feet, and see how the moon and starlight had played on Ariel's skin. Had he been there with a woman he didn't even know, embracing her more intimately than he ever had anyone?

"Found plenty," he said, forcing his attention on work again. "Just not a bug." Shifting the phone from ear to ear once more, he added, "I'm just looking at the first slide."

Taking it from the immersible rack, he slid it under the microscope. And stared. His breath caught.

"What have you got, Rex?"

He wanted to lie. He wanted out of Bliss in the worst kind of way, but professional ethics made that impossible. "It's not the virus, Jessica," he whispered. "But it's trace." Just a hint of material, the casing of the virus. He glanced at the picture drawn in Szuzi and his pulse quickened. "It looks like something similar to the South American bug."

His mind started clicking. Bliss had a long history of periods when the town had gone silent, usually only a week or two, starting in 1790. While Szuzi's written history was hardly as sophisticated as in the States, their oral tradition easily vied with American textbooks for accuracy, and they'd lost time, too.

"Judging by this sample," he said, looking into the microscope. "The bug's not live. No one's being currently infected."

"You're sure?"

He shook his head. "Not so far. But I have to go through all the samples." Then he'd look for the connection between Szuzi and Bliss. Bugs of any kind always had to travel. Still holding the phone, he stared harder into the lens, studying the dark, looping chains of the organism—or what was left of it, after it had died. "Judging from the molecular setup, I don't think it destroys the cells it enters." When many viruses invaded, their own genetic material took over the cell, and after they died, only a dry husk was left.

"Look at the rest of those samples," Jessica said. "Call me as soon as you find something that's still alive."

If he did. "Will do," he said, already reaching for another slide, not knowing whether to laugh or cry. If he found a live, traveling virus, the World Health Organization would be here by nightfall. If he found substantial evidence the population was infected, the military would arrive and quarantine the entire population. He grimaced, hating to think of Ariel's career being affected in any negative way.

But whatever the outcome, it meant he couldn't leave Bliss.

REX HESITATED, THEN KNOCKED on Ariel's door, his heart skipping a beat when her husky voice sounded. "Who is it?"

"Rex."

There was a long pause. "Come in."

She didn't sound particularly happy to hear it was him, and when he swung open the door and entered, he realized she didn't look all that thrilled, either. The first thing he noticed was the notes for her human-interest story spread over the bed, as if she'd set to work the second he'd left. Unwanted annoyance coursed through him, even though he knew she'd meant to plan her story throughout the week, talking to people, targeting those she most wanted to show on camera. Still…hadn't their night meant anything to her?

Maybe it had, he realized, because her crystal eyes were red-rimmed, the irises swimming. The covers were mussed, the piled pillows marked with indentions as if she'd flung herself into bed and wept. Her long hair was usually so straight that she could have ironed it, but now it was crimped, curly looking, and disheveled beyond hope.

No, he wasn't flattering himself, or soothing a wounded ego, he decided, as she hopped from bed, smoothing down a lightweight dress. She'd really been crying. But over him? Just as his heart missed beats, he felt blood pooling when he saw the yellow dress she was wearing. It was so lemony it could have made his lips pucker. Warm sunlight streamed from behind her, illuminating curves of legs and an outline of panties. A long silk ribbon to the halter top of the dress bodice hung in front, over a bare shoulder, and the end looked like a curl of blond hair; it brushed the tip of her right breast. He wanted to cross the room, lower his mouth to a bud, sponging her through cloth until she was as wet as a river.

Without thinking, he closed the door, then wished he hadn't. "I…don't want to let in the cool air," he found himself saying, the explanation sounding ridiculous, since he didn't really care about the air-conditioning, only about being alone with her. But now the room seemed stifling, despite a breeze from open windows that made the white curtains ruffle. She turned abruptly toward the windows as if to be closer to the rustling air.

Rex followed, feeling drawn. Ariel Anderson engendered a craving, like an addiction. The pungent, heady scent of August leaves and flowers didn't help; it melded with scents of sex. His eyes skated down, over the swell of her breasts and belly, and his throat tightened.

Her voice was infuriatingly indecipherable. "I thought you left."

She'd said it as if she didn't care, but the puffy eyes claimed differently, just fueling his sense of the way things between them ought to be. "I came to tell you I need to stay a few days."

She turned toward him. "You..."

Bands were swirling around his chest, just the way silk ties had bound his wrists the previous night. He tried but failed to push aside memories of how she'd pranced around him, strapping him to the bed. He'd never felt that level of pure sexual frustration. "Found trace in the water," he managed to explain.

A blond eyebrow arched. "Trace?"

"Evidence that the bug's been in the water. Not live," he clarified. "But I found virus casings. Just remnants. Particles." Feeling like he was rambling, he continued filling her in. "I need to take more samples. See if I find anything live. Do some interviews with the community, and then look for a connection between Bliss and Szuzi, the infected village in South America." He shook his head. "There could be antibodies in some of the blood samples. I might be able to tell if anyone's been infected in the past."

Ariel's eyes widened. He could see traces of salty tears on her cheeks and wanted to lick them off. "Do you think people here are infected?"

"Maybe."

Her eyes lifted, locked to his and held, and then it hit him like a freight train. The two of them might be infected. They'd joked about it, sure. But now that he'd found trace evidence…Why hadn't he been more careful?

"I'm going to be here a few days. I'll…" *Stay out of your way.* The words were a lie. His mind hazed when he thought about touching her, sliding his hand along the long length of her arm. Even now, he could feel the crashing pulse at her wrist. "I'll have to draw a blood sample from you."

"Just me?"

He shook his head. The way he felt, the first tube he intended to draw was his own. "Everybody's. And I've got to contact Studs Underwood." He paused, his eyes sharpening, as if to assure her that he'd rather not. "We need to hold a town meeting, to let everyone know we're running tests, but that the bug's not lethal. Otherwise, we'll keep things quiet. Bliss doesn't have its own news station, so…"

"You don't want coverage?"

Despite her concern, her eyes were flicking over him, making him aware that he was still wearing the lab coat he'd pulled on over his jeans. He wanted to take it off. He shook his head. "Not now. And I'll be careful not to cause any hysteria. If there is an infected area, though, and people travel…"

"I see," she murmured, her eyes returning to the window and the staggering view they'd enjoyed last night— the now cloudless blue sky shimmering above a lacy canopy of green leaves.

Frustration was making him antsy. Against his better judgement, he reached, almost gasping when his fingers touched the smooth skin above her elbow. Startled, she turned more fully toward him. A jolt shot into his fingertips and they instinctively tightened, curving around her arm, his thumb settling on a vein in the hollow where soon he'd be drawing her blood, to find out if...

They were infected.

"See what?" he asked, his voice gruff. He could see the rapidly beating pulse in her neck that deserved nothing less than the attentions of his mouth.

Silence had fallen. It was full of tension. The breeze lifted the skirt of her dress, and his hand flexed, tugged. When she stopped short of his chest, he felt a rush of annoyance. Angling his head down, he moved to cover her mouth, intending to kiss it until it was stung and swollen. But she turned and his lips brushed her cheek instead. He registered the smoothness, tasted the salt.

"Dammit, Ariel, you were crying," he murmured.

"No," she denied.

He circled a hand around her neck, tilting her head and bringing her eyes to his. "Liar."

She edged backward, but with the window behind her, there was nowhere to go, and he used that for leverage, sighing in relief as their bodies collided. "You wanted me to go," he found himself muttering. "Because all you care about is your reputation." He paused. "And your story."

Oh, he'd taken it all in. He hated the people who'd hurt her, too. But it was the past. "You want your relatives to think you're a good girl," he continued. "The whole town to understand what that bastard of a sheriff did to you—"

When those heart-stopping eyes implored him, he realized she could have pushed him over with a feather. "Do you blame me?"

"No," he said, his fingers softening, strumming at the pulse point, glad it announced excitement she'd rather hide. "Yes," he then muttered, changing his mind, his voice husky with accusation. "You care too much what people think."

"You're wrong about that," she defended herself. "Didn't you see me dump that jerk in the spring?"

"Yeah. But you didn't toss his wife out this morning." His eyes said the rest…how they could have lain there instead, naked. "Why should you still care?" he demanded softly, need infusing his voice, pulling it down octaves. "Can't you see how far you've come? How much you've grown?"

She eyed him. "Ah. You're telling me I can never go back home again? Well, thanks for the advice."

Maybe she hadn't wanted it, but he continued. "These people are history." Arguing seemed foolish, since she knew what he wanted. Why he was bothering to argue. She wanted the same. As he leaned nearer, his head spun, and when he doused the creamy column of her neck with his tongue, he muttered, "Forget about all of them. Let them go."

"Maybe I should."

Her heart beat against his chest. "Team up with me," he urged. "Who knows where the story's going to lead. If World Health and the military show up, you'll be ready, Ariel. You can deal with Studs. And these people. Work with me to organize things while I run tests."

He glanced toward the bed again, sorry her notes were strewn over the sheets. More than anything, he wanted to grab her hand and urge her to lie down with him. He dragged a hand through his hair, shoving it back, and when his gaze returned to hers, her expression was unreadable.

"Do you think that will happen?"

"Will the World Health Organization show?" He shook his head. "I don't know. But you need to know what's happening...for your story."

"I...thought we'd leave it at last night. It was so..." She hesitated. "Perfect."

So, that's what she was thinking? His heart staggered like a crazy drunk in his chest. "Today can be perfect," he muttered. "Tonight."

As if to prove it, his mouth was on hers in a flash. Like lightning, his tongue darted, then rolled like a thundercloud, turbulent and forcefully convincing. "We can do it again," he whispered, powerless to ignore the assault to his senses as her tongue engaged in a quick, hot battle that threatened to turn into a war. Her arms circled his neck, and he could feel her limbs turning languid and pliable, and think of a thousand ways to bend them further.

She exhaled shakily. "You mean...keep having sex while we're both here working?"

"And then I'll leave," he whispered.

She kissed him again, saying yes. They'd be bedmates, and at the agreement, a scalding wave washed over him, but it didn't satisfy. "What are you afraid of?"

"I'm not afraid," she said.

But she was. "I'm not them, Ariel. I'm nothing like the people who hurt you."

She didn't look so sure.

Suddenly, he tightened the embrace, pulling her closer. The wall and window frame grounded her. He rolled his hips, meeting her pelvic bone and felt pleasure blind him. His words were strangled. "Admit it, Ariel. You want this." His hands raced down, cupped her buttocks and pressed her against his erection. "This," he clarified, muttering against her mouth, his lips dampening hers.

"Yes."

"Let's forget everything else," he said. Already, the words sounded mangled. "Let's get back in bed." His eyes fixed on lips he'd already savaged. Just looking at them, so bruised and slick, he felt unsteady, as if the floor had ceased to be solid. It had turned to water and begun to flow.

"But…" she whispered.

"No buts," he whispered back.

"Rex…what if we really are infected?"

He knew he should fear that what was happening between them wasn't real, at least not in the usual sense of the word, but he didn't give a damn. The pressure against the fly of his jeans was excruciating. Stretching his arms down, his fingertips grasping the dress hem, his hands whirled like a wild wind, rustling up her skirt. A heartfelt sigh came from someplace deeper than her throat… deeper than her chest. It shuddered up from her belly and was released in a hot utterance as his fingers stroked her thighs.

Quickly, he stripped down her panties, and as she stepped from them, he kicked off his shoes. His hand found the snap of his jeans, flicked it open, then jerked down the zipper. Then the pants were gone. He hadn't bothered with briefs.

"The door," she said, sounding unbalanced.

He didn't want to leave her, since he was afraid she'd change her mind, but he did. Locking it, he returned, lifting a condom from the dresser as he passed. Luckily, she'd kept some, and now he hesitated to think what might have happened if one hadn't been handy. He was so sexed up. He readied himself as he approached. He was almost there when she parted those gorgeous legs. Settling hands on her waist, he lifted her and she felt as light as a feather as she circled her legs around his back. He'd meant to head for the bed. But it was strewn with papers, and besides, there was no time. Reaching between them, she quickly guided him in, gasping.

Ecstasy exploded as his mouth found hers for the greediest kiss they'd ever shared. Had he really been about to leave? What had he been thinking?

His muscles strained, but he braced her weight, his buttocks clenching as he arched. She stretched, every inch of him merging into her. Melting. He moaned, a hand hitting the wall above her head, and his shoulders hunched, curling as he drove his hips to hers, her soft pants telling him he wasn't alone in passion.

"I didn't want to leave," he muttered, sucking breaths between his teeth as he thrust deeply inside.

"I didn't want you to, Rex."

Against his neck, the words were hoarse. He found her mouth once more and kissed her. Over and over, his tongue parted her lips like a river. Lower…well, that was a river, too—unfathomable. He was taut now. Fingers were shredding his back. As the nails dragged down, taking skin, he shuddered, shutting his eyes as they raked his backside, making him cry out. She was getting tighter, slicker and hotter around him. Through the condom, he could feel every sensation. Pushing, he slowly drove apart each tight inch of her, registering her whimper as gloved fire fisted him.

She suddenly bucked—wild, brazen. Then silence took them. Everything shattered into heartbeats. Breaths. The pound of hips and the focus of the climb. He tunneled, racing. And then she clenched, spasms rocking her. A shaky exhalation fluttered in his ear.

"Come inside me," she whispered urgently.

"A siren's song," he muttered, the words lost in a kiss, his tongue feeling too big for his mouth as her breathless command became a last push that sent him reeling another mind-bending inch to release.

A heartbeat brought him back. Maybe hers. Maybe his. Either way, Rex knew he'd been crazy to think he could drive away from Bliss without a backward glance. On one pretext or another, he would have returned. She was still shaking with climax, and he almost smiled, realizing it was just as likely Ariel Anderson would have come looking for him.

12

ARIEL HOPPED OUT of the passenger side of the mobile lab, and as Rex locked his door and circled around, she rearranged their gear in the seat—their notebooks, syringes and the tray for blood samples. Keeping the door open, she grabbed Rex and spun him close, into the shade cast by the vehicle. She slid her hand over his backside, exhaling a deep sigh as she did so. Then another, as he leaned for a quick, thorough kiss.

Then she glanced over his shoulder at the jammed gravel parking lot of the Outskirts Motel. Most visitors to Bliss stayed near the spring, but the main venues—the Ivy Terrace, Rustic Inn and teahouse—had quickly filled because of the Harvest Festival. Now some were forced to stay farther from town, at a motel appropriately named the Outskirts. Four low-slung buildings were arranged in a square, the parking lot was in the middle.

Earlier in the week, Rex had drawn a blood sample that he'd found interesting from a man staying here named Lawrence Nathan. Because the man had left the interview early, Rex wanted to draw another tube of blood and to question him further, since he'd said he was interested in wild habitats and rain forests.

Rex said, "Ready?"

She shook her head, reaching on tiptoes for another kiss that infused her with tantalizing heat. "Hmm," she whispered, feeling his warmth mingle with the mid-morning sunlight; it seeped through his lab coat and jeans to her pale lavender suit.

His gaze flicked over her, approvingly. "You're sure you can take another day of this?"

The week had been flying by. She'd been on hand as Rex had taken blood samples and conducted interviews, and through that, she'd been able to question people herself. She was very clear on the direction she wanted to take for the story. She smiled, thinking of their nights of passion. "Do I look tired to you?"

He shook his head. "Nope."

"This is the last interview, anyway," she reminded him.

Tomorrow was the Harvest Festival. Thinking of it brought a touch of depression. After all, the recipe book hadn't yet been found, and her mother, Gran and Great-gran were beside themselves. All the more reason Ariel figured she'd wait until after the festival to have a heart-to-heart with her mother.

"Later, I'm going to help my relatives pack up stuff to take to the festival," she said, murmuring the words against Rex's lips. Already, the booths were set up at the fairgrounds. "You're going to have fun," she promised.

"Watching guys play saws and display prize pigs?"

"You might get to eat some ramps," she said.

"Huh?"

"Wild onions."

When he grimaced, she added, "Snob."

She knew he really wasn't, though. "Are your notes

done?" he asked, although his tone told her countless things other than her human-interest story were on his mind.

She nodded. "I'm still toying with the new angle on it."

"Jack and Ryan said it was a go?"

She nodded once more. After serious thought, she'd decided to contact her bosses one more time, regarding the story. She hoped, with the permission of the CDC, to introduce the mystery of the possible love bug and to explore the history of the town's blackouts in a light, fun, upbeat way for her fifteen-minute spot.

"If it works out," she said, "people will love it."

"It'll work out," he promised. "Jessica okayed our end."

Regarding Ryan, she'd been surprised when he'd engaged in their usual flirtation. She'd realized light-years, not days, had passed since she'd seen him. Looking into Rex's blue eyes, it was hard even to imagine the other man now…his sandy hair and brown eyes. Had his professional air really made her feel he'd be a good partner? Next to what she'd shared with Rex, Ryan's flirtation was tame. Child's play, she thought now. She and Rex had found something so much more elemental, a passion strong enough to weather life storms.

"I think everything's together," she finally said, enjoying the feel of his arms wrapped around her. She wanted more right now, though. She could take it, too. He'd taught her that in the past days. She didn't care how passion made her look, either. After Joanie had stormed out of the house, Ariel hadn't been surprised at the renewed disdain she'd been met with in town. In the hardware store, some of Joanie's ex-high school friends had made a point of moving their conversation to another aisle. And in Jack's Diner, Studs and one of his buddies had snubbed her and Rex, pointedly lifting their check from the table and leaving. Even Elsinore Gibbet had been cool.

She'd seen it all coming, which was why she'd flung herself across the bed and wept when she'd thought Rex was gone. She'd lived this too many times, so she'd known exactly what was coming down the pike. So far, as usual, Ariel had done nothing but push Studs into the spring, fully dressed. Still, when she was with Rex, none of it mattered any longer. One touch of his mouth, and the past really did seem to recede, like a bad dream almost forgotten. Shifting her weight, she brought her hips to his, igniting a spark that almost took her breath.

"Careful," he murmured.

But the lift of his hips and glint of awareness in his eyes undercut the warning. So did the firm mouth that smacked against hers. The kiss, like his body, was warm and as she parted her lips and greeted the tongue that slipped inside, she was achingly aware of memories of their nights together.

All at once, she was down on her knees, taking the heated length of him into her mouth…then lying on her tummy, raising her backside. Even now, a shudder rocked her because she could feel his trembling hands on her lower back and hear his chesty moan as he entered her from behind, the movement slow and deep. *That's right, babe, open for me. Let me in.*

Yes, it would be easy to drag him inside the mobile-lab unit, pull the curtains and lock the door.

She broke the kiss and glanced hungrily into his eyes.

He looked as tempted as she was. "We've got to finish interviewing," he reminded her, the huskiness of his voice making clear that he'd rather be back in bed. Or on the floor. Or against a wall.

She forced her attention to the previous subject. "You were asking about my taping tomorrow," she said to jump-start the conversation. "When I actually begin, I imagine I'll need to make adjustments."

"You're doing interviews live, right?"

"Right."

"What about your cameraman?"

"I touched base this morning. We talked about what I'll need from him. His name's Don. He seemed smart. Really on top of things." She'd been worried that something might happen, causing him not to show. "I'd hoped to bring someone with me from Pittsburgh, so I wouldn't have to worry about their reliability."

"He'll show," Rex promised.

After speaking with Don, she had no doubt that things would run smoothly, but she smiled. "What?" she asked rhetorically, shooting him a sexy smile. "Do you have ESP?"

His mouth found hers and his tongue flickered, the pointed hot spear of its tip working wonders. Pulling away, he said, "About certain things." He flashed a smile, his teeth looking as white as moonlight against his tan skin and in the dark shadows cast by the mobile lab.

"Like?"

"The fact that we're going to have sex real soon."

"You should open a shop. You know, buy some crystal balls and tarot cards."

"Your relatives already did that," he teased, his breath

hovering closer before his tongue traced her lips again. "And given the way I feel, I suspect it's you who stole that recipe book, lady."

She widened her eyes in mock surprise. *"Moi?"*

He nodded slowly. "You've given me one of those potions that Matilda used to make for her lovers right before she killed them."

Sex was thrumming through her now. "Maybe," she agreed. "I'm feeling sexy enough that we probably should call in the World Health Organization."

"The military, at least."

She was glad neither had come to Bliss.

"You should definitely be arrested," he added.

She couldn't help but laugh. "Not by Studs," she begged.

He chuckled. "I reserve all rights to handcuff you, Ariel."

"Too bad there are no toy shops in Bliss."

His voice turned throaty. "What would be your pleasure?"

She thought of all the things she'd seen, over the years, in magazines and the windows of such shops— the fancy vibrators, flavored paints and ribbed condoms. She could only shake her head. "We'd just have to experiment."

"That could be arranged."

She really wished there was such a shop nearby. After the way Joanie had barged into the house, Ariel better understood her own reactions in the past. Maybe it hadn't been the best way to respond, but some people here were so narrow-minded. It was hard to suppress the urge to fight back, however counterproductively, by shocking all of them. Even the nicest girl in the world would want to walk down Bliss Run Road naked, if she had to put up with all these prudes!

When her lips touched Rex's again, the thoughts skated backward, skittering to some lost, tucked away, far-off corner of her mind. Every inch of her was humming. Breaking the kiss, she tilted back her head and surveyed him for a long moment. If the truth be told, she could do so for hours. Days and nights had passed, and the passion had seemed endless. Everything else had become a blur. A town meeting had been called and she'd helped Rex, as well as herself by working on the story, but she lived for the moments they were in bed.

She'd heard some scandalous tales, too. As it turned out, not everyone in Bliss was a prude. Antibodies to Romeo had been found, but only in the blood of people who'd lived in Bliss in the late seventies, including her mother, Gran and Great-gran, which had led Rex to believe there had been an outbreak in the summer of 1977. The results had led both he and Ariel to test themselves, and they'd come up clean, with no antibodies at all.

Surprisingly, the summering visitors seemed unperturbed by the possibility of an outbreak, especially once they'd understood that the bug caused no harm, and that, in the worst case scenario, they might only become less inhibited and experience an improvement in their sex lives.

Only Jeb Pass had shown undue concern. The teenager had pulled Rex and Ariel aside, adamantly saying he was sure the town was infected. He'd declared that's why there hadn't been mass hysteria at the possibility of an outbreak. He'd demanded to know everything Rex could tell him about the case. Because a live bug hadn't been found in the water or blood tests, Jeb was sure this proved the CDC's testing methods were faulty. In careful detail, he'd talked about his friendship with a girl named Michelle, who'd come to Bliss with her family every summer. This year, he'd said, had begun like every other, but in the past few days, everything had changed.

"We went to the movies," he'd begun, glancing around the front room of the library where Elsinore Gibbet and Carl DeLyle had insisted the interviews be conducted. Because the mobile library, despite being a trailer, was the only edifice besides Stud Underwood's office that qualified as a public building in Bliss, the choice had seemed logical, and Rex and Ariel had gone with it.

"Go on," Rex had said.

"Michelle was…all over me," Jeb had continued. "I mean…" A blush had crept into his cheeks. "She was rubbing my legs and kissing me, all during the movie." Pausing, he'd swallowed hard, the red in his cheeks deepening. "Do you…uh…need more detail, sir?"

Taking mercy on him, Rex had said, "That's enough. The important thing is that you feel Michelle's behavior has changed."

Looking relieved, Jeb had nodded. "That's affirmative," he'd said, making Ariel bite back a smile. She suspected he'd heard the response on episodes of *Star Trek* and had waited to say the words himself for years.

"And you say this happened recently?"

Jeb had nodded. "Again, affirmative. All at once.

Overnight. Uh…" The lump had seemed to lodge in the boy's throat again, and he'd swallowed around it. "Not that I really mind," he'd said.

Rex's lips had twitched. "Judging by the hickey on your neck, I think that goes without saying."

Watching Rex take notes, Jeb had flushed more darkly at the comment, then added, "That's why I think something's wrong with your tests. Maybe they can't detect the virus now. Maybe it's mutated, so it doesn't look the same as it did in South America. Did you think of that? I mean, maybe it's…oh, I don't know, become invisible or something. Smaller. So, equipment can't detect it." Jeb had been thinking out loud. "Viruses do mutate. Don't they, Dr. Houston?"

Rex had nodded. "Yep. It is in the nature of the beast. The proteins in viruses form an envelope in which material from other cells can grow. So, they can do just about anything."

Jeb had swiftly bobbed his head. "That's what I was thinking. Marsh and I—he's my best buddy—have been reading about them. And like I say, I think that's what's happened, Dr. Houston."

Once more, he'd glanced around, then lowered his voice. "Can't you see?" he'd plunged on. "Michelle is all over me. And Marsh and I had to deliver Jay Jones's paper route. And I noticed something else suspicious that I can't talk about yet…."

Rex had squinted, his mind back on the first comment. "A paper route…?"

Jeb was getting more agitated. "Yeah. And well, you have to know Jay Jones. He's always on time. Never forgets his homework. Head of the chess club and class president. But Marsh and I found him at the spring, practically doing it with one of the summer visitors. He was right there in front of everybody! And the bag of newspapers was just lying in the grass!"

"So, you delivered them?"

"Yeah. And…" His voice had dropped as he'd jerked his head to the side. "Look at Chicken Giblets, I mean Miss Gibbet." He'd paused significantly as Rex and Ariel's gaze had followed his. "She's never married. She hates men, especially Mr. DeLyle. But look at how she's laughing and smiling, talking to him now."

Rex had nodded once more.

"They usually hate each other," Jeb had repeated.

Ariel had spoken for the first time. "That's true."

"Only love songs are playing on the local radio station, and the Bliss theater's only showing romantic movies." Jeb had glanced toward Ariel, his cheeks turning another shade pinker, if that was possible. "And your relatives. The uh…"

"Witches of Teasdale's Terror House?" Ariel had suggested, her lips twitching when she'd suddenly realized that this boy, too, had probably heard all the crazy tales about her overactive sexuality. Shoot, maybe they had a point. No one could miss the sparks flying between her and Rex.

"It's okay," she'd coached. Even though it was probably a lie, she'd felt compelled to add, "You can say anything, Jeb. You won't offend me."

Jeb had swallowed hard. "They're wearing floral-print dresses. And your great grandmother was in town, wearing pink and talking to Eli Saltwell. You know that's weird."

She was just as confused about it as Jeb. She'd nodded, glancing at Rex. "Maybe he's right. Maybe there is an infection, and the tests aren't picking it up. What if Romeo really has mutated…?"

"It's possible. Still, I'd probably have seen something under the microscope," Rex had countered.

She'd shrugged. "You think so. But isn't that the point of mutations? Some new strain of a virus evolves that's stronger and more resilient?"

Rex had considered a long moment. "There was a camouflaged bug found in West Africa once," he'd admitted. "It mimicked the outer husk of normal cells so well that, at first, researchers didn't realize the seemingly normal cells were really carrying the virus."

Jeb had sighed. "I know I'm onto something here, Dr. Houston."

"You're a smart kid," Rex had commented.

"Yeah." Jeb had looked sheepish. "I'm an underachiever. I skipped a grade, too. But I hate to study. Anyway, I've got a good eye for detail. And my granddad—they call him Pappy—has taught me lots." Looking stricken after a moment, the boy had slowly shifted his eyes between Rex and Ariel. "Uh…that's why…well, pardon me for pointing this out to you, sir. I mean, you are a doctor, and you're with the CDC…."

"Feel free to say whatever you want," Rex had said.

"Well, with all this going on," Jeb had continued insistently, "how could you really trust people to give accurate reports about their own behavior? And if you were affected by a mutant virus, how would you know you're attending to all the necessary details?"

Rex and Ariel had surveyed each other a long moment, then had looked at Jeb again. "Are you suggesting," Rex had murmured, "that we might be infected, but because we're so happy, we just don't know it?"

Jeb had shrugged. "I'm no scientist or anything," he'd ventured diplomatically. "But you have to at least consider the possibility...."

Ariel had. But then, seconds later, when she'd looked at Rex again, everything had just slipped from her mind. Besides, the idea of a camouflaged bug just seemed so farfetched. Like something from a TV show or movie. And then, at that precise moment, Rex had leaned and kissed her again, so she'd barely even noticed when Jeb had sighed loudly, stood and left the room.

Now she blinked, realizing that, once more, she and Rex had been staring at each other. She took in how sunlight hit his blond hair, turning yellower strands to white. Hunks were tucked neatly behind his ears, but a stray lock had tumbled onto his forehead. His blue eyes looked like starbursts, she decided.

Once more, she blinked. "We'd better check out Lawrence Nathan." She frowned. "What was so strange about his first blood sample?"

Rex shook his head. "Just some trace. I'm not sure. I just want to look again." He reached down, grasping her hand as he lifted the supplies from the passenger seat of the mobile lab, slammed the door and locked it. He handed her the notebook she'd been carrying, in case she heard something of use for her human-interest piece tomorrow.

"I think we entered the zone," he murmured as they headed for room twelve, Lawrence Nathan's room.

The zone. It was the phrase he used to describe the lost time he experienced when he was hard at work.

Ariel was the same way. When deeply involved in writing a story, or researching a topic that might become of interest to the public, she, too, entered the zone. Hours could pass or a phone could ring right next to her ear, and Ariel would never even notice. She would simply realize she'd been swept away.

Other things did that to her, too. Riding horses in the snow on the mountains around Terror House. Swimming in the spring. She glanced beside her and thought, making love to Rex.

He stopped at the door to room twelve, his eyes focusing when he glanced at his watch. Then he looked her way, quizzically, concern crossing his features. "Didn't we leave the house at nine-thirty?"

She considered. "Yeah. What time is it?"

"Eleven."

How long had they just stood in the lot, gazing at each other and kissing? Trying not to worry over that, she took a deep breath, pushing away any thoughts about the implications of what Jeb had said. "The zone," she said simply.

"Right," he murmured. "The zone."

As he knocked on the door, he said, "I never entered it with somebody else."

"Me, neither."

But now they had. Somehow, they'd reached a special place that nothing could penetrate. As the door swung open, Ariel was determined to concentrate on the matter at hand. "Mr. Nathan," she began, taking in the spry man in the doorway. He was probably sixty, but looked ten years younger, with his long silver hair pulled back into a ponytail. He had a mustache and a well-trimmed beard that hung a few inches below his chin. There was something noticeably vital about him, energetic and alive. His blue eyes danced as he studied them, making Ariel flush, since she suspected he'd seen them from the window. Given that she and Rex had been in the zone, it was hard to say just exactly how deep their kisses would have looked to an onlooker.

"Dr. Rex Houston, CDC," Rex said, shifting his supplies into one hand and thrusting out the other. "We know you're expecting us. We're sorry to bother you on your vacation, too, but we only want to draw another blood sample, if you don't mind, and then ask a few questions. It'll only take a minute. We were really glad you showed up at the library, at the beginning of the week, but know you had to leave before the interview was complete."

The man stepped back. "Come on in."

ANGUS LYONS THRUST OUT his arm, then pumped a fist as Rex tied it off, his eyes never leaving the young woman he suspected was his daughter.

"This will pinch a little," Rex said.

Angus wasn't feeling a thing. He wasn't even noticing the low-rent accommodations. Everything in Bliss had been booked, and staying at the Andersons' bed-and-breakfast had been out of the question. The only room left was one at the Outskirts, which the proprietor had initially declined to rent, saying a crew he'd hired this winter hadn't managed to finish remodeling before summer. Angus had slipped him a few extra dollars, though, and secured the place.

Unlike the other rooms, it was unrenovated, all right.

The worn brown carpeting was half ripped up, grout was missing from the bathroom tiles, and extra furniture was stored haphazardly in a corner. The lumpy bed made pine needles in a mud hut feel like heaven, and the smell of disinfectant didn't help. If there was a love bug in town, Angus figured he was a good candidate to be counted among the uninfected, since this place didn't contain one iota of romanticism.

At least until he looked at Ariel.

She was the spitting image of the woman he'd met in the paradise of Bliss twenty-nine years ago. She had his Sammy's bewitching blue eyes, and clear, perfect skin, but her hair was blonder and straighter. Definitely, she was an Anderson. He'd known that the first day she'd hit town when he'd watched her nearly mow down Elsinore Gibbet in a Honda. And then, when he'd shown up at the library last week, right after the town meeting announcing they had to have blood tests, he'd seen her again. He'd hoped to be the first to be tested and miss seeing anyone who might recognize him.

The first day, he'd recognized that old bitty, Elsinore Gibbet, from years ago, too. His sweet Samantha, whom he'd always called Sammy, had said Elsinore was as nosy as a summer day was long. According to the proprietor of the Outskirts, Elsinore was the resident who'd called the CDC, too, which figured. After all, years ago, it was Elsinore who'd first found out about the machinations of Angus's father from Eli Saltwell. She'd told Sammy's mother, who in turn, had told Great-gran....

And, of course, Sammy had already suspected.

Definitely, this was one small town. When Angus had seen Elsinore for the first time in nearly thirty years, he'd quickly slipped away, even though he'd been hoping to catch sight of Ariel or Samantha. Instead, he'd seen Great-gran, and if she'd seen him, that would have been the kiss of death. She'd been outside the hardware store, arguing with an older man.

Great-gran was one of the few people who'd still recognize him. Oh, he looked nothing like he had years ago, when he'd first come to Bliss with his father to convince the community to sell their property for development. Now, watching his blood fill a glass vial, he wondered what he'd been thinking all those years ago.

Maybe he'd never know. He'd been born rich, after all. The Core Coal Company was only one of his father's many businesses. And if the truth be told, he'd only been thirty himself when he'd first hit Bliss. Sure, it was old enough to be an adult and think for oneself, but he'd never had much occasion to question the way his old man had conducted business. At least not until he'd met Sammy.

Angus had always worked for his father. He'd attended business school, then had walked right into the family business. Still, there was no excuse for his naiveté. He knew that now, and he'd paid for his oversights. He'd been so myopic. But then, his father had never considered that his plans for Bliss were wrong. When he'd begun making deals to buy land, he'd done so under the name of his land development company, Bright Futures. According to the logic of Lyons Sr., he'd simply gotten a better idea. Before Bright Futures did as promised and built resorts in the area, why not have his coal company reap even more profits from the area by strip-mining the rich coal reserves first?

When the lush vegetation grew back, then he'd build hotels and condos around Spice Spring. The location had been perfect. Central to the Northeast and Washington, D.C., and an easy hop from New York. The spring was pure, the land gorgeous. It offered swimming, fishing, hunting and riding. Hotels here could easily compete with the nearby famous Greenbriar Hotel, by catering to upscale clients seeking a getaway.

Of course, Angus's dad had overlooked the simple fact that the people didn't want their land strip-mined, and that it would take years for vegetation to grow back. Angus's father had even argued that the locals would also benefit financially from mining, more than the resorts, so they'd accommodate.

Slowly, over the years, Angus had realized that his old man's promises never materialized. And the people suffered. After realizing what his father had intended for Bliss, he'd never worked for his father again. Instead, he'd traveled the world, trying to repair damage done to the earth by industry.

"Are you okay?" Rex asked, his voice breaking the reverie.

"Can I get you something to drink, Mr. Nathan?" Ariel asked, obviously concerned that the loss of blood was making him feel faint. "Juice maybe?"

Her voice was like Sammy's, too. It had a husky quality that steered a man's mind toward bedrooms. And she was his, he thought. He could see himself—in her gait, the point to her chin, the tall angularity of her body. He could see his own father, too.

For all their disagreements, he missed the old man. He'd died seven years ago of a heart attack. Not long afterward, Angus had lost his wife, a woman he'd loved, but not in the same way he'd loved his Sammy. His wife had never known about her. It hadn't seemed fair to tell her since she'd only have been hurt by the idea of him loving another woman.

Here one day, he thought now. Gone tomorrow. That's how his own relationship with Sammy had ended years ago, abruptly. He'd felt as if his heart had been cut out. Finally his eyes meshed with Ariel's and he shook his head. Glancing between her and Rex, he recognized that they were lovers. He'd been watching them from the window. Their love was palpable, something as natural as the air. Just like what he'd shared with Sammy.

He found his voice. "I'm fine."

She didn't look convinced. "Are you sure, Mr. Nathan?"

Hell no, he wanted to say. Your mother never even bothered to tell me you existed, even though she was right not to. That was the hardest thing. His lovely Sammy had been right to cut him off. Once she'd learned of the real agenda of his father's company, it was all over between them. His own unwitting part in the deal wouldn't have mattered. Sammy loved this town. She'd been a part of the mountains and the spring. The prettiest, most popular girl in town....

When he looked at the clock, he hoped Rex and Ariel would get out of here quickly. Samantha was supposed to be here at any minute, and she had no idea why she'd been asked to come. He'd sent a note by one of the local kids, asking her to meet him here. He'd used the name Lawrence Nathan. He still didn't know exactly what he was going to say.

This wasn't how he'd imagined seeing his Sammy again, either. No, he'd imagined asking her to some elegant restaurant. Or to some quiet, beautiful place outdoors, under an arbor of trees. But he wanted privacy, too. And this happened to be the only room in town. She could be further harmed if anyone recognized him and saw them together....

Maybe she wouldn't even come. Why should she go visit some man she'd never heard of before, named Lawrence Nathan? His heart missed a beat, and he eyed Ariel once more, wishing he could just tell her. And yet, he had to ask Sammy and make sure Ariel was really his, even though he knew the truth in his heart, already. Besides, after all the trouble he'd caused, he'd never simply appear in Ariel's life, not even if he was her father and had a right to do so.

Rex Houston started asking him questions, and Angus shifted his attention from the thoughts of Ariel and Sammy to Rex. Angus had liked him immediately. He was direct. Forthcoming. Didn't play games.

After answering the first questions, Angus said, "I'm sorry. I really only have a few minutes. I'm expecting someone."

"Only a couple more questions," Rex said. "Just what we weren't able to ask in the first interview. Have you ever been to Bliss before this trip?"

Angus hesitated. Possibly, this was leading somewhere that would require him admitting his real identity, which he couldn't do just yet. But then, this was a CDC issue. "Actually," he said, "yes."

Rex's gaze sharpened. "When?"

His heart skipped a beat. Only older people in town

had seen him years ago, and only a few newspaper pictures existed that had been taken during his first stay in Bliss. Though, judging from the call he'd gotten from Jack Hayes, while he'd been still in Peru, Ariel had read about the Core Coal Company, and from what Sammy had said in the past, armchair town historian, Elsinore Gibbet, kept clippings galore about Bliss.

"Mr. Nathan?" The young woman who was probably his daughter was talking to him again. "Are you sure you're all right?"

She really thought he was about to pass out because of the blood Rex had drawn. His throat tightened. "I'm fine, Ariel," he said, speaking her name for the first time. "I was here…in the late seventies."

Rex prodded. "And this was in regards to…?"

"My work. Like I said when we first met, I preserve natural habitats. Places such as Bliss." Both statements were true, he thought, pleased with himself. He had come to work. And he did preserve habitats. Now, anyway. With any luck, his answers would leave a false impression that would distance him from connections to Core Coal.

Rex continued. "Have you ever been to South America?"

Angus shrugged. "Actually," he said again, "yes."

"Where exactly?"

Angus squinted, having no idea why Rex was asking. "All over the place." He looked once more at the clock, silently begging the fates to be kind. The last thing he needed right now was for Samantha Anderson to walk in and find him with her daughter. *Their daughter.* "I…work to save untouched places," he repeated. "Natural habitats, as I said. That means I spend a lot of time in rain forests." Pausing to take in Rex's and Ariel's excited expressions, he rattled off a list of villages, ending with Szuzi.

"Szuzi?" they echoed in unison.

Lawrence Nathan nodded.

Rex Houston whistled.

And then Ariel whispered, "We just hit the mother lode."

13

JEB WAS STARING through binoculars, lying on his belly on top of one of the buildings at the Outskirts Motel with Michelle McNulty on one side of him and Marsh on the other. Marsh had borrowed his dad's truck, pulled it to the back of the building, and they'd all climbed up to a roof, using one of the ladders Marsh's dad kept in the bed for contracting work.

"It's hot up here," Marsh whispered.

"I'm burning up," Michelle agreed. She waved the microfiche printout of the news article showing Angus Lyons's picture in front of her face like a fan.

"The door's opening," Jeb suddenly said. "They're coming out." Pressing the binoculars more firmly against his eyes, he tried to concentrate, but it was hard when the girl who'd let him fondle her breasts last night was lying next to him, wearing tight jeans and a halter. Heat was warming Jeb's skin, and it had little to do with the steamy heat outdoors. When Marsh had seen the hickey on Jeb's neck, he'd just rolled his eyes as if to say, "Another one bites the dust."

Jeb was hardly the only one. His grandmother had forgiven Pappy for whatever mysterious transgression had been the root of their quarrel, and now he and Hammerhead had moved out of Jeb's folks' house again. He was back at home with his wife. Of course, that hadn't stopped everyone from coming over to Jeb's for breakfast this morning, which meant they'd seen the hickey. Chuckling, they'd exchanged glances, but hadn't said anything. Still, Jeb had wished the floor would open and swallow him. Shaking his head as if to clear it of confusion, he concentrated as Rex, Ariel and Angus Lyons stepped outside.

"I'm sure it's Angus Lyons," whispered Michelle excitedly.

By snooping in the motel office, they'd discovered that he'd registered as Lawrence Nathan. Focusing the lenses, Jeb sharpened the image. Angus's eyes were scanning the lot worriedly, as if he didn't want to be seen. Then he waved goodbye to Rex and Ariel, who started walking to the mobile lab, carrying notebooks and blood samples. Jeb glanced from the lenses to the picture in Michelle's hand, then gave her the binoculars.

"He's changed a lot," said Michelle, now passing the binoculars to Marsh.

"It's him," Marsh said. Then he added, "Wow. Look at Dr. Houston and Ariel. They're really going at it. Guess everything they always said about her and Sheriff Underwood was true."

"I heard those stories in the diner," countered Michelle, as Marsh gave the binoculars to Jeb again. "And I think they're just rumors."

Before an argument could begin, Jeb shifted his gaze from the couple, but it was difficult. They were going at it hot and heavy, and when they broke the kiss, it was only so they could get into the mobile lab and drive away, probably to the nearest bedroom.

"That adds a whole new meaning to burning rubber," Marsh commented as they zipped out of the parking lot.

Jeb's thought exactly. Suddenly, his fingers tightened on the binoculars. A car was approaching from the opposite direction, and while Jed wasn't sure, he thought...

"Samantha Anderson," Marsh murmured as she steered into the parking space vacated by the mobile lab.

Jeb watched as she got out of the car and slammed the door. "The witch is wearing a white dress," he said, feeling surprised. It was printed with tiny pink flowers, and she looked good, too, sprucing herself up, as if expecting some action—checking her lipstick in the sideview mirror, smoothing her windblown hair with a manicured hand and straightening the skirt of her dress. She'd scarcely reached room twelve when the door opened. It was too dark to see inside but Angus Lyons seemed to be inviting her in.

"What's Angus Lyons doing in Bliss again, after all these years?" Jeb wondered aloud.

"And why is one of the witches visiting him?" asked Marsh.

Michelle spoke decisively. "All this looks suspicious. We'd better go find Sheriff Underwood."

WORDS COULDN'T HAVE EXPRESSED what passed between their eyes. After a long moment, Angus said, "I'm sorry to surprise you this way, Sammy, but if I'd told you it was me I was afraid you wouldn't come."

She pressed a hand to her heart, as if that might stop it from beating out of control. "I thought it might be...I mean, Great-gran told me she thought she'd seen you in town last week."

He should have known. He'd tried to hide from Great-gran, but she had the vision of a night owl. He eyed Sammy. "You haven't changed a bit," he said, the words seeming all wrong for the moment, too superficial, but he didn't know what else to say. His breath caught. His Sammy had the same long strawberry hair and bright blue eyes that sparkled with wit and intelligence. She weighed a few pounds more, and the wrinkles etching fine lines around her eyes lent her an air of wisdom. But then, she'd always had that, even in her youth.

"You haven't changed, either."

They stood there awkwardly. Two people who'd meant the world to each other, who'd hurt each other, then had lived oceans apart. Her hands were trembling, held loosely at her sides, the pink of her nails matching the tiny flowers on the fabric. He wanted to believe those fingers were itching to reach for him. He wanted to pull her into an embrace and squeeze tightly, wrapping her in his arms.

But neither of them moved. He didn't know how to ask what was uppermost in his mind, so he just said the words. "Is she mine?"

His Sammy drew a sharp breath. "You knew?"

He nodded, quickly explaining the call he'd received from Jack Hayes. "I only found out recently." And now, he wasn't sure what he was feeling. Anger, yes. But even after all these years, he loved and trusted Sammy. He was the one who'd shown himself to be not good enough for her, after all, not the other way around. Not a day had passed that he hadn't thought of her.

Her expression was hard to read. Guilt, concern, relief, anger—all those emotions played on her face. "I wanted to tell you," she said, speaking slowly and deliberately, as if well aware each word counted. "I...was angry for a long time, and I thought you might come back. I wanted to shut the door on our time together and forget."

She inhaled deeply, then plunged on. "Ariel asked some questions, but I...I guess I was never really as forthcoming as I told myself I'd been. I only told her I'd had a relationship that hadn't worked out, but that it was worth it because I'd gotten pregnant with her. But..."

She paused, then continued. "Everyone in town suspected you were her father. I mean, the older people, the ones who were around when..."

"My father and I tried to fleece them?" he finished.

Without asking, he could imagine the rest from the pained expression in her eyes. Samantha Anderson had been the shining light of the community, after all. Bright and beautiful. An honor student and homecoming queen. She could have married any local boy, but she'd soiled herself by nearly running off with him. And then, just as her grandfather, Eli Saltwell, uncovered Angus Sr.'s real motives, so had Sammy.

"Eli and Great-gran haven't spoken since," she said. "At least not until this past week. She said she was talking to him when she saw you in town...."

Pain knifed through him. "I'm so sorry, Sammy."

She shrugged. "Those two always fought like cats and dogs. Probably, something else besides our relationship would have broken them up. And you knew my mother liked you. For years, Gran and I have snuck into town to see Pop, from time to time. But as much as it pains me to say it, my grandfather isn't the most pleasant of creatures. Great-gran always had a handful with him."

Maybe. But the final rift was caused by fights over Sammy taking up with a well-dressed, fast-talking Northerner. Great-gran and Gran, Sammy's mother, whose husband had passed on, had said Sammy should marry whomever she pleased, and Eli Saltwell, otherwise knew as Pop, had said he intended her to marry a local boy and make her life in Bliss.

"You can meet Ariel. I think…she'd like that. You're on her mind right now. I think…she's trying to find someone to settle down with right now, and maybe she wants that part of the past resolved."

He shook his head in contemplation. "I'm surprised she didn't ask you more questions."

"I think she wanted to," Sammy admitted. "I know that now. I tried to tell myself it didn't matter, that she was happy and didn't care to know you identity, but now I realize my manner put her off." Her voice broke. "I feel terrible about it…to think of her wondering all these years and feeling that she couldn't talk to me, her own mother!"

"Don't be so hard on yourself," he murmured. Judging from her expression, she'd missed him fiercely.

"Probably, I should talk to her first."

"She was just here, but I didn't tell her…."

Sammy's eyes widened.

"She didn't know," he explained. "They came to draw another vial of blood. The man she's seeing, Dr. Houston, thinks there may be a connection between a virus in the spring and one found in Szuzi, a South American village where I stayed after leaving here. She's beautiful, Sammy. All grown up. You did a good job. I can tell. And he seems like a nice guy."

"He does, doesn't he?"

He nodded…then felt the moment slipping away. She'd suspected he was here, and she'd come dressed to the nines. Surely, she'd come for herself, not Ariel. Suddenly, his voice caught. "I've thought of you, Sammy." She'd never know how much. Whole nights. He'd lain awake, especially after his wife had passed, knowing he should be thinking of her, not his Sammy. Countless times, he'd tossed fitfully on narrow cots in a jungle or a rain forest, the sweltering heat or his own memories of her turning the sheets damp. He'd stare through the mosquito netting of the tent door, into the impenetrable dark and wonder just exactly where he'd gone wrong, or stare at shimmering blue seas, knowing she was out there somewhere, whole worlds away.

She said, "I googled you."

It was the last thing he'd expected, and a silver eyebrow raised in surprise. "You did?"

She nodded. "I almost didn't recognize you. And I couldn't believe the work you've done all over the world." She hesitated. "I saw a picture of you and your wife."

All this time, his Sammy thought he'd been married. He shook his head. "She passed a few years ago."

Her eyes filled with pain, and her voice lowered with compassion. "I'm sorry, Angus. I really am."

It was the first time she'd spoken his name. He wanted her to do so, again and again. He shrugged. "Me, too." He paused. "Did you…"

"Marry?" At that, she smiled, looking surprised, almost as if she'd never thought of doing so. "No."

Pain sliced through him again, feeling like too much to bear. "You should have," he found himself saying hoarsely.

He shook his head, wishing things had unfolded differently in the past. "I hate to think of you alone...."

Her eyes found his in the dim light. "I'm not now, Angus," she said. "You're here now."

A second later, he was in her arms.

"NOBODY'S HOME," said Marsh, putting his hands on his hips and staring at the yard. It was littered with kids' toys—a red bicycle with training wheels, two yellow trucks and a Wiffle bat. The name Underwood was painted on the mailbox beside the front door in red-white-and-blue letters.

Jeb pressed the bell a third time and stepped back. "Well, where else can we try?" The sheriff's office in town had been empty, except for the dispatcher who took calls while he was gone.

"Maybe somebody will come," said Michelle. "The door's open."

"There's no car in the driveway," Marsh pointed out.

"A lot of people around here leave their doors open in the summer," Michelle offered, shoving a hand into the back pocket of her jeans. "Still, it probably means the Underwoods didn't go out for long."

"And they took their kids," said Marsh.

Jeb sighed. "I just wish we knew what Angus Lyons is doing in town."

"Whatever it is," said Marsh, "it can't be good."

"Especially not if one of the witches is visiting him," Jeb agreed.

Michelle sighed. "I think those ladies are nice."

That sounded more like a woman taking up for her own kind, but Jeb didn't think it was in his best interest to point that out to Michelle, so he didn't. "We've got to tell Sheriff Underwood he's here. The sooner the better."

"He might be down at the festival grounds," Michelle said, "watching people put the finishing touches on the booths. Tomorrow's going to be a big day. Or maybe he's following up on the missing recipe book."

"You'd think the dispatcher would know," said Jeb, his gaze drifting over Michelle. For a moment, he entirely forgot the matter at hand. Come nightfall, he wanted the matter of Angus Lyons to be off his plate, then maybe he and Michelle could skinny-dip in the spring. He blew out a long, slow breath, then glanced away, wondering if she'd want to keep in touch after summer's end. In only a few days, after the Harvest Festival, she'd be gone.

"The dispatch did put in a call," Michelle pointed out.

Marsh considered. "Yeah. But he didn't pick up."

Not a comforting thought. "What would happen if we had a real crime here?" Jeb said rhetorically.

"We did," returned Michelle. "The recipe book was stolen."

"I meant a murder or something," Jed said

Michelle's eyes met his and seemed to sizzle. "Things seem pretty tame around here."

The flaring heat in her eyes carried a different message, as if to say that there was nothing tame where they were concerned. "For now," he murmured with significance. Later, he'd definitely like to break a few laws with her.

Marsh was getting antsy. "I guess we can wait here."

"I think we ought to keep an eye on Angus Lyons, though," said Michelle. "He's probably up to no good."

"We can leave a note here," Jeb suggested.

"No paper," countered Marsh.

There hadn't been any in the truck; they'd already looked. Jeb shrugged, then cast a glance toward his friends as if to make sure they were on the same wavelength. His eyes lingered on Michelle once more, and he fought the flush warming his cheeks. It was making him look stupid. Like some dumb schoolkid. He couldn't believe he'd really put his hands under her shirt and...suddenly, he forced the thoughts away. If he wasn't careful, he was going to get aroused. Knowing he'd better find a distraction fast, he leaned and tried the doorknob again. When it turned, he said, "There's probably some paper inside. Under the circumstance, I don't think Sheriff Underwood will care if we get some, so we can leave a note."

"Especially not when he realizes why we came," agreed Michelle, as she and Marsh followed him inside.

She said, "Let's fan out."

"I'll check in the living room," Marsh said, already moving to his left.

Michelle turned right. "And I'll look in the study. That looks like Sheriff Underwood's desk."

"Hello?" Jeb called, preceding straight ahead in a long, dim hallway toward the kitchen. "Is anybody home?" Not even an echo came back. Next to the phone, he saw a yellow tablet. Just as he opened a drawer, hoping to find a pen, he called, "I got it!"

Michelle's return sounded ominous. "You guys had better come here." She paused, then added, "Right now."

Jeb pivoted and went toward her voice, not bothering to take the pad. Marsh was already in the study, standing next to Michelle, staring at something behind the desk, seemingly on the floor.

Jeb circled around. "What…"

"Hammerhead's bandanna." Just as Marsh leaned, starting to pick it up, Michelle's hand stayed him,

"Leave it. It might be evidence."

"From what?" Jeb said, but then the pieces clicked into place. It was evidence from the Andersons' crime scene. He frowned. "But Sheriff Underwood came by the other day, and questioned Pappy about Hammerhead's whereabouts at the time of the theft," Jeb said.

"And I don't see how Hammerhead could have lost the bandanna," Marsh continued. "You know how tightly Pappy always ties it, and besides, he's such a lazy dog. He'd never hoof it all the way up to Teasdale's Terror House."

"Exactly," said Michelle. "And why is it here, instead of at the station if it's evidence? That's why I called you guys. I opened this drawer—" she leaned to indicate which "—trying to find some paper and pencils. And look!"

Jeb followed the trek of her pointing finger. Then he gasped, barely able to believe what he was seeing. In the open drawer was an ink pad and a joke gift from a novelty shop—a stamper shaped like a dog's paw print. And… "Matilda's recipe book," he said.

"In Sheriff Underwood's drawer," Michelle said, her voice lowering in surprise.

"He must have found the book recently," said Marsh, confused.

"No way," argued Michelle. "He took it." She glanced at Jeb. "That's why he didn't bother to question your grandfather about Hammerhead. He knew the dog had never been in the root cellar."

Jeb considered. "But why would he…"

"He wanted the book," said Marsh. "So he decided to frame your granddad."

Jeb couldn't believe it. Even less when Michelle said, "Or you guys. I mean, I've heard people have tried to steal the book before. Maybe he meant to cast suspicion on you, but then act as if he couldn't find enough evidence."

"Trying to turn attention away from himself," said Marsh with a low whistle.

"What should we do?" Jeb asked, suddenly glancing toward the door. "We'd better get out of here," he added, "In case somebody comes back." Now that they'd found the book, he didn't exactly want to stick around.

Gingerly, Michelle shut the drawer.

Marsh said, "Let's go. I don't want to be here when they get back."

"I think we should call Dr. Houston and Ariel," said Michelle as they headed for the hallway. "I mean, the book belongs to the Andersons, and since Sheriff Underwood works alone, we can't call his deputy. It wouldn't be right to involve the dispatcher, and if we go to a town outside Bliss, the sheriff will have time to move the book."

Marsh sighed. "My dad's cell's not in the truck."

"We can stay long enough to use the phone," Jeb said nervously, now moving toward the kitchen. He stared into the drawer he'd opened earlier, found a pen, then started to lift the receiver. Changing his mind, he grabbed a dish towel first, then covered the receiver.

"Good idea," Michelle said in such an approving

voice that Jeb's pulse raced. "No fingerprints. This really is breaking and entering, isn't it?"

That hadn't been their intention, but Jeb nodded. In the instant before the information operator came on the line, he felt his knees weaken. Michelle's red hair was swirling around her bare shoulders, and waving strands licked creamy skin. Through her top, he could see the outline of the breasts he'd touched the previous night. He'd give anything to see her fully naked, swimming in the spring.

The operator clicked on. "What number please?"

"Anderson residence. Mountain Drive," he said, still thinking of Michelle's nude body, glowing under moonlight. He cleared his throat, since it felt as if he'd swallowed something mealy. Even worse, his voice had hitched and broken when he'd spoken, sounding as high as a soprano. Color flooded his cheeks, and he turned away, hoping Michelle hadn't noticed. Then he tensed, thinking he'd heard a car approaching.

Marsh ran for the door. "It's somebody else," he called. "A Chevy's passing the house. But hurry. I'm going to move the truck. That way, if anybody comes back, it won't be in the driveway. We can wait at the other end of the block."

Jeb could hardly make public phone systems move faster. Feeling relief when the operator came onto the line again, Jeb scribbled the number hurriedly on the yellow pad he'd found earlier, then he depressed the dial-tone button, disconnecting the call, and released it for another tone.

As he dialed, he could only hope Ariel Anderson was home.

ARIEL KICKED BACK and stared at the house where she'd grown up. It was really beautiful, full of strange nooks and crannies, old pantries and long dark hallways that looked as if they could be inhabited by ghosts. And they were, she thought now. Or they had been. Until Rex had come along. Rising from the passenger seat, she headed for where he was leaning over the microscope and stood a pace away, not wanting to disturb him. She liked watching him work. He looked incredibly sexy with his overly long blond hair almost brushing the shoulders of a lab coat. His eyes were squinting into the lens.

"You look like a mad scientist."

He glanced from the scope, his expression momentarily distracted. Then he took her in and his blue eyes darkened, warming.

"The zone," she guessed. Before he could answer, her eyes flickered over the blood samples next to the cell phone on the makeshift desk. "What's Lawrence Nathan's sample look like?"

He looked at her a long moment, something indecisive in his eyes. The pause stretched a moment too long. "It's fine."

"I thought you said he had more trace evidence of Romeo in his blood than others who were here in seventy-seven. And this is the connection to Szuzi...right? I mean, he said he'd been here before, so he must have taken the bug with him when he traveled. He must have infected Szuzi." Right after Rex had realized Lawrence Nathan had been in Szuzi, he'd continued questioning him, and he had found the man had been to Bliss, also. On business, he'd said. According to Lawrence, Bliss had found a special place in his heart, and he wanted to keep it green.

Rex still hadn't said anything, and the strangeness of his expression was starting to unnerve her. It made her feel as if their perfect synchronicity was being broken. Just as she moved closer, wanting the reassurance of his arms, the phone rang and he turned away to answer it.

"Houston," he said.

Simultaneously, she realized two things. First, that it wasn't Lawrence Nathan's blood Rex had been studying under the scope, it had been her own. And second, Matilda's book had been found. Her ears perked up. "Somebody found it?"

"C'mon," Rex said as soon as he clicked the off button. "Help me secure all this stuff."

"Who was that?" As he moved the blood samples, she quickly forgot about her own. She locked the microscope into position, as well as the roller chair.

"Jeb," Rex returned. "He, Marsh and Jeb's girlfriend, Michelle, are at the Underwoods's. They've been trying to find us. They called the house first, and since I gave the number to your relatives, he got my cell number."

Her mind was still trying to catch up as he headed for the front seat. "What are they doing there?"

Rex turned the key over in the ignition. "They say they just found Matilda's recipe book in Studs' desk drawer."

Ariel sighed with relief. "He found it?"

Rex shook his head as he pulled from the lot. "Uh…no. It looks like he stole it."

Ariel could only shake her head. "Why would Studs steal Matilda's book?"

"Beats me. But I bet we're about to find out."

14

"Now," said Sheriff Durham, pushing open the driver's side door of his cruiser just as Studs and Joanie entered the house. "We're ready to move."

Thankfully, the Underwoods's children weren't with their parents. That made it easier to arrest Studs. If that's what was about to occur, Ariel thought. Somehow, this seemed to be too good to be true, though. Had the jerk really stolen the book, as the teens claimed? Was he finally about to get caught at his own nasty games? And why? Did he really hate her that much? Had he done so to put a damper on her relatives' good time at the festival? Surely, he knew how much the book meant to them and how cherished it was. Had he stolen it out of spite?

Ariel only hoped it was in the house and unharmed. She could almost see its worn, yellowed cloth cover. Because edges of the brittle pages threatened to crumble and blow away, it had to be handled with the utmost delicacy. The recipes had been recorded years ago, in crimped writing with a quill pen, and the ink had faded, so that it almost blended into the paper. If the book ever got wet, it would be ruined.

That's why it had been stored in the cellar's safe. Unlike most root cellars, the one at the bed-and-breakfast wasn't damp, but rather, it was the driest part of the house, almost hermetically sealed. Ariel's relatives claimed Matilda had once grown tea leaves on the mountain and that she'd built the cellar for the purpose of hanging leaves to dry.

Now Ariel glanced from the windshield to Sheriff Durham. He was tall and lanky, so his angular arms and legs, clad in a short-sleeved tan uniform, seemed to unfold like a shirt from cardboard as he got out and stretched his legs. Only a wide-brimmed ranger's hat kept his shaved head from soaking up the sun and reflecting it like a headlight beam. As he stared toward the house, he hiked his slacks and rested a hand on his gun holster.

As soon as Rex and Ariel had called, the young law officer had driven over from the next town, and now Michelle, Jeb and Marsh tumbled from the back seat. Sheriff Durham had parked a half block away from the Underwoods's home, under the cover of a weeping willow, and now, stepping around the hood, Ariel felt her pulse quicken as she saw the couple enter the small, two-story house. Her eyes trailed over the yard, taking in the toys strewn over the grass, and she realized two things—first, this sort of life would have been hers if she hadn't left Bliss, and second, she'd have felt unchallenged and unfulfilled.

She hated to think it, but for the first time, she wondered if Studs and Joanie hadn't felt some jealousy toward her, as much as they'd never admit it. Sure, she'd had it rough, but that had driven her to develop skills, hobbies and talents, and in the end, she'd gotten out of town. She was still young, her career just beginning, and if the past week was any indication, her love life was more promising than ever. If her human-interest piece for the Harvest Festival went well, she might wind up as a television producer before her thirtieth birthday.

Studs and Joanie had landed in a very different life, and while many Bliss residents loved what living in the country had to offer, Joanie hadn't looked particularly happy the day she'd stormed into Ariel's bedroom. No more than she had moments ago, walking toward the house, wearing black shorts and a black T-shirt, as if she were dressed for a funeral, with her lips pursed and her arms crossed tightly over her chest. Studs had looked equally disgruntled, preceding her.

"Stay back," Sheriff Durham coached now. "Sheriff Underwood's in civvies. So, he's not carrying right now, but he's got guns in the house."

Dutifully, everyone kept a few paces back, and when they reached the porch, they stood off to the side as Sheriff Durham rang the bell.

"Dean," Joanie said, opening the door. "This is a surprise. What brings you into Bliss? Come on in." As soon as she stepped back to admit him, everyone else circled the corner of the house and crowded in behind, pushing over the threshold.

"What's going on?" Joanie said, taken aback.

Despite the sheriff's warnings, Michelle took charge. "The book's in here."

Studs was in the study, standing near a window, staring into the side yard, and when he heard the ruckus, he turned. Ariel's lips parted in surprise; his eyes were slightly watery, and while it was hard to tell, she could swear he'd been crying. Michelle went straight for the desk, grabbed a drawer handle and began to pull it.

"No," Studs said simply, moving toward Michelle. "Don't open that."

Then everything happened at once. Studs reached for Michelle, clearly hoping to stay her hand before she could finish opening the drawer. The second his beefy fist closed over her upper arm, Jeb released an animal grunt, charged with pure testosterone. Rushing forward, he lunged at Studs, catching him around his paunchy waist and shoving him backward. Studs slammed into the wall next to the window through which he'd been staring.

Joanie screeched, "What's going on here?" Racing forward to protect her husband, she grasped the back of Jeb's T-shirt, attempting to pull him away while Ariel edged across the threshold and into the room with Rex on her heels.

"He stole the Andersons' recipe book," Michelle announced triumphantly, as Sheriff Durham came forward, covered his hand with a rag from his back pocket, then lifted the book from the drawer.

"And the festival is tomorrow," Marsh said. "The Andersons always have a booth, selling teas, and he made sure that was impossible for them this year."

"He wanted to frame Marsh and Jeb," Michelle said as she shook off Studs's arm. Seeing that she was safe, Jeb released his hold from around the man's waist and glanced at Sheriff Durham, who was placing the book into a transparent evidence bag.

"Will my relatives be able to get their book back before tomorrow?" Ariel asked, her eyes studying it from its place inside the plastic.

"Of course. I only want to dust it for prints. It will only take a few minutes, once we're out of here. You can come with me, or if you can just trust me with the book for an hour…"

"Be careful," said Ariel. "It's very old and fragile. A family heirloom." But she did trust Sheriff Durham with it. Just like she trusted Rex. She cast a glance beside her, surveying the man who'd loved her so senselessly all week long. He was incredibly handsome, with his blond hair tucked behind his ears and his bright blue eyes intent on Studs. He looked as if he could chew the man up and spit him out without ever breaking stride.

"My husband didn't take that book!" exclaimed Joanie now, her jaw becoming rigid and intractable. "He's been working on the case, trying to find that book, despite how…" She paused. "How that tramp has chased him all these years."

"Even if I was a tramp," Ariel said, "which I'm not, I and my family pay taxes. Solving crimes is your husband's job."

"And those are my suspects," said Studs, staring at Marsh and Jeb.

"You're crazy," said Jeb.

"We're not criminals. We came to talk to you about Angus Lyons," Marsh quickly said. "We saw him at the Outskirts Motel, but you weren't home, so we looked for some paper to leave you a note, and—"

"Angus Lyons?" Ariel said, gasping. "What's he doing here?"

"That's when we found the book," said Michelle, ignoring Ariel and picking up on what Marsh had said. "And this!" She nodded toward the ink pad and stamper.

"He put paw prints around the safe in the root cellar," Marsh accused.

"And who would know better how to crack a safe than a sheriff?" asked Michelle. "We heard the safe wasn't blown open, so whoever broke in knew the combination."

Ariel sighed. "A few years ago, my mother turned in the combination to the sheriff's office, for security purposes, along with an inventory of valuables in the house. She was redoing the insurance policy, and the agent suggested that the paperwork be filed in town, also."

"Looks like you've been caught red-handed," said Sheriff Durham, unhooking the cuffs that he wore attached to his belt.

"Those kids planted the book," Studs said, eyeing Sheriff Durham as he approached. "Don't you see that what they've done is breaking and entering! They admitted as much! They were snooping in my house! And you're going to arrest me?"

"Sorry, but I'm going to have to," said Sheriff Durham, coming to a standstill a foot away from Studs. Ariel followed the action, still wondering about Angus Lyons. Had the kids really seen him at the Outskirts?

Suddenly, she thought of Lawrence Nathan's skittish behavior, how he'd seemed to be expecting someone. The idea that the men were one and the same came in a flash, like a buried insight that surfaced all at once. He was about the right age, and he'd been the first to show for a blood test, saying he wanted to get it out of the way. Maybe he'd just been afraid townspeople would recognize him.

But why would he return to Bliss? Everyone here hated him, if only by reputation. Stories about the near takeover of the town had circulated for years. If Lawrence Nathan was really Angus, was that information she could use in her story?

She tried to remember the pictures she'd seen of him while researching possible angles for her Harvest Festival piece. When she was a kid, she'd seen news articles; most kids in Bliss had been shown news stories about Core Coal. Elsinore Gibbet had made sure of that.

The long-haired man she and Rex had met was around the same age as Angus Lyons. Though, his style was completely different. He was a hippie, wearing loose khakis, a T-shirt and Birkenstock sandals, with socks no less. Hardly the short-haired businessman she remembered from the photo. In a three-piece suit and standing next to his father, he'd looked every inch the corporate raider. While Jack and Ryan hadn't wanted her to focus on the Core Coal material in her story, fearing the land development angle would detract from small-town human interest, the resurfacing of Angus Lyons might yield some angle they'd allow her to use....

"They entered my residence when I wasn't home," Studs was still protesting when Ariel returned her attention to him. "And they looked in my drawers."

Ignoring his arguments, Sheriff Durham drew a card from his back pocket and began to read Studs his Miranda rights. "You have the right to remain silent..."

Before he had a chance to click the cuffs around Studs's wrist, Joanie edged between them. She stared at her husband. "You told me those boys took the book," she said. "So why didn't you arrest them yet? Or talk to their parents? And why is the book here, not at the station? And what about that ink pad and paw-print stamp? And Hammerhead's bandanna?" Her voice rose. "I'm sick of this, Studs Underwood. Sick of you! You contribute nothing around here. I do all the cooking, cleaning, taking care of the kids. You won't even let me go back to school! And now this!"

"You're not going to get out of this one," Sheriff Durham said. "Not unless you confess and can offer some reason for what you've done. Then, if the Anderson women are nice enough to take pity on you and not press charges, seeing as their property doesn't look harmed, you might be set free."

"Don't count on it," Ariel said. "As much pain as this jerk has caused us, I can't imagine not pressing charges. So, no confession will be necessary. I think we can rely on the evidence."

She felt a rush of pleasure as Rex's hand curled around her elbow. Heat suffused her. All at once, she wished they were somewhere other than here. Like in bed. Time was running out, the festival was tomorrow, and she wanted to spend every last possible moment with him.

Glancing beside her, she surveyed how the T-shirt hugged his muscular chest. Her gaze dropped, then took in the tight fit of his worn jeans. The fly curved over him, molding the unmistakable bulge. As she blew out a breath, she took in the hard muscles of his thighs. And dammit. As usual, it was Studs Underwood who was in the way of what she wanted!

If not for the sheriff, the recipe book would still be stored in the safe, her relatives wouldn't have been worried all week and could have been busy preparing specialty tea blends to sell tomorrow. Now, they'd be up all night, hard at work on pouches of teas for the booth. Which meant she'd be busy, too. Suddenly, she saw all her best-laid plans for lying naked in bed with Rex tonight going up in smoke. "Definitely, we're pressing charges," she burst out.

"Now, Ariel, honey," Studs began, a pleading look coming into his beady brown eyes.

The look alone was enough to push her over the edge. "I hope you rot in jail. Ever since high school, you've been spreading rumors about me all over town." She stared at Joanie. "And they are rumors. Frankly, I wouldn't touch your husband with a ten-foot pole. Who would want him?"

"All that was lies!" Jeb exclaimed.

She whirled on him, not about to mince her words just because of Jeb Pass's age. After all, he'd already heard it all through the grapevine, anyway. "What?" she said, the laughter coming from her lips undercut by her steely gaze. "Do you really think I had sex with him in the parking lot of Jack's Diner? Or drove into Charleston with him, just to get it on with another woman in a skanky motel room?"

Before Jeb could answer, she plunged on. "Now, look at me, Jeb Pass. And look at him. Me. Pretty, smart and working for a television station in another city. Him. An overweight thief."

"Well, uh, Ariel...put that way..." Jeb began.

She almost smiled with satisfaction. Yes, maybe she should have defended herself years ago, but she'd known no one would listen. And now, since he'd been caught red-handed, stealing from her family, she had leverage. Since Michelle worked at Jack's Diner, the news of this would probably be all over town before sunset.

Marsh gasped. "What a jerk!"

"Arrest is too good for a man like him!" said Michelle.

Ariel was staring at Joanie. "So, don't you ever—" She paused "—And I mean *ever* come looking for your husband in my bed again. It interrupted me. And it interrupted our guests who pay good money to have a pleasant stay and vacation!"

"Well said," commended Rex.

Not that Joanie heard. "How could you?" she said to her husband.

Ariel almost felt bad about what was happening. The pain in Joanie's expression was apparent, but then, none of them were kids any longer. Pushing aside a twinge of guilt at hurting them, she said, "I'd feel sorry for you two, but you've caused a lot of trouble."

"Why?" Joanie asked, her eyes on her husband's, imploring.

Studs hung his head in a way that would almost have been comical, if not for all the havoc he'd wreaked in Ariel's life. "I…wanted the recipes for myself," he admitted, trying to keep his voice low enough that only his wife could hear. "And I wasn't going to ask the witches for it."

"Only because I was up there," Ariel said. "And you know I wouldn't give you a damn thing, Studs. What do you have against me and my family, anyway? Did you do this out of spite?" Only now did her mind really register that he'd said he wanted the recipes.

He lifted his gaze, as if to meet hers, but his eyes stopped shy of hers. He exhaled a long breath. "C'mon, Ariel. Tell him to let me go." Now his eyes did meet hers, and the uncharacteristic honesty in the gaze made her heart lurch. Then she reminded herself that Studs was only being nice so he wouldn't go to jail.

"I took the book. I admit it. And…" His eyes shifted

to his wife. "I made up those lies." All at once, his voice cracked. "Joanie baby," he continued. "It was for you. You'd get so jealous when you thought I was with Ariel, and then you'd come running to me, doing all those sweet things, trying to make sure I loved you best. But you've been so unhappy lately…" He swallowed hard, then continued. "I couldn't ask the Andersons for any specialty teas, but I figured if I borrowed the book for a few days, maybe I could find a tea that would…"

Joanie's voice was hard to interpret. "Set things right between us?"

He nodded.

Ariel could only shake her head in stupefaction. "This is his motive," she muttered, unable to believe it. Surely, Joanie would leave the jerk now. Already, she was unhappy in the marriage, and now her husband had been exposed as the most dangerous kind of gossip, as well as a thief.

As if reading her mind, Michelle muttered, "Leave him in the dust."

Instead, Joanie grasped her husband's hands and brought them to her heart. "Oh, Studsy," she whispered. "You did all that for me?"

Ariel uttered a strangled sound. Could this possibly be happening?

"You know how much I love you, Joanie," he said.

Had Ariel's whole life been dogged by rumors, just so Studs could make Joanie jealous? Joanie was smiling through tears. "Well, you know they're saying something's in the water, so maybe we should…"

"Kiss and make up?" Leaning, Studs offered a wet, sloppy kiss.

Ariel's eyes felt as if they were going to pop out of her head. "I really don't believe this," she said, stunned.

"They deserve each other," said Michelle.

"Don't you dare show mercy," Rex put in.

"Throw the book at him," Jeb said.

"Ditto," added Marsh, sounding astonished.

"I wasn't about to let him off the hook," Ariel assured.

Swiftly, as soon as she nodded, Sheriff Durham stepped past Joanie, grasped Studs's wrists and cuffed him. As he moved toward the door, Ariel felt Rex's arm slip around her waist, guiding her in the same direction. Her whole side warmed, and once more that telltale heat washed over her, urgent and undeniable. As they walked toward the front door, their steps were in perfect tandem, and she wanted to feel Rex against her, skin to skin.

"C'mon," he urged, leaning so close to her ear that his breath feathered over the lobe. "Sheriff Durham can handle the rest. Maybe we can get some alone time before he returns the book to you. After that, we may be busy all night, helping your folks get ready for the festival."

And she had to sleep, unfortunately. Tomorrow was such a big day. The cameraman from Charleston would be here to greet her by seven in the morning. Most of the real work would take place in the editing room in Pittsburgh, but Ariel wanted to make sure the story wound up having the exact right approach. Since Jack and Ryan had said she could use the material about the CDC looking for a love bug in Bliss, she was sure the piece could be humorous, quirky and heartwarming. That's what she wanted, at all costs.

"I think we can steal a couple hours," she whispered huskily to Rex, already feeling his fingers on her thighs, parting her, and the rush of sensation as he filled her until she was sure she'd die from the pleasure of it.

They'd reached the yard when, from behind her, she heard Marsh say, "Maybe we ought to tell Sheriff Durham about Angus Lyons."

"Yeah," Jeb cut in excitedly as Ariel turned to look over her shoulder at the others. "We saw him," Jeb continued. "I recognized him from an old newspaper clipping that Chicken Giblets, I mean Miss Gibbet, showed us in school. I thought it was interesting, so I read more about the Core Coal takeover. Anyway, it's definitely him. He's back, and he's staying at the Outskirts Motel."

Studs's voice sounded then, the tone as sly and crafty as a snake. "That's another reason I've been so busy lately, honey," he said to his wife. "I've been staking out Angus Lyons. He's registered at the Outskirts under a fake name, Lawrence Nathan. I've been watching him and his ex-lover."

"Oh, honey," commiserated Joanie, as if her husband were Perry Mason and Sherlock Holmes rolled into one.

His eyes skated to Ariel's, and now, although he was wearing handcuffs, the gaze held a gleam of ugly triumph. "Now that you've gotten me arrested," he said, his mouth slowly broadening into a Cheshire cat's grin, "you have a free afternoon stretching before you, Ariel. So, why don't head on down to the Outskirts Motel and meet your daddy?"

15

"MY DADDY?" ARIEL SAID in shock, clutching the dashboard as Rex drove. She glanced beside her. Feeling uneasy about what she saw in his expression, she added, "What?" as he pulled into the parking lot of the Outskirts.

Rex hesitated, then said, "Nothing."

She squinted, inviting further commentary that didn't come, then she glanced around the lot. "My mother's car's here," she murmured, her hand already on the door handle. Her mind was still reeling. Maybe her mother had had an affair with Angus Lyons years ago, after what appeared to be an outbreak in Bliss. Then after he'd left town, he'd carried the bug to Szuzi. But was she, herself, a result of their union?

Angus Lyons, she thought now. Impossible. And he'd seemed like such a nice man. Maybe that was the worst thing. She'd taken a liking to him both times they'd met. *No wonder he was looking at me in such a strange way. Almost…as if he knew me.* Had he and her mother kept in contact? Why hadn't her mother said something about him? Had she known he was in town? And had he known about Ariel?

Whatever the case, she hated that the information had

come from Studs. Anger surged through her as Rex turned off the vehicle. Not waiting for him, she hopped out of the mobile lab, slammed the door and headed for room twelve, having no idea what she might find.

Rex's hand grabbed her from behind. "Maybe you'd better take a deep breath, Ariel," he murmured. "Don't go in there half-cocked."

Even though she knew he was right, she wasn't about to wait. She'd been wondering about her father her whole life. "I'm fine," she said, her voice a mere croak. Her lips had gone dry. She licked them and realized she could still taste Rex's kisses. That calmed her some. "Okay," she said, seeing the concern in his eyes. Dutifully, she made a show of inhaling deeply, then exhaling.

A slight smile toyed with his lips, and it brought a twinkle to his eyes. His voice grew husky. "Kiss me first."

Her arms circled his neck quickly, drawing him near, and his arms wreathed her back. Mouths and hips locked at the exact same moment and sparks of fire passed between those two pressure points. She tilted her hips upward as his tongue plunged deep, meaning business. She gave him a payoff, a slow thrusting that got the juices rushing inside her. A second later, her mind cartwheeled into the abyss.

He went with her, she could feel it in his response. She was falling into the wet heat of his mouth, spinning over a waterfall, riding a current of relief.

The past hour had been so strange. But this man was grounding her. Gliding her hands from his neck, she cupped his powerful shoulders, then flexed her hands, drawing him yet closer…and then wanting him closer still. She wouldn't be satisfied until he was thrusting deep inside her again.

Rex's grip around her back grew tighter, as if he had every intention of pulling her right down onto the burning concrete and loving her, here and now. The sun was strong, and when she opened her eyes, she saw sunspots. Blinking, she found herself looking into his eyes, which were as blue as the sky. When he tilted up his chin, she could see clouds reflected in the irises.

She squinted. "What?"

He shook his head. "Hmm?"

"You're looking at me funny."

He hesitated, and once more, just as in the car, she was sure he was withholding something from her. He shrugged. "It's nothing."

Whatever it was, there was no use trying to find out. Turning, she slipped an arm around his waist and headed for the door. Nothing more than the knock of his hip against hers made her knees weaken. When they reached the door, she lifted a hand and rapped.

A man's voice called out. "Who is it?"

Her hand curled around the doorknob. "Ariel."

Would he know who she was? Yes. She was sure of it. He'd watched her earlier with such awareness. He had to know she was his daughter. But maybe she was wrong. What if all this was just fantasy? But that's why she'd come here, wasn't it? To put the past to rest, so that she could move on.

From behind the door came a rustling sound, whis-

pers. No one said anything, though. They were in there
together, trying to decide what to say, she thought, turning the knob. The door wasn't locked. After a second's
hesitation, she pushed it open, then realized she
shouldn't have. Inhaling quickly, she glanced around the
room. The man who'd previously called himself
Lawrence Nathan was bare-chested and quickly donning
his pants. Her mother was blushing, her cheeks bright
red, and she'd clearly just slipped her dress over her head.

Ariel was so stunned she could only gape. "Sorry,"
she managed to say. Then added, "I guess it's true."

The color that had flooded her mother's cheeks now
drained until they looked chalk white. "You heard...
How? That's impossible."

"Sheriff Underwood found out that..." She hazarded
a glance at the man who was probably her father, and
was thankful for the strong wall of Rex's back, which
she could feel right behind her. "That, uh, Angus Lyons
was in town," she said. "And we found the book. The
sheriff took it."

Her mother squinted. "The sheriff?"

"Long story," Ariel said simply. "He wanted the recipes,
to heal the relationship with his wife. Sheriff Durham arrested him and took the book to dust it for fingerprints.
We'll have it back in an hour." She could barely believe
the words coming from between her lips. There were so
many other more important things right now. And she
wanted to know about her father... "Is it true?" she asked.

Her mother came forward, caught her hands and
looked deeply into her eyes. "I'm so sorry," she said.

"You always asked questions, but I was very hurt by how my affair with your father ended, so I didn't really want to talk, and I pretended you didn't really need to know."

"Maybe I didn't," Ariel said quickly, venturing another glance at Angus Lyons. He looked so still. Not a muscle moved. Even his gaze seemed stationary, just fixed on her face, and she had no idea what he was thinking.

"I've been happy," she forced herself to say, hating the pain she saw in her mother's eyes. And the love. Over her shoulder, Ariel could see the mussed covers of the bed, and a lump formed in her throat. If she hadn't met and made love to Rex, all this would be playing out differently, but now she knew how passion could rock a woman to her very soul. Her mother, too, might have lost her head and experienced the kind of loving Rex had shown Ariel. It would make people do things they never would otherwise.

"I know you've been happy, honey, but…" Her mother took a deep breath, then the story poured out, and Ariel listened with growing understanding. Her mother and Angus had met when he'd come to town with his father, to buy real estate, ostensibly for land development. The affair had started during a late summer such as this one, and they'd spent an idyllic time, becoming lovers, even though Samantha's grandfather, Eli Saltwell, didn't approve.

"He didn't approve of big business," she explained. "He'd worked in the coal mines in his youth, and had lived through some of the more violent strikes down in the southern part of the state. He remembered when that part of the country was kept peaceful only under marshal law, and he'd seen how chemical waste from the mines had destroyed the rivers and streams."

Ariel's mind couldn't catch up. "Eli Saltwell was married to Great-gran?"

"Still is," her mother said. "They never divorced, and now I believe they're starting to make amends. Of course, who knows if it will last. Those two were oil and water. Passionate and fiery, but they couldn't carry on a civil conversation." Her gaze shifted briefly to Rex. "If you need any proof there's something in the water, that's probably it."

From behind her, Ariel heard his chuckle. "I think I've found my own proof."

"Angus was in the dark about how his father operated," her mother went on. "And while he was here, he started to wise up."

"Because I fell in love with your mother," Angus clarified, now coming to her mother's side. His voice was soft, almost silken, and seemed to strum with feeling. Ariel could hear the love in it. "I found..." He paused, his eyes drawing Ariel's to his. "Things in Bliss I'd never imagined. Your mother bolted me out of the world I'd always known and made me see things in a whole new way...."

Ariel squinted. "What happened?"

"Your mother found papers in our rooms regarding the land deals. My father and I, as well as other members of the coal consortium, were staying in the bed-and-breakfast," he explained. "And she was tidying up.

I…there's no excuse," he began. "But I guess I bought my father's sales pitch lock, stock and barrel. I figured he really did intend to turn Bliss into a tony resort, initially, but then began crunching numbers and realized that the coal business would bring more revenue, which was why people from Core Coal had come into town to meet us. I also believed he'd make good on his promise to the town later, and develop the resorts after Core Coal had mined."

Ariel's gaze shifted to her mother. "And you told Eli…."

Her mother shook her head. "No. I sat on the information. I wanted to ask Angus about everything first. So, I left the papers."

"And then Eli found them?" Ariel guessed.

Her mother nodded. "He drove through Bliss like a bat out of hell, telling everyone who'd already sold land that they'd been conned, and everyone who was considering selling not to do so. Then he headed to Charleston and brought back a good attorney."

"When your mother asked, I told her everything I knew. Like I said, I still believed my father's lies." He shook his head. "My father believed his own lies, you see."

"Rationalizations," put in her mother.

He nodded. "So, to me, it seemed natural that we might have a change of heart and mine the land first. I'd grown up in a business-oriented family, and from our point of view, such development always looked like positive growth. In terms of revenue, it would have been good for the town, but the land would have suffered."

"So, I told him to get out." She flashed him a quick look. "But I didn't know I was carrying you then, Ariel."

"So he left...." Ariel prodded.

"That woke me up," he said. "I understood what we were really doing here, how it could affect people. But it was too late. Your great grandfather and great grandmother were fighting like cats and dogs. Gran, who'd just lost her husband, that's your grandfather, to a hunting accident—"

"A hunting accident?" asked Ariel.

"You knew that," said her mother.

Yes, but that had been only one of so many rumors about her family. Sure, her relatives had told her that her grandfather had died while hunting deer one autumn.

"People in town blamed me," her mother put in.

"She was the prettiest girl in town," Angus clarified. "A homecoming queen. Everyone loved her."

"But they thought I'd fallen in love with someone who wanted to harm them."

Angus's voice hardened. "And she did."

"But you didn't know, not really," said her mother, then added, "after that, I left town for a couple years and lived down in Charleston. By the time I came back, Gran and Great-gran had sort of started keeping to themselves. And I guess with no men around, we got a little stranger and dowdier, only going into town once a week, or when we absolutely had to do so, for odds and ends."

"But people in town knew..."

Her mother shrugged. "Older people probably suspected you were Angus's child, but they weren't sure. And because he was the wrong sort, as far as they were concerned, I suppose I got a reputation. You know how people can be around here," she said. "They don't have the benefit of running an inn, so they don't meet so many fascinating people from other places."

Ariel had never thought of it that way. She swallowed hard. Her own mother had been the victim of gossip, just like her. "You'd think I would have heard the stories," she said.

"About you belonging to Angus?"

Belonging. The word made her heart turn slowly over in her chest. Suddenly she wouldn't believe this was happening. She nodded.

"People were put off by us after that. Like I said, we kept to ourselves. And I guess, as often happens in such experiences, everyone made a silent pact just to keep quiet about whatever they suspected." Her voice softened. "I didn't really want to talk about the whole ordeal," she explained. "I believed then that Angus had meant to fool me, that he thought I was a stupid country girl who could be taken in by his lies."

"I told her differently," he said.

"But I didn't know what to believe."

"So, I just took off," Angus said. "Left the country. I had to think things through on my own, without my father's influence. I've always loved him. I always kept in touch. But after losing your mother, I...well, I can't say I blamed him. But I learned that I had to chart my own course."

"He's worked all over the world," her mother said. "Saving rain forests and trying to slow development that would ruin the earth."

Really, Ariel thought, no one was at fault. And yet she wanted someone to be. Maybe that was the worst kind of tragedy, she decided, when at the end of the day, there was really no one to blame. Angus had grown up in such a way that he'd bought into his father's rationalizations, and her mother was only trying to get the whole story from her lover before telling anyone. And Angus had seen the error in his ways and relented.

"So, you didn't know about me?"

Angus shook his head quickly. "Of course not. And don't blame your mother for not telling me. I married a few years after that. She was trying to forget the past."

Of course he'd been married. Her mother would have had every right to move on, also. "How did you…"

"I was in Peru when I got a call from Jack Hayes a little over a week ago," he said.

Ariel was shocked. "My boss?"

He nodded. "We were at Harvard together. So, when you said you wanted to—"

"Do a story that might involve you and Core Coal," she finished, the pieces falling into place, "he called you."

"Yeah. I recognized the name Anderson, got your age and I…"

"Came?"

He nodded. Tears suddenly stung her eyes. He'd come running the second he'd suspected he had a child. He hadn't seen her mother for years, but he'd come where he'd heard about her. He'd come for her!

A silence fell. Everyone took a deep breath, then exchanged glances, as if wondering where to go from here. Ariel felt wrung out, since all this was overwhelming. Moments ago, when she'd come through the door, she'd had no idea how things would play out. She'd imagined tearful accusations, or maybe furious explosions, but not finding her mother blushing and in bed with Angus Lyons. "Will you come up to the house for dinner?" she asked.

He glanced toward her mother. She nodded. Then he said, "Okay. But only if your mother calls Great-gran first."

"I will," said her mother, looking tremendously relieved to have the encounter over with. No doubt, she'd been concerned about how things would go from the moment Ariel had knocked on the door. "And we'll see you there."

Leaning, Angus Lyons touched her shoulder and his eyes sought hers. "We'll get to know each other," he promised.

Ariel almost smiled as she turned away. After all these years of wondering, the whole scene felt absurdly anticlimactic, and yet it was the wondering, perhaps, that had made it so. She'd imagined meeting her father so many times that there were few scenarios for which she hadn't prepared herself. And what had just occurred was the very best—a normal, sane, mature conversation and a promise to talk again.

"Angus Lyons," she said as she stepped into the sunlight. How could she have imagined the identity of her father? Hugging her to his side, Rex headed for the car, and he must have sensed her mood because he silently opened the door, then circled to his side and simply drove away, letting her process everything.

As they climbed up Mountain Drive, she blew out a shaky breath. She really did feel weak from the past hour. Studs had gone to jail, the rumor mill had been informed that she and Studs had never really been an item, and she'd found her mother in bed with Angus Lyons, who just so happened to be her father. If she received just one more realization, she'd doubtlessly go right over the edge. Her nerves felt wired tight. Wound up but with nowhere to go…except bed. Yes, she wanted to go straight upstairs, rip off her clothes and Rex's, then fall onto the mattress.

Definitely, that would break through this strangely surreal feeling that was haunting her. When he pulled into a parking spot at the house and turned off the motor, she said, "Wait a minute. I've got to get my jean jacket. It's in the back."

As he got out, shut his door and locked it, she skedaddled into the lab area and lifted her jacket from the back of the roller chair. And then she frowned. *The slide.* It was still settled in a tray in a wire-mesh wall pocket. Lifting it, she read the label. *Ariel Anderson. AB Negative.* Squinting, her heart suddenly missing a beat, she rifled her fingers through the tray and found what she was looking for. *Lawrence Nathan. AB negative.* And then… Angus Lyons. There was a slide smeared with blood, labeled with her father's real name.

All the pent-up emotion she'd been holding back came to the surface, and she gripped her jacket and charged toward the open passenger side door. She stepped down, right into Rex's waiting arms, but she pushed him away, barely able to believe what he'd done. Hurt recoiled inside her. She'd been so open with him. And not just with her body. "You knew," she accused softly. Why hadn't he told her? So, that's what he'd been withholding earlier, on the drive to the Outskirts.

His lips parted, as if in protest, but none came out because he was guilty. And scared. She could see that in his eyes now. He was afraid of losing her, and he should be, she decided. As much as she'd loved their sexual relationship, she didn't go out with liars.

"I...did," he finally said.

How could he! She hauled off and hit him with the fist gripped around her jean jacket. The muffled thud fell ineffectually against his shoulder, and he grasped her arm when he felt the punch, as if to steady himself, even though it had clearly hurt his heart, not his body. "How long?" she demanded, staring into his eyes. "When did you suspect?"

"The first day—"

"The first day!"

"You both took blood tests. The blood type's unusual, but that doesn't mean much. Still, there was something about him that was..." His voice trailed off and he shrugged. "Suspicious. He was the only visitor who wasn't with his family, and when I checked with the motel owner, he'd taken a room that wasn't finished, paying extra for it, insisting he had to come to Bliss immediately.

"I checked the records for his flights, and since he'd

come from Peru, I realized he'd been close to Szuzi. So, I checked back through all the records for Americans who've been to Szuzi, from the year of the outbreak on. The CDC has pretty intensive access to records for things such as flight information. I found no Lawrence Nathan listed, but there was an Angus Lyons. He looks different from his pictures in the old Bliss papers, but I did a Google search for him, and…"

"But you didn't interview him again until today."

"I was still researching the facts, and I didn't want to confront him. I wanted to see what he said. That's how we're trained to research. Sometimes, we have to play people a little, to find the truth. I'm an investigator, Ariel. I didn't know how much he knew, whether he came to see your mother, or knew you were his daughter."

He was so clinical about all this, she thought. That was the most unnerving thing. "And you didn't tell me?"

"I was going to," he said, leaning nearer, his breath hot on her lips, his eyes turning more intense.

"When?" She was reeling again, just as she'd been on the drive to the Outskirts. How could he have lain so close to her and listened to her talk about the past, knowing she'd never known the identity of her father.

"I'm sorry," he murmured.

"Sorry?" she repeated, stunned. "That's all you have to say? You knew what I'd been through in this town as a fatherless kid, and you know how people saw my relatives, but when you found out what was really at the root of it all…"

"I wanted to check my facts."

"Bull," she said, leaning forward, almost on her tip-toes, to better look straight into his eyes. "Look at me," she demanded. "And tell me you had any doubts."

His silence said it all.

"You knew it was true," she said again.

He nodded. "Yeah."

"Sex," she found herself biting out before she could think things through; the end of the week was looming and tomorrow the weekend festival was beginning. "That's all this was to you."

His grip tightened on her arm. "That's not true, and you know it." The settling of his mouth on hers seemed to say otherwise. His tongue followed, a burst of heat that flashed like the sun in her eyes before she shut them, giving in only momentarily to the sensations. She had to fight not to stretch her arms around him, because she didn't want this kiss…no, she didn't want it at all.

But it went deeper. He drove his tongue down, hard, thrusting over and over, as if he was afraid to let her have a breath. Maybe she'd walk away, so he had to use desire to hold her. He was drinking her in as if drowning. He was kissing her, as if for the last time, and she felt almost faint from the assault.

"If anything," he murmured, "I didn't tell you because I thought I might ruin our time together."

"That's so selfish," she whispered, looking for the right words. "I…let you *in*." She emphasized the word *in*, as if to say how deeply.

"I let you in, too," he said, his voice husky, his eyes glinting with answering anger and hunger, his lips just inches from hers.

"Oh, right," she muttered, nodding her head up and down, still furious that he'd kissed her like that, so possessively. This was the wrong time. "You let me in by knowing my father was in town all week at the Outskirts Motel. But then..." Her throat constricted. She eyed him a long moment. "You have to play people sometimes, don't you, Rex?"

"That's not what I meant."

"How did it feel to play me?"

"You're angry right now," he said.

"Maybe so. It's been a long day. But withholding information from me on that level..." She shook her head. "It's just not right, Rex." In fact, this was feeling like the worst kind of replay; during a similar summer, her mother had fallen in love, only to find she'd been played for a fool. Just like this, it had been no accident. The lover, who'd come into her life during what had probably been an outbreak in seventy-seven, really had lied to her. He'd come into Bliss with every intention of selling out the townspeople.

"Dammit," he muttered, hauling her nearer. "I didn't know what to do. I had a job to do here, can't you understand?"

"Your job's done now."

"And I didn't feel right intervening in family matters."

That hurt the most. It shouldn't have, and she tried to fight the feelings, but she felt a knife of pain slice into her. He hadn't wanted to intervene? And here she was, the whole week, letting go of herself with him, feeling closer and closer....

Until she'd fantasized that he was her family. She could admit that now. They hadn't talked about what would become of their relationship after the festival, but she'd imagined them moving to the same city soon; she'd wondered if she could get a job in Atlanta. She hadn't realized how attached she'd become to him, not really.

But it was only a fantasy. A week of pure bliss.

"I want you to go," she said.

"Fine," he muttered, glaring at her. "But not without this."

His mouth settled on hers again, the firm, implacable lips forcing hers open. The touch was too much and her arms did lift this time, circling his neck while she wondered if this was really goodbye. Memories of how he'd held her, that first night on the dock, came racing back as his hand found her jaw. Using it to steady her, his tongue plunged. She tried to tell herself they lived in different cities and that he traveled all over the world, so he wasn't even on the continent most of the time. No, it never would have worked, anyway, she told herself as his tongue teased out feelings and heat, making her arch.

She released a moan against his lips, but the kiss captured it. Her mind tumbled into somewhere too dark to fathom. They whirled like stones in a polishing cylinder, brightening until they glowed like midnight moon. One moment, they'd been fighting. Now she wanted Rex in bed. And yet he'd lied to her. She twisted away. His eyes looked glazed, his mouth damp and slack. "I gave you my body," she found herself whispering thickly. "Everything," she repeated.

"I gave you my heart," he said, dragging a frustrated hand through his hair, thrusting it away from his face.

"By lying to me?" She shook her head. "What we had was great, Rex, but you should go," she said.

And then she watched him wordlessly circle the front of the mobile lab, get in and start the motor. A long, tanned arm stretched and he grasped the door handle, slamming shut the passenger-side door. That was the thing about Rex Houston, she thought, as she watched him drive away. He was used to traveling light, which meant he could leave things behind, such as his suit-cases. Or a woman he'd met.

She pictured him in the driver's seat then. She was sure he never glanced into the rearview mirror as the lab unit lumbered over the top of Mountain Drive. No, Rex Houston would never look back.

16

"WELL, AS YOU CAN IMAGINE, we were scared half to death when Matilda's book was stolen," Great-gran said. She was standing behind a shelf in the Andersons' booth at the Harvest Festival, wearing a pale blue dress and talking directly into the camera, which Don held steady.

"Then to find out the sheriff had stolen it!" exclaimed Gran, smoothing down the skirt of her airy yellow dress, the hem of which was blowing in the wind. She circled a row of jars containing mixtures of tea leaves, then glanced at the rows of booths dotting the crowded fairgrounds, containing everything from cotton candy to prize goats and pigs. "Why, we were up all night long," Gran continued, "putting the finishing touches on all our jars."

And they had been. After Sheriff Durham had taken one of Studs's prints off the recipe book and returned it, Ariel had gone into action, gathering with her relatives and Angus in the teahouse kitchen, mixing and measuring tea leaves meant to cure everything from back pains to menstrual cramps. She'd tried to forget Rex, swearing to herself that he didn't matter. She did what she'd always done, pushed aside the pain. She was a doer. Always had been. When the kids had ridiculed her in the past, she'd drawn pictures, ridden horses and planned a future. Besides, she wanted to get to know Angus, and there had been so much to be done before the festival in the morning. It had been long past midnight when Ariel had gone to bed... alone.

"Usually, we're all done with the preparations at least a week before the festival," Gran was explaining now.

Ariel's mother shook her head. "But this year our book was stolen! And just so the sheriff could fix a love potion and work things out with his wife! He could have simply asked for the tea!"

"Tea sounds good to me," said Angus, who was puttering about the booth, arranging jars. Smiling toward the camera, he lifted one. "Matilda's love tea," he announced.

Ariel's mother took it from him. "Why, I think I'll fix some," she teased.

Jeb Pass and Michelle sauntered into the view of the camera. "We might take a cup, too," Jeb said.

Michelle laughed. "And make it strong."

"I'd like a pouch of leaves for arthritis, if you ladies have got it," said Pappy, who sidled next to them. "Mine's not bothering me now, but it will, come winter."

Marsh appeared, carrying some cotton candy. "I'd like something to help beef up muscles," he announced. He glanced around the booth. "You all look like you're dressed for summer. No black?"

Great-gran tittered. "So, you noticed?"

"I think the whole town noticed how you're dressed, ladies," said Pappy.

"Well," said Great-gran, "here comes Eli. He's my husband, and he always hated a dowdy dress. Blue's his favorite color. He says it matches my eyes."

"So, you're back together?" asked Pappy, surprised.

"Time will tell," Great-gran said, clearly not sweating it.

"Now, about that love tea…" began Michelle.

Ariel's mother grinned. "For you, we'll even use springwater. It's been one of those special summers, so the tea should have extra potency." She looked over at Great-gran. "Of course, Great-gran swore last night that she has bottled water left over from the outbreak of seventy-seven, but she can't remember where she put it."

"That would make a potent tea, for sure," said Angus.

Ariel turned toward the camera, glad she'd chosen to wear her new pale blue suit to tape the footage, knowing she looked exactly the part she was expected to play. Jack Hayes and Ryan were going to love this. Even though her heart was breaking, she smiled. "Thanks to Atlanta's Centers for Disease Control and Prevention, this has been a particularly wild season for Bliss, West Virginia. Just recently, a CDC researcher, Dr. Rex Houston, was lured to Bliss—"

"I'm the one who called him!" Elsinore Gibbet stepped next to Ariel, nearly edging her out of the frame. She was wearing a peach dress and straw hat, the brim of which was decorated with flowers, and she was being squired around on the arm of Carl DeLyle, who looked dapper, himself, wearing a three-piece, gray-and-white striped seersucker suit.

Carl DeLyle patted her arm. "What would Bliss do without you, sweetie?"

They looked so happy together that Ariel felt a sudden surge of emotion. Her mother and Angus were just as happy, and Great-gran and Eli. Pappy and his wife were back together, and Jeb and Michelle couldn't keep their hands off each other. Only days ago, that same happiness had been hers. Tears pushed at her eyelids, but she shoved aside the thoughts. Rex's leaving didn't change her professional circumstances, after all.

She faced the camera again. "So, my family would like to thank Elsinore Gibbet and Dr. Houston." She plunged into a spiel about the history of blackout periods in Bliss, then said, "After Miss Gibbet called the CDC and Dr. Houston arrived, he tested the water and interviewed all the citizens. And that..." She smiled as Angus stepped beside her. "Is how I came to find out the identity of my own biological father...."

"BRILLIANT," JACK HAYES SAID days later, hitting a button on the remote in his hand, then Play again. "Truly, it's a wonderful piece," he said, standing and preparing to leave the conference room.

But it wasn't. "Rex should have been in it," she apologized. That was the only thing that kept the story from going right over the top, into excellence.

Loosening the brown-and-silver tie he wore with his three-piece suit, Ryan shook his head. "Are you kidding? Jack's right. It's great."

"It's got humor," agreed Jack. "Small-town quirkiness. He smiled. "Loads of sex. And I've got good news for you."

She raised an eyebrow. "Hmm?"

"NBC picked it up. They want to use the long version on a news-magazine show. Also, they may edit it down for a two-minute spot at the end of the NBC nightly news."

Her heart lifted, but only for a moment. And…then what? she thought. More stories, more editing, more traveling. More pastel-colored suits that made her look like a bona fide talking head. For the first time, the idea made her feel weighted down and burdened instead of excited. Usually, she imagined herself striding through airport concourses, pulling a roller bag behind her, running to catch a plane to a new location for a shoot. Now, she imagined an endless life on the road….

And for what?

Inside her, something had changed. Although things hadn't unfolded as she'd planned, her confrontation with the past really had set her free. Studs had gotten out of jail on bail, but until his trial for theft, he was no longer able to function as sheriff. If he was convicted, which he would be, he'd never return to office. News of what had transpired had swept through Bliss like a brush fire, and now, especially with the history regarding Angus out in the open, including his separation from his father, the Andersons' reputation around town would surely improve. The human-interest piece would do exactly as she'd hoped, too. It would put Bliss on the map.

"Good going, kid," Jack said again, patting her shoulder as he passed. "And I can't believe Angus turned out to be your dad. When I called him to tell him about your interest in him, that was the last thing on my mind."

"I'll bet," she said. That piece of her life still felt anticlimactic. But then, not knowing the identity of her father had led to fantasies about him and an incredible buildup. It was going to take them years to deflate. But they liked each other. Not that he wasn't larger than life, of course, she thought with a smile. After all, he was quite an adventurer. A worthy object of her fantasies. He'd been all over the world, and now, it seemed, he had plans to take Ariel's mother with him.

"So, sugar cakes," said Ryan as soon as Jack left the room. "It looks like you're moving to another department. Jack gave me carte blanche to offer you the promotion into production. You'll be working with a woman I think you'll like. And you'll be able to begin pulling together other stories. Whatever you want. You're the idea man now." His voice lowered. "And you'll be on another floor...."

Which meant they could date. Probably why he'd just called her by the unlikely nickname of sugar cakes. She stepped back a pace as he stretched a finger, meaning to catch the edge of her jacket, and she studied him for a long moment. He was good-looking, with sandy-brown hair and soft brown eyes that usually carried hints of amusement, and he had a square jaw that she'd always thought of as "very Kennedy." Definitely, he was the kind of guy she'd imagined might...lend her respectability.

And that's what she'd needed, just a week ago when she'd driven into Bliss, hoping for this exact moment—

a triumphant return and a situation where they might start seeing each other. But now, every inch of her body seemed touched by sizzling hot handprints. Respectability paled, as far as she was concerned, next to hours of heat and heavy breathing. Desperately, she needed to feel that again…the tingling at her core, the wild, disjointed thoughts shattering into sharp shards as Rex plunged into her depths.

Warmth suffused her cheeks. The office seemed to vanish, and in her mind's eye, she was bucking, her legs circled tightly around Rex's waist. Feeling her nipples constrict, she tried to tamp down an unwanted rush of heat. The sudden need for Rex was almost painful. Only he would know what she wanted right now…know exactly what to do. He'd cup her breasts and squeeze with just the right amount of pressure, until she was gasping for breath. Yes, she needed him—pulsing, hard, engorged. She could feel him enter, burning as she opened for him….

"Ariel?"

She snapped to attention. "Hmm?"

"I was saying Jack gave me carte blanche with regard to your next career move. After I take you upstairs, to meet your new boss, you can work on whatever you like. You'll have a healthy expense account for travel…."

As he explained the package, she began to drift again, her core melting, her senses splitting into hairlike filaments.

"Ariel?" he said again.

"I think I might want to do a follow-up to the Bliss

story," she said, swallowing hard, realizing what she wanted to do.

"Where?"

"Atlanta."

"PUBLIC RELATIONS wants to know why you aren't in this piece." Clicking a button on the remote, Jessica muted the sound on the videotape and straightened in the chair behind the desk. She glared at Rex, whose gaze shifted to the picture.

Ariel looked so damn happy. He really couldn't stand it. She was standing in front of the teahouse booth at the Harvest Festival, grinning and holding up a jar of specialty tea. It was illogical, but he hated that every man in America would be staring at her, dressed in that fancy blue suit. Of course, she looked professional, but he spied lace beneath her silk blouse. Besides, legs to die for were exposed, and even if she was dressed, he knew exactly what lay beneath every stitch.

A slender, tall, willowy body that called out for his hands, he thought. One touch and he knew she'd be quivering for him, moaning as he unbuttoned that blouse with his teeth. He'd rip down her stockings. Maybe he'd just dig a hand into the hosiery and tear it to shreds. Her panties, too. Then he'd shove up that pretty, delicate silk blouse…just shove the bra over her breasts, not even bothering with the straps, so he could clamp down his mouth onto one of those sweet buds and suckle….

"Rex?"

He looked up to see Jessica tossing her auburn hair

the way a lion might his mane. It was one of her power gestures. Now she let the hair swirl softly around her shoulders as she glared at him, coming in for the kill. "I demand an explanation, Rex."

Maybe there was no use in lying. "I…met someone."

Her lips tilted as if she might smile. "Her?"

He hated that Jessica now knew he'd bedded Ariel Anderson. It was his private business, but he said, "That's why I called and asked to be on the next plane to Timbuktu." He paused. "You did send me to investigate a love bug."

She took a deep breath, then nodded. "Public relations would have been thrilled to see you on this spot. A network has picked it up, and they're going to use it on a news magazine and maybe cut it for a human-interest spot on NBC nightly news. They say it humanizes the CDC."

"Good for her," he said. He was glad for Ariel, but that didn't make him rest easier about the way they'd left things. And yet, it seemed right. After all, they'd been under the influence. Even if their blood had tested clean, what Jeb Pass had said was exactly right. Viruses mutated. Most probably, they'd been infected, but tests hadn't picked up the virus, something he'd discussed with Jessica.

"I want to work in the lab with the samples," he said now. "The equipment's better than in the mobile unit, and we may be able to find evidence of a mutation." Then he'd have proof that the sensations he'd experienced were only a biological response to something beyond his control. Then he could let go of his memories.

No woman could make a man feel that good, not by natural means. Unwanted pleasure pooled in his belly and his groin tightened.

"First things first," Jessica said.

He raised an eyebrow. "Hmm?"

She slid a ticket across the desk. "A ticket to Timbuktu," she said. "Or Szuzi, as it were. I want you to get more samples."

PARADISE, REX THOUGHT, except for the one annoying fly he batted from his face as he capped a last tube of water and put it into a tray. And the heat, he added silently. Steam rose from the trees and waters. He looked around the cove. It was utterly silent except for a vaulting waterfall rising a good fifty feet from aqua water below and plummeting in a rush of white water over boulders.

Arches of lush green leaves tumbled all around him, creating a gorge, and grapevines, moss and monkeys hung in trees with fronds larger than a man; wild orchids bloomed, too, nestled in joints of branches. Some looked like the famed ghost orchids, almost transparently white, the petals as thin as air.

He could barely breathe. The air was heavy with mist, so much so he almost felt he'd stepped into a dream. It was thick with heat, too, heavy with scents of flowers. As he inhaled, he thought of Ariel again and wished he hadn't.

He glanced behind him, half expecting his Jeep to be gone. Definitely, there was something surreal about this place. It was almost spooky. And it reminded him of

Bliss, too, which was something he could do without. Why, he wasn't quite sure. Maybe it was just the lushness of the vegetation. Or the silence. Absolutely no one was around, but then people from the nearest village were working.

"The hell with it," he suddenly said, unsnapping his cargo shorts, trying not to think of how it had felt to swim with Ariel in Spice Spring in Bliss. It was too hot not to swim before he headed to base camp in the village. His hand settled on the pull to the zipper, and then he imagined for a moment it was her hand, not his. It was she, not he, who was dragging it down....

The pang to his groin came swiftly. Heat surged. Trying to deny the pulsing need, he pushed thoughts of her from his mind and jerked down the zipper, then kicked off his shorts. He'd worn briefs, a real no-no most of the time, and especially in this weather. Glancing down, he felt his heart stutter, missing a beat.

He really was getting hard. Drawing a breath through clenched teeth, he couldn't help but cup a hand over the beginning erection. He shut his eyes, sighing at the contact, the warmth of his hand teasing the stiffening ridge through cotton, but it was her long, slender fingers...

They circled the head, a thumb teasing the underside, brushing over where a drop of moisture beaded. A trapped sound stirred in his throat as she curled her fingers around his length...then glided them all the way down until she'd cupped his balls. She tested the weight, slowly jiggling them in her palm, then she squeezed in a way that threatened to take him to a point of no return, engendering heat so intense that he knew he'd better stop. Otherwise, he really would be out here, stark naked by a waterfall in the back of the beyond, jerking off to memories.

"You're really losing it, Rex," he muttered, opening his eyes. He wasn't going to kid himself. The relationship was over. She'd been grinning like the Cheshire cat on the news. She'd come into Bliss to do her piece. It was her past she'd wanted to put to bed, not just him. And his main agenda had been, just as now, to collect samples for the CDC.

The rest…well, everything else was just the kind of lies people uttered in the heat of the moment. Hearts and flowers. Undying love. Promises for tomorrow. Not that they'd said all that, not in words. But every touch had carried a message. Still, if he'd been infected by a mutated version of the bug, he figured it would have worn off by now….

He shook his head to clear it of confusion. The heat, isolation and silence was getting to him. None of the villagers even spoke English. It had been days since he'd felt connected to anything, except fantasies of her. Hooking thumbs under the waistband, he eased the briefs down, then pushed them aside with his foot.

A soft chuckle sounded. What was that old line from the Tom Waits song? he wondered, willing it back to memory. "Oh right," he muttered. "Harder than Chinese algebra." That pretty much described his state. Taking a deep breath, he pushed off, doing a surface dive into the shallow water, his nerve endings singing with relief when he hit the water. Relatively speaking, it was cool.

Then he gasped as he surfaced, moving his feet. Something in the water had stirred….

Hands circled his calves. Slowly, feeling as feathery as palm fronds, they rose, molding each inch of him. Higher and higher…until they reached his thighs and he could see the top of her head beneath the water. "Ariel?" he murmured as she surfaced.

She'd come straight up from the depths, approaching like some fantastic, beautiful lagoon creature. Her hair fell straight, the water turning the blond strands darker, so they looked the color of sand against her china, rose-tinged cheeks. She'd gotten some sun. But how long had she been here? Why had she come?

The questions died on his lips. She was as naked as he, and judging by the reddened tips of her nipples, she was at least as aroused. Just looking at her made his mind blank, and his heart started telling him everything he needed to know. He roped his arms around her, pulling her flush against him. She cushioned against his chest, her belly pressuring his, bringing relief to where he ached.

"Wouldn't want you to be left playing with yourself alone," she murmured huskily.

So she'd been watching him. "Ariel," he murmured again as her arms wrapped around him. "Ariel… Ariel…" His lips were in her hair, kissing the damp strands, then sprinkling her cheeks until their mouths meshed, hovered, locked and held. He'd caught her bottom lip between his, and now he clung, nibbling with passionate hunger.

"Why'd you come?" he whispered against her ear.

Her voice was a slow, sensual purr that was asking for more. "I called your boss," she said. "Actually, I had to do a little background checking while I was editing my piece—"

"It was great—"

"Thanks. But…" Her eyes met his. There was a lump in her throat; he could see her work hard, trying to swallow. "I missed seeing you in it, Rex. You should have been there."

"It killed me to see you on TV," he admitted hoarsely, his lips skating over hers, the warmth coursing through him undeniable now. She was so close…so naked…so hot. His mouth suddenly covered hers in a kiss burning with their desire. "You looked so good," he whispered, his voice catching. "I wanted to make love to you while I was watching it."

She blew out a shuddering breath. "You did?"

Nodding, he glided his splayed hands down her sides, which were slick with water. "Wanted to touch you," he said thickly, as if his tongue were suddenly too big for his mouth. "Here…" Lifting a hand, he gently plucked a nipple, rolling it slowly between a thumb and forefinger before squeezing her breast. "And here…" Flattening his hand, he trailed it slowly down her tummy until it teased her curls. "And here…" His hand curled to the lower contours, cupping her and flexing his fingers, his mouth falling to hers once more when he felt how her juices were flowing for him.

"I…wound up telling your boss everything."

His eyes found hers. "Jessica?"

"Sorry. Everything just kind of spilled out."

He understood that. "It's okay, but…"

"She told me where you'd gone."

His breath was in his throat. "We never talked," he said simply.

She shook her head, her hands cupping his shoulders to brace herself. "But we said a lot."

"I missed you," he whispered.

Words didn't seem to matter. The heat they shared said it all. Slowly, he watched as she lifted a hand from his shoulder, brought it before his eyes, and with a flick of her wrist…a small foil packet appeared between her fingers.

He couldn't believe it. He shifted his gaze to hers. She was smiling back. "Now where'd that come from?" he asked.

She shrugged in a way that lifted her breasts higher, as if for his eyes. "Magic," she returned, her voice a scarcely heard rasp. "Trick of the family trade." She chuckled. "Just in case I'd like to love a man to death, then bury him up on the mountain. You know," she teased, "like all my other lovers."

"Believe me," he promised. "I'd die with a smile on my face and know I'd already been to heaven."

Her hand found his and she began leading him toward the bank, out of the cool water and into heat as steamy as their bodies. "I brought a picnic lunch," she said.

And she had. Behind a copse of trees, a blanket lay open on the ground. He saw grapes, fruit, bananas and bread, and in an ice bucket, a bottle of champagne chilled, with two long-stemmed glasses beside it. It amazed him to realize that he'd been so lost in fantasies about her that he hadn't even heard her approach.

"But first," she said, lowering herself to her knees. Reaching into a basket, she withdrew a slender silver Thermos and gingerly began pouring the contents into two Dixie cups. Whatever it was looked brown, murky and unappealing. He frowned as she handed him a cup.

"As it turns out," she explained, her hungry eyes drifting over him, "Great-gran bottled some water during the outbreak of seventy-seven. This is Matilda's home-brewed love tea made with the springwater."

It was the last thing he'd expected her to say. And she was definitely the last person he'd expected to see here. His shoulders shook with laughter. "You're not joking."

She shook her head, sobering. "I mean...we didn't know whether what we've shared is real or not, right?"

He shook his head, wanting to say that it hardly mattered now. She was so beautiful, like a wood nymph surrounded by abundant green vegetation, naked and on her knees, with her wet hair falling wildly around her shoulders.

"If we drink this," she assured. "Then we'll know we're infected."

He laughed. "It'll be nice not to have that question hanging over our heads." As he studied her, his heart felt like it was stretching to breaking. Suddenly, he said, "You forgive me?"

She nodded slowly, then said, "But you can't do it again. I won't have lies between us."

"I didn't know how to handle the situation," he admitted.

"You should have talked to me."

"I know that now."

She paused, struggling for the words. "It was you saying that you didn't want to intervene in my family that hurt the most. I..." Color came into her cheeks and he could see the risk in her eyes, a sheen of what was either emotion or tears. "I...felt you were my family, Rex. Being with you, I felt like I'd really come home. And that the past just didn't matter, because you were the future, but..."

He hadn't seemed to share the feelings. "Oh, Ariel," he said, moving to set down the cup. "It's not like that. I..."

A finger on his lips silenced him, and he could only wish it was her mouth. "The tea," she whispered. "Let's just drink it. Okay? We don't have antibodies. You checked, so..."

Offering a quick nod, he lifted his cup in tandem with hers, and like her, kicked it back, downing the contents. It was even worse than it had looked, as brackish and sour-tasting as a dirty river. They both came up sputtering.

"Now we know we're infected," she managed to say on a hiccup.

"What a guy won't do for love," he muttered.

Suddenly, they were both laughing. The sound bubbled in the silence just as the nearby water. And then they were rolling, too…into each other's arms, onto the blanket, readying themselves for the dive over the waterfall, into the heady, dark abyss. He found the condom, put it on, then he was on top of her.

Catching her hands, he drew them over her head, his heart missing beats when he saw how open she was to him. Her blue eyes were bright; her breasts were bare and exposed. Shakily, he lowered a hand and pushed apart her thighs, feeling her flesh leap in his hands. Instinctively, he knew there would be tomorrows, and that they'd talk about all the intricacies of their relationship, catch up on pleasantries and decide where they'd meet in the future. But now…

Angling his body inward, he edged closer. Suddenly, he arched, thrusting up…in… As slippery fire enveloped him, he watched her well-kissed lips slacken and those gorgeous eyes roll back. Fingers dug into his shoulders, urging him deeper, and only after he thrust fully into her and she'd cried out, did he pull slowly out…all the way out…then thrust again harder, deeper, faster.

"I love you," she whispered as she shattered.

"Yes, love me, Ariel," he whispered back, arching for all she had to give. "Promise you'll love me."

She did then, in earnest, answering in ways words could never say, with her hips and lips and hands. It was a way of talking he understood and all he would ever need to hear. Love had entered his bloodstream, just as it had hers, and as he captured her mouth in a kiss, he felt it running as he knew it always would, like the spring in Bliss from its mysterious, eternal source, hot, wild and free.

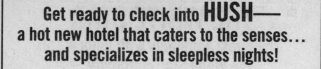

HARLEQUIN® *Blaze*

Get ready to check into **HUSH**—
a hot new hotel that caters to the senses...
and specializes in sleepless nights!

Room Service
by
JILL SHALVIS

It should be simple. All TV producer Em Harris has to
do is convince chef Jacob Hill to sign on for her new
culinary show. Only, when she sets foot in Hush, the
sex-themed hotel where Jacob works, she knows she's
in over her head. Especially when she develops an
irresistible craving for the sinfully delicious chef...

A linked story to
HOT SPOT by Debbi Rawlins (Book #220, December 2005)

Shhhh...
Do Not Disturb!

If you enjoyed what you just read,
then we've got an offer you can't resist!

Take 2 bestselling love stories FREE!

Plus get a FREE surprise gift!

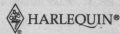

HARLEQUIN®

COMING NEXT MONTH

#231 GOING ALL OUT Jeanie London
Red Letter Nights
Bree Addison never dreamed that landing in Lucas Russell's yard would change everything. Who knew that her rescuer would be bent on having a sizzling affair with her? And who could have guessed that her nights would suddenly become one big sensual adventure? Only, adventures aren't meant to last....

#232 ROOM SERVICE Jill Shalvis
Do Not Disturb
It should be simple. All TV producer Em Harris has to do is convince chef Jacob Hill to sign on for her new culinary show. Only, when she sets foot in Hush, the sex-themed hotel where Jacob works, she knows she's in over her head. Especially when she develops an irresistible craving for the sinfully delicious chef...

#233 TALL, TANNED & TEXAN Kimberly Raye
24 Hours: Island Fling
After years of trying to make cowboy Rance McGraw notice her, Deanie Codge is taking action! Two weeks at Camp E.D.E.N., a notorious island retreat, will teach her to unleash her inner sex kitten. The next time she sees her cowboy, she'll be ready. And it turns out to be sooner than she thinks....

#234 SINFULLY SWEET Janelle Dension, Jacquie D'Alessandro, Kate Hoffmann
A Decadent Valentine's Day Collection
Sex or chocolate. Which is better? This Valentine's Day, join three of Blaze's bestselling authors in proving that, in both sex *and* chocolate, too much of a good thing...is a good thing!

#235 FLIRTATION Samantha Hunter
The HotWires, Bk. 3
EJ Beaumont is one big flirt. Not exactly the best trait for a cop, but it's an asset on his current computer crime investigation. He's flirting big-time with a sexy online psychic who—rumor has it—is running a lonely-hearts scam. Only problem is, as a psychic, Charlotte Gerard has EJ's number but good!

#236 HIDDEN GEMS Carrie Alexander
The White Star, Bk. 2
Jamie Wilson thinks his best friend, Marissa Suarez, is dating the wrong men—his wanting her for himself has *nothing* to do with his opinion. When Marissa's apartment suddenly becomes a target for thieves, Jamie steps up to the plate. Maybe Marissa will finally see the hidden gem he is—inside the bedroom and out!

www.eHarlequin.com